DOCTORS IN HELL

HEROES IN HELL: THE GREATEST SHARED UNIVERSE OF ALL

created by **JANET MORRIS**   edited by Janet Morris

by   Chris Morris

with the diabolical assistance of the damnedest writers in perdition

Perseid Press
P. O. Box 584
Centerville, MA 02632

Doctors in Hell

Cover: Pandemonium, John Martin (1789-1854), circa 1841, oil on canvas; from private collection

Cover Design: Sonja Aghabekian
Cover copyright: (c) Perseid Press
Interior Design: Sarah Hulcy

Trade Paperback, ISBN-13: 978-0-9864140-9-1, ISBN-10: 0986414093
ePub, ISBN-13: 978-0-9964289-0-3, ISBN-10: 0996428909
Kindle, ISBN-13: 978-0-9914654-9-6; ISBN-10: 0991465490

Published in the United States of America

10 9 8 7 6 5 4 3 2 1 Weston, A Moment of Clarity

ACKNOWLEDGEMENTS

Janet Morris and Chris Morris, The Wager
Chris Morris, The Cure
Andrew P. Weston, Grim
Deborah Koren, The Right Man for the Job
Nancy Asire, Memory
R.E. Hinkle, What Price Oblivion
Richard Groller, In the Shadowlands
Matthew Kirshenblatt, Let Us Kill the Spirit of Gravity
Bill Snider, Pavlovian Slip
Joe Bonadonna, Hell On a Technicality
Michael H. Hanson, Convalescence
Paul Freeman, Hell Noon
Jack William Finley, The Judas Book
Janet Morris and Chris Morris, Writer's Block
Andrew P. Weston, A Moment of Clarity

DOCTORS IN HELL

TABLE OF CONTENTS

The Wager

Janet Morris and Chris Morris

"Let's make us med'cines of our great revenge,
To cure this deadly grief."

—Shakespeare, *Macbeth*

The armchair generals of the 20th and 21st centuries were mustering their troops on the plain below. To the left of each battalion, a long white tent with blood-red crosses gleamed balefully in the sanguine light of Paradise, its doctors ready to tend the casualties.

As Altos, hell's only volunteer angel, watched from a lofty precipice, fools in bright uniforms gathered, parade-ready; flaccid souls who dreamt dreams of unlimited power strutted like peacocks, each dressed in the manner of a real soldier he'd idolized in life.

If there was a sadder spectacle in hell than these flabby souls, their arrogance and pride worn like medals of honor, Altos had never seen it. He swung his sandaled feet slowly, back and forth, back and forth, and stared down on all these who embraced war as a test of manhood, a solution for disagreement, a way to distinguish oneself in bravery, to impose one's superior view of the world upon lesser fellows.

Beside Altos sat Satan himself. The conjunction of these two above the battle plain on the jutting spur of rock they shared was in itself a singular event, their meeting an indication that more than a battle between weekend warriors and sky-diving wannabes would soon be joined here.

For the devil and the angel had made a wager, and the heart of the wager was this: The devil insisted that modern souls in hell—the New Dead, as they are called—were so vicious, self-centered, hubristic and morally bankrupt that they would punish themselves, if given a chance, more horribly and thoroughly than hell's bureaucracy could contrive to do.

Altos had leapt at the chance to prove the New Dead worthy of salvation—or at least deserving of leniency, to show themselves no worse than their predecessors or successors. So the angel invited the devil to set the terms of the wager.

The devil had stared at Altos from glowing, slitted eyes and said, "This, then, if you agree: the militarists of the 20th and 21st centuries will combat one another in battles fought exclusively by volunteers: armies manned by voyeurs of violence who find vicarious thrills reading of heroes who never were, fighting villains who never could be. If we hold this war and nobody comes, or the doctors of the damned heal the wounded and save the plague-ridden, then, Altos, you will win, and I shall soften my heart unto the New Dead and forestall the purge you know I am readying."

Despite the risk of death, maiming, dismemberment and disease, many, many had come, wearing white masks on their noses and second-hand uniforms, as if they were dressed for a costume contest. Since death in hell is fleeting and torment eternal, Altos had counted on the fear of purge and plague to keep most damned away. It hadn't.

Plagues brought to hell on the wings of Erra, the Babylonian plague god, now visited all the hells with pestilential misery. This mysterious new purge of Satan's promised further torture, which Altos hoped to help the teeming damned avoid. Hell is hell, and the damned must suffer, but the devil was furious about Erra and his auditors sent from heaven to prove hell insufficiently hellish.

Altos was not privy to the specifics of Satan's threatened purge—and did not want to be. The angel longed to save the doomed of perdition, forfend more horrendous torment of crippled souls too foul to find within themselves one bit of grace.

Steam issuing from his every orifice, the devil had told the angel: "If they want war, they will have it. Have it until the slaughtered make a stairway to heaven, until their viciousness becomes an object lesson of nightmare proportions, until their thirst for blood is quenched, until the Sea of Sighs rises to a floodtide swollen with their corpses. I will even restrict their access to the Mortuary. Their resurrection by the Undertaker will be slow and painful, and the hell they find upon their return to afterlife will be one devoid of comfort."

The angel did not doubt that Satan could do all he said. Between now and final judgment stretched time enough for Satan to remake all the hells of latterday humanity into whatever shape he chose.

Altos had been in hell since infernity began. He'd volunteered when all the hells first formed from every nightmare dreamed by every primitive culture Earth had ever spawned; when monsters had roamed its dusty streets and half-human creatures tortured quivering wrecks of humanity without a moment's respite. He'd been here when the Judges and the Lords of Hell were chosen; and when Satan and his fallen angels, numbering a third of the stars in the sky, fell into the Deep to languish in the dark, in the cold.

Over eons, the hells had multiplied, and changed, and changed again, until the netherworlds numbered as many as mankind's sins. Part of hell's nature ensured that it metamorphosed to suit those it incarcerated.

All societies created the hell they deserved, if left to their own devices. And the devil moderated the creation of the New Dead's societies, so that no one group took power, intent on preserving the balance that made the underverse an equally uneasy resting place for history's manifold modern damned.

In all of time, Altos had never seen Satan so outraged. Even today, when the devil had come to the precipice to view the sporting event upon which they two had wagered, his fury was palpable: his body odor pungent, sulphurous; his breath so vile it caught you by the throat.

For Satan had taken on human aspect today. No longer did his wings glow white or black; no longer strode he beauteous or baleful across the underbelly of creation. Now he waddled, short-legged, paunchy, pimply, pale, and goateed. His soft rosebud mouth pursed in a perpetual sneer. His pasty hands twisted in his pillowy lap. He sat a long time in silence beside Altos as the ranks of New Dead combatants trudged onto the battleplain.

And they were a multitude.

Their bayonets shone. Their helmets gleamed. Their battle standards waved high. Their aircraft buzzed the field, spewing colored smoke, piloted by souls who'd never before piloted more than a computer simulation.

Beyond the armies lining up to face each other across a steaming chasm that would return the slain to the Mortuary, bands played a discordant cacophony of marching songs. To Altos' right, where the Sea of Sighs met the plain, huge battleships test-fired tracer rounds, the HSMS *Perdition* among them.

Between the seashore and the armies, infernity's press corps gathered amid doctors and nurses under awnings outside the red-crossed triage tents where white flags flew high.

Altos wanted to weep. To forestall the devil's vengeance, he had agreed to this test of New Dead souls and now regretted it.

He should have told the devil that so many novices would skew the result, but he had not. He should have demanded that, to be valid, such war must be waged by a preponderance of combat veterans. He had done neither of those.

Satan had cowed him, intimidated him. On the devil's turf, no emissary from on high enjoyed immunity to schemes concocted by the Father of Lies.

The devil never would have agreed to fairer terms; even Altos knew that war was waged as much by men like those anxiously gathering on the plain, laughing and boasting, as by men who should know better.

Altos had already lost. Worse, the New Dead had lost. With the first shot fired, more than the battle for the Plain of Just Deserts would commence: When the bugles sounded, the devil would begin a war against the denizens of New Hell which could have but one winner: Satan.

To avoid catastrophe, Altos knew, was impossible: it was too late. Yet he must salvage something. So he said to the devil, "Satan, let me go down among the soldiers and make sure the damned know what they are about to do here. Let me go among the doctors and find the unselfish who minister to the dying. Surely putting up posters, offering 'Spoils of War to the Victors' isn't quite fair. Surely I deserve an equal chance, if not equal time, to remind these doomed play-actors they are about to slaughter the souls of their own allies."

"Go ahead, Altos," grinned the devil. "Go ahead. Go among the troops. Go among the physicians. Speak your mind. It won't change anything. These are not the fighters; these are the proselytizers of war and peace, the enfamers, the moral cowards, the holier-than-thou: these are the writers of war novels, movies, TV shows, and commercials. These are the 'Physicians without Borders,' sure that their moral rectitude will protect them. These are the would-be martyrs. These are the lame and halt who couldn't make it through basic training. These are the privileged and the spoiled and the willfully under-informed. Among them, you will find xenophobes and racists of all sorts, those who do not like others whose eyes or skins are a different color, or whose ideology or religion or even sect is different from their own. These are not fighting over matters of import. These are fighting for bragging rights or because they think war in hell will be like watching a war movie, not like being in a war. These are those who wish to force others to their will for the sheer power it gives them, who mistake power for morality or moral authority; might for right—who come here because war is sexy. What you see before you, Altos, is the pornography of violence."

"Surely they were lured here under false pretenses," Altos argued. "Placards saying 'Real heroes fight for their rights' weren't any part of our agreement."

"Our agreement—our wager—said nothing about means. And no poster makes fools of souls already damned. It is in them. These are the filth of modern times. These are those who have never truly suffered enough. They are proof that I must tighten my grasp here, else you would have won, because no soul with the wisdom of a 'dumb' animal lines up to risk being slaughtered for the mere chance of doing murder and mayhem upon his fellows—or exhorts his peers to do likewise. Admit it, you have already lost: by their gaiety, by their posturing, by their eagerness for the battles to be joined, they prove themselves unfit for mercy."

The angel hung his head and a tear welled in one golden eye. He blinked it back. "I will go among them. I will talk to the generals and tell them what is at stake. I will talk to the medics and warn them that hubris is a sin, that souls who play god impress no one but themselves. Otherwise, our wager is only a wager—it proves nothing. These souls don't realize that the future of all hell is at stake here."

The devil stuck out his neck and made a face, aping Altos' obvious concern. "You are stupid. You depress me. You should learn a lesson here, Angel. All humanity is not worth saving. Some, perhaps. But the filth? These?" He spread his pasty hands. "Go on, they won't listen. All these souls want is the thud of their hearts beating fast, the excitement of battle, and to be able to curl up afterwards with a beer and tell exaggerated stories of their prowess to men who don't tell such stories because they have real prowess. Remember, these are the unbloodied, the untested and the rear-echelon warriors, nonentities compared to the fabled heroes they hope to emulate. For every one of these, transient death and rebirth on the Undertaker's slab seems worth risking in exchange for a taste of glory." The devil smirked, showing perfect teeth.

"Then," said the angel morosely, "with your leave, I'm on my way." Before the devil could respond, Altos rose, unfurled his wings, and pushed off into the sky over the battlefield.

That battlespace echoed with martial strains, and above the noise Altos heard the devil call out: "Just hurry, if you don't want to miss the opening salvos! You have less than an hour before the battle cry sounds and the carnage begins." The devil was absolutely chortling.

Over the massing ranks flew Altos, until the wind had dried his tears. There was no arguing with Satan's evil, honed through millennia of congress with humanity's worst souls. But the angel yet had a chance, if a slim one, of persuading those assembled below not to make war on one another. He must try.

Although his first priority was the devil's own rehabilitation, Altos could work as he willed among the damned. The Almighty had decreed that infernity always offer hope.

Altos would make the most of the time he had left before the battle joined. He circled over the ranks of World War I and II armies, their horses and jeeps and lorries, and found himself repelled by the blood-thirsty legions he encountered there.

So he flew farther, while men looked up and some took potshots at the high flying dot that he was. He flew until he reached the ranks of the latter twentieth century. There, some who had not fought in Korea or Vietnam or Beirut or Afghanistan or Africa or Bosnia or Kuwait or Somalia were calibrating electronic warfare gear in their helicopters, booting hand-held computers, and shrugging into Alice packs. Others taped banana clips together and checked their phosphorous and fragmentation grenades.

Down among these troops, many of whom were still reading inch-thick manuals and trying to accustom themselves to the complexities of their tanks and personnel carriers and drones and electronic counter-countermeasures, the angel descended until he reached command headquarters, far to the rear of the incipient fighting.

Here Altos learned the awful truth of Satan's clever plan and bold prognostication. The New Dead's rear echelon was composed of damned souls such as never had risked their persons in the field: movie producers and video stars; comic book artists and book publishers; toy makers and news directors; "veterans" of wars who had never been incountry but fought from their hometown desks—all dogged by reporters never embedded with a forward unit, busy scribbling down notes for hell's posterity.

None of the damned whom Altos saw were familiar to him. Here were none who'd earned commendations carrying their fellows out of fire zones; here were no souls whom Altos had been told to watch because they had done nearly as much good in their lives as evil. In fact, here crowded only weaklings who misremembered the wars they'd fought from behind the lines, and adolescent souls who'd never fought any wars they couldn't end with a keystroke or the push of a button, or abandon by sliding into their vehicles and returning home.

Here stood no damned who had ever distinguished themselves in any mortal combat. Here were those who were sure they knew exactly how the war—and this infernity they now inhabited—should be run and were busy telling everyone else about it. Here were pundits who spoke in capital letters about Honor, Bravery, Duty, and Righteousness.

Not one soul here behind the lines, so far from harm, felt concern that this enemy was not unlike himself. And that, to Altos, was the saddest thing of all. The devil knew his damned. These New Dead were willing to slaughter their fellows, remotely, in a multitude—were looking forward to it, in truth, back here where it was doubtful that harm could reach.

But Altos knew that harm *would* reach here: that this was what the *Perdition* and her sister ships were here for. Their shells would fall short of their purported targets, inaccurate as ever, and land upon these fools so puffed up with the excitement of their picnic-table war.

Thus it was to the picnic table before him that the angel strode, as angry as an angel can get, and pounded his fist upon it. Three men looked up, each paler and softer and rosier-cheeked and more artfully quaffed of head and facial hair than the last.

Altos said, "Who's in charge here? There's still time to stop this."

"I am," said the first, in a German accent . "I am Moe Annenberg. In life I published the Daily Racing Form. If you want to bet on a winner, you still have time."

"I am," said the second, a wild-bearded Hungarian. "I'm Doctor Edward Teller, from Livermore. Wait until you see the lethality we shall deliver to this battlefield today. It'll be hell on earth . . . er, hell!"

Before Altos could respond, a third roly-poly fellow got up from his folding chair—a soul who looked remarkably like the devil Altos had left on the precipice, and this one stomped over to Altos and looked him in the eye.

"*I* am the commanding general here." The man pointed to his chest, glittering with ribbons bought in New Hell's pawn shops. "I'm in charge of all the others." On his shoulders, rusty stars gleamed. "What can I do for you, lady?"

Altos was shocked. His hair hung long, but he looked nothing, to his mind, like a woman—or even like a doomed soul. Of course he was wearing a long, flowing, white robe. "I'm an angel, not a woman or a man or the soul of either," he said.

"Of course you are, honey," said the general. "And I'm a famous book publisher." He gave his name, which Altos did not recognize, and continued: "But there's no room for women around here. Not yet." He leered suggestively. "When we've kicked the shit out of those low-tech grunts over there, there'll be plenty we men can do for you ladies. So go wait in my trailer, why don't you?"

The general summoned his aides with a snap of his fingers.

Altos looked at the two big, blank-faced souls who didn't know enough to be worried. Each had an earbud in his left ear and wore mirrored sunglasses.

The angel said, "Generals, sirs. I've come to warn you: do not engage this enemy. If you do, the result will resound throughout the underworlds. Satan has decreed that, if this battle takes place, all in hell will suffer more than they've ever suffered before."

"You don't know what you're talking about," said the commanding general.

"Please," said the angel, becoming desperate and rushing on as he realized the other generals were listening. "What is the reason that you fight your fellows? Why, in hell, must you war upon your brothers—on the New Dead, so many of them your countrymen?"

"Why?" echoed the commanding general, his face turning red. "Because it's got to be settled, that's why."

"What?" Altos demanded, "What has to be settled?"

"Whether the armies of Woo Woo Two can kick our butts for us, that's what. Whether the modern fighting man has any balls, that's what."

"Then why not go into battle yourself? To the front line, and call out the commanding officer of your so-called enemy, and decide this matter in single combat, or with the toss of a coin, or through some other means?" pleaded the angel.

"Decide something this important on the flip of a coin? I thought you were an angel. Isn't betting a sin? Anyway, honey, this is men's work. Women never understand war games. Now go away, sweetcakes, until I've got some stories to tell you."

"But there's no reason for this, not when you're risking hell's very stability!"

The commanding general's aides put huge hands on Altos' shoulders.

"There isn't? The reason is that we're defending what's right. First we have this li'l war game; then, with a standing army that's proved itself, we take on the Ivans, the Ragheads, the Chinks, the Hellamic State, the eco-terrorists and cyber-terrorists, the fundamentalists of every flavor. . ."

The general's eyes were gleaming. "It's the righteous way, ma'am. That's what we're protecting, our primacy. The perception of might *makes* right. We gotta win. We can't have it any other way."

"In *hell?*" asked the angel as the aides began forcing him away from the commanding general.

"I'm a hero, honey, wherever I am. Hell, schmell."

And it was hell, as soon as the big guns from the ships started booming, and the front-line troops surged into each other's lines.

When the shelling of the command post began, Altos was able to slip out of the trailer where the aides had taken him to wait, since his guards had run away.

The angel walked through the camp where the damned writhed on the ground, screaming, or clawed after blown-off limbs, or tried to hold their guts in their skins, and he wept. He could not even give comfort, not to these, not when they'd knowingly done this to themselves, and worse to others. Nor could the doctors. No ambulance screamed its woeful song. No medevacs came down from the sky in a buffet of helicopter blades. Not a single white-coated medic labored here among the dying: they were still in their red-crossed tents, waiting for the shelling to end.

Through the smoke from the fires and the muddy, bloody camp, wandered the angel, dazed and mourning. Nowhere did he hear a single soul call upon the Almighty, but only one another. And: "Doctor! Doctor!" so many cried. "Get me a medic!"

But no doctors nor medics or nurses would come.

Eventually, sick at the sight of eyes splattered upon cheeks and bones protruding from skin and portions of the damned crawling over the ground to nowhere, from nowhere, Altos took wing.

He flew over red-crossed tents flattened by explosions and burning, the few remaining doctors ministering to one another. He flew to the far side of the battle plain, hoping to find some mitigating factor among the rear echelon of the World War II contingent. But there was no difference in the quality of those souls or the fate they had bought for themselves.

So at last the angel flew back to the precipice, weeping as he soared above the pitched battle. Wherever his tears fell, bodies were healed, but there were too many maimed and not enough tears. Selfishly and unreasonably, for egotistical reasons of their own, these had inadvertently volunteered to be the proof that Satan needed to make hell an even worse place for souls to bide.

When Altos reached the outcropping of rock, the devil had changed from human form into his rufous-winged, formidable aspect and now sat crosslegged, poking at a computer tablet with one long, black claw. His cat/bat familiar was rubbing around his legs, drooling while it purred. Satan himself hummed as he tracked the carnage with its rising body count.

When Altos alighted beside him, the devil showed his fangs. "Welcome back, Angel. Good job, I'd say. Let's work together again some time."

Altos hadn't the strength to frame a retort. Hell would need him, its single un-fallen angel, very badly for a while. He sat down beside the devil, his immortal enemy, the Adversary who had tricked the angel into participating in—or at least not actively obstructing—the start of a war in hell such as none had ever seen.

Sorrowfully, he helped Satan number the fools dying on the plain below.

The battle didn't end until every weekend warrior, every armchair general, every doctor and nurse, every relief worker, and every pornographer of mayhem had gotten a taste of the real thing. By then there was nothing left moving on the plain but demons, come to clean up the mess.

In the Sea of Sighs, the tide was rising.

The Cure

Chris Morris

And that must end us, that must be our cure:
To be no more. Sad cure! For who would lose,
Though full of pain, this intellectual being,
Those thoughts that wander through eternity,
To perish, rather, swallowed up and lost
In the wide womb of uncreated night
Devoid of sense and motion?

—John Milton, *Paradise Lost*

"Reserved and destined to eternal woe, you say? You think. You crow. As for those of us who were chained in the fiery lake, you think the Deep was not better? You think the cold, the dark, respite from the godly light did not ease our burning flesh, Master Milton? You think those days of all four rivers pouring into a flaming lake shall not come again? Look you then. Look you now." Satan pointed at the dark unformed heavings of the Deep, whilst a torrent of black fire between them rose, whilst Pandemonium's ramparts rounded in on them, a lofty prison, listing inward, enclosing all until the fundament itself shivered and bucked and cowered, then settled askew: "From here, there is no escape but forward. Across the stones on foot for you. For me, the wailing winds will bear me, hot and cold and slapping hard, trying to bat me from the air and into hungry fires."

With a whoosh the Archfiend's wings appeared, rustling and bating.

"I think," said Milton, "that what's ahead for me, trying to cross a flaming cataract of woe, and what's for you, soaring over all, is the difference between damned soul and fallen angel." This creature of blazing talent groped for words, looking askance at Satan, downcast. "I wrote a dream of this day and called it *Paradise Lost*, mighty lord. 'Twas a dream of four infernal rivers disgorging into the burning lake their baleful streams: 'Abhorred Styx/ the flood of deadly hate,/ Sad Acheron of sorrow, black and deep;/ Cocytus, nam'd of lamentation loud/ Heard on the rueful stream; fierce Phlegethon/ Whose waves of torrent fire inflame with rage.' Now here they are. So was it a dream you sent me, or did you bring me here in sleep so long ago, infect my soul while yet I lived back then?"

Fear you a warning from on high, unheeded? An omen from Above? Yet and still you wonder, John Milton, my best and truest bard. "Once the beauty of our torment did enthrall you. Then you feared no end, but sang a song for me, arms out to embrace your vision coming true. So now it is nigh, why are you struck dumb?" The Archfiend scoffed. "Then? Now? Time rises all the same to me—what happened, happens; what was, is and ever will be. No difference unless you lie chained upon the rocks of that flaming lake and burn—then you crave some end to eternity and a hope of infernity. Only to you afflicted creatures of Almighty dalliance is there a difference between yesterday, today, and tomorrow. It's your comfort, this madness that creates amnesia for what will come. Else your puny minds and hearts would burst. Now do me this, if you prefer not to cross the flaming lake this day."

Milton shook his dark-haired head, so young at Satan's pleasure, comely for a mortal, full of longing and homage to the Deceiver's fate and world in all its awful glory. "What? I'll do whatever—"

"Yes, you will. So go you to Marlowe, who abides with Shakespeare. Give unto Christopher Marlowe your dumbstruck ear, your frozen heart, your emptiness profound. That fool has put himself between Shakespeare and me one time too many. When their writing together ends, their loving time together will stop as well."

Seething with jealousy, empowered by rage, Satan's aspect turned red as the flowing rocks of Phlegethon, which shone dark, not light, upon Milton and upon the ruler of all the latterday hells.

"But, great Satan, how can I? I am a lowly soul, wandering; no magic have I anywhere—"

"You know that all the netherworlds stagger under Erra's plagues of boils and phlegm and suffering. Know you more: know that I begin a purge of souls who find their afterlives too vexing. You will give Marlowe this eternal woe, take away what Marlowe loves the best, as easily as a plague is spread by kiss or handshake. Ask Marlowe this, the question of questions—what is the cure for damnation?—which when he hears it will truss his tongue and evacuate his wit, for in its answer lies the undoing of every soul who overcrowds creation."

The Archfiend drew a deep breath, hot with brimstone and magma's dark perfume, so that overhead the clouds veiling Paradise from Satan's sight bent down to hear his words. "Tell Marlowe you have learned the difference between oblivion, impossible in my domain, and obliteration, which a soul can claim be he brave enough: obliteration—complete and sweet: Not only 'not to be,' but to be expunged as if he'd never been at all. That will make an end to his playwriting and poetry, and an end to his affair with Shakespeare."

Milton, Satan's certain messenger, saw the clouds between worlds part once and then again, and gasped. "Say *that*? I wish I'd never heard it."

Yes, there is a way out of hell, John Milton, a way which none will freely take—obliteration: the sure undoing of everything that makes a soul worth keeping. "But you know it's true, Milton. You knew in life what awaits a blemished soul. You wrote it. Now, unless you can define the meaning of 'rowling' from thine own works, go you now and tell some truth to Marlowe, and see how truth undoes the boldest soul."

"'Our cure, to be no more; sad cure!'" whispered Milton, Satan's best, feared by every soul in hell who had a mind left to protect. "I wrote it, but writing is not believing."

"Is it not?" With a flap of wings, Satan cast off his demonic visage and rose, white-winged and glorious to behold, high above.

"Believe this." And from those heights, a finger described the shape of Milton, and lifted him up and away from the edge of the Deep, to where the ordinary damned of the newer hells should dwell.

These words carried *the* cure Satan had striven so long to bring to bear. The delusional, corrupted damned of hell were manifold, far too numerous for Satan or any other lord of hell to discipline, soul by soul. From Above, those on high sent their worst, their dross, their deeply flawed and unrepentant, to the netherworlds for discipline. As if discipline could keep a predator from prey or a murderer from his sport.

Thus here they did what they'd done in life, but did it more, and did it worse, and did it longer. Did it until the powers Above mixed in, sending heaven's auditors, sent Erra, god of pestilence and mayhem and his Sibitti, seven personified weapons, to adjudge hell insufficiently hellish and force the doomed and damned to repent.

The problem with the Almighty, as it always had been, was that the First Cause could not be wrong, nor admit an error, nor correct a flaw.

Satan had waged war against the sanctimony on high—and lost.

And ended here, in the fires, in the cold, in the Deep, in the dark with his loyalists, who served him still. Of all the flaws in hell that were not flaws, part and parcel was this one soul, John Milton, who had seen what humanity should never see: the abyss, Satan's lordly seat.

And since great revenges take long to foment, sending Milton to poison Marlowe, using words more sure than hellebore or hemlock, would serve as an amusement and make Shakespeare surrender. More pleasurable than battle or oppression was this prospect.

Meanwhile, the cure would slowly become known; it would swallow souls whole; it would rot reason; it would eat like acid into the hopes of the damned; it would be the cause of riots and looting and warfare, of weeping and every sort of lamentation and misery, for these doomed souls would finally know the way out of hell, but not one would dare take it: to be expunged, erased, unmade.

Under the cover of Erra and his plagues, the Son of the Morning was instigating wars of class and color, of witchery and calumny. Thus obliteration grew closer day by hellish day.

Over the flaming lake fed by Phlegethon, its fire casting darkness, not light, Satan now flew, and over his own ramparts, where Pandemonium stabbed heaven's underbelly. He flew a path that circumscribed his domain, wrathful and dolorous, and harkened to the moaning choirs of the damned.

When he reached Pandemonium's adamantine heights, Samael, angel of death, and six stalwarts who'd battled beside Satan against a demented heavenly host all caught up to him, soaring and hovering above, below, on his left, on his right.

They flew as they'd flown when first cast down, into the dark and the Deep, as they'd flown for millennia while denied a place to land.

And when at last they did alight in majesty on Satan's ramparts, the dark lord and his cadre resumed their own special torment—waiting. For until no damned soul remained must they tarry here, caretakers of the Almighty's detritus.

For eons had pious cruelty bound them round. They had fought for a better heaven, so they thought, and lost—lost the glorious, the light—inheriting in its stead this abyss where they must bide until the last damned soul was no more.

Now anticipation awoke in the devil and his angels, for he had apportioned words of perfect measure to the damned soul Milton, words of purest inspiration—Satan's sovereign formulation, a vaccine against hope, which itself would spread like a plague of obliteration throughout the underverse: words to expunge the damned, unmake heaven's mistake, the cause of Satan's own transgression.

Wherefore those words might yield a cure for even the plight of fallen angels. More than purge and punishment and penance, more than wars and calamity, this cure whispered of an end to angelic sorrow and woe that mankind could not know.

With words the key and obliteration the cure, the lords of the latterday hells might themselves go free.

*

Far off course, the slow and silent stream called Lethe rolled through New Hell City this day, while the fundament did shake. Buildings quaked and toppled and leaned askew, while those who drank her waters of forgetfulness climbed over one another, their fear of a plague from heaven forgotten with all else: with misery and grief, remorse and pain. Then those who never drank a drop rioted and fell to looting, jealous of the oblivious. They beat those who had drunk, wiped their smiles away, cut off their smirking heads and stuck them on pikes all over New Hell to remind the populace that in this city tribulation and malfeasance still ruled. Those burdened with hateful memories roamed in gangs, screaming, "Purge! Cleanse our streets! Plague-bearers! Rid New Hell of these wretches!"

Then Lethe recalled herself, her graceful course that led her back to Elysion, and poured away home, leaving New Hell convulsing in her wake, its streets wet and wild with water and bile.

Here Milton picked his way across muddy streets where the desperate licked damp pavings for a taste of Lethe's oblivion, and the jealous destroyed all comers for imputed guilt or apostasy, until he reached New Hell's Old Rogue Theatre.

There he paused and read a placard advertising *The Witch and the Tyrant* by William Shakespeare and Christopher Marlowe, and a notice askew across it: *'Matinee Performance Canceled Due to Plague.'*

In this Elizabethan neighborhood the rank stench of necrotic flesh stopped his nose and caused his eyes to tear; most souls he saw wore white paper masks hooked round their ears. A charnel house smoked nearby, choked with rotting cadavers piled before it, tags on the toes of those who still had toes.

One yawning crevasse in the street contained so many bodies that Milton was tempted to walk across them. He didn't; he went around, picking up his black robe's skirts and giving the newly dead a wide berth. Soon enough, at the pleasure of the Undertaker, these husks would be returned to life. Milton studiously avoided making enemies in hell, where grudges festered perpetually.

Nevertheless, this Sadderday he must and would make an enemy or two, or slight his unholy patron, His Infernal Majesty.

With matinees canceled, if Marlowe and Shakespeare were not rehearsing today, they'd be working behind the Old Rogue playhouse, here at the heart of New Hell's Londonopolis district between the Third Globe and the Rose of Thorns theatres.

Once he'd pounded thrice on the stage door of the Old Rogue and no one came, misgivings filled him: Were the two playwrights dead? Ill? Plague infected? Hiding? Had word of Milton's mission somehow spread? Or were Shakespeare and Marlowe simply . . . elsewhere?

But Satan had delivered Milton here, to the theatre district where thespians were legion, not to Tartaros or Arali or Dis. . . .

The stage door had a peephole. It flicked open, then shut. The big door creaked, pulled inward far enough that Milton saw Will Shakespeare in a claret doublet open over a stained white kirtle, strapping a bodkin on his hip. In life, Shakespeare had died when Milton was but eight years old, yet they looked of an age this day.

"Good even to you, Master Shakespeare. 'But wherefore thou alone? Wherefore with thee came not all hell broke
loose?'" said Milton, quoting *Paradise Lost* in his opening
salvo. Shakespeare and Marlowe loved their quote game;
to give back in kind, Milton came well armed: Shakespeare
knew that Milton was asking the whereabouts of Kit Marlowe.

"Hail, prince of poets. How dost thou, sweet lord?
Kit's here, but we're not rehearsing, just writing a bit of this
and that," said Shakespeare, eyes narrowing. "So we have
naught to offer, if you've come about a role. If you've come
about some civil disobedience, we're innocent." His goatee
turned up with his grin. "Come in, would you?" And, turning: "Come you out of hiding, Kit. Here stands John Milton, blackest humorist of us all. Let's write some comedy….
Laughter does any soul some good."

*Innocent? Never. Laughter, when evil rides astride me,
straight to your door? You both know me, what I wrote,
whom I serve.* "Come in? Yes, I will," Milton agreed, before
the bard could change his mind.

Shakespeare bowed with a flourish and stepped back,
closing the door and barring it. "What brings you out amid
plague and pestilence?"

Within, great disarray met Milton's eyes: boxes and
cloth and props and dust—and now Marlowe, throwing on a
shirt, then pulling up his hose: nearly naked at this late hour.
And how to respond? "I'm come for a word or two with Kit
that he'll be better for hearing." *Truth, the telling weapon in
any battle.*

Pulling on boots, Kit Marlowe said, "A word or two is what we need, great Milton. Finish this with us, John: we've been working at it all the day long." Suspicious, quiet Marlowe—brilliant ruffian and rakehell, a spy who'd been killed in a brawl with another agent of the Crown, the murder weapon a bodkin like the dagger Shakespeare wore—began to sing in a voice so sweet that Milton blinked:

"He that has a little tiny soul,/ With hey, ho, the wind and the rain,/ Must serve in hell till time's last bell,/ For the rain it raineth every day. . . . Now we need one more couplet . . . What say you?"

So Milton thought, both their eyes on him, then sang tunelessly: "And when I first awaked in hell/ With hey, ho, the wind and the rain,/ I found my soul's last place to dwell/ And the rain it raineth every day."

Shakespeare looked at Marlowe, who shrugged. "Not bad. But I'd hoped for better—with your vaunted reputation, good my lord."

Will said, "That's not why you're here, John—to help write ditties."

"No, but my words are for Kit: politics and subterfuge and risky business—all of which you abhor, do you not, bard of Avon?"

"I do. I'll find us some food upstairs. 'Twill take but a blink, and we'll feast."

"Aye," agreed Milton, relieved. "You two still have food without maggots, and drink without urine, since you're rehearsing plays for the Archfiend; 'tis well known. And I'm famished." *Go carefully, now. The deed is nearly done.*

As soon as Shakespeare's green-hosed legs disappeared up the stairs, Marlowe's face changed from youthfully handsome to deadly dire: "How now? Felicitations to your devilish master. What scheme is this? I'm far past 'the devil will come and Faustus will be damned.' Yet and still I stand by this: 'you must be proud, bold, pleasant, resolute,/ And now and then stab, when occasion serves.' What occasion have you to seek my counsel?"

That quote spoke by Marlowe, from his own *Edward II*, startled Milton. But he recalled his visit of late with the Archfiend, the blazing lake, and the stones throughout with their chains. Thus he said, "Occasion? Not occasion, but your nature: You might be the very model from my poor *Paradise Lost*, which came after your time, so in truth you may not know it: 'th' unconquerable will,/ And study of revenge, immortal hate,/ And courage never to submit or yield/ And what is else not to be overcome?'"

"Outside's a plague, if you haven't noticed. Not something bravery can fight, nor fools attack, nor poets glorify. Quick, now. Speak, before Will comes down those stairs, if what news you bear has import."

Milton sighed, the field prepared, the animal brought to the sacrificial stone, festooned with flowers and ribbons. "I saw the Prince of Darkness, eye to eye. And he was as I once imagined: lost happiness and lasting pain torments him."

"That's no news. So you saw the devil on the wing? We see him far too much round here, and crave to see him less," came Marlowe's famed bravado.

"But listen and learn. His Infernal Majesty told me the true truth: a way out of hell does exist. A cure for damnation far more sweeping than this capricious plague or that cruel torment, both circumscribed. So I thought to bring the news to you, since you'll use it well and tell it widely. . . ." He stopped, assessing his intended victim, and met eyes that glittered.

Kit Marlowe said, "A way out? At what cost? Many would give a goodly portion for such news."

"No cost, but the knowing of it. Hear me now?"

"Now." Marlowe crossed arms over chest.

"Hear this then, for it changes everything for a soul damned as you or damned as me: Obliteration is the one and only cure for all the damned. Satan told me once before, long ago, and I wrote it down but scarce believed. Now I do: 'And that must end us, that must be our cure: To be no more. Sad cure!'"

Kit Marlowe took a deep breath. His jaw worked. "That's true, then? Lose all? The devil said this, not you?"

Milton nodded and took his chance, strode to Marlowe, who hadn't moved, embraced him, then whispered: "All. But from mine own verse, here's the rub: 'For who would lose,/ Though full of pain, this intellectual being,/ Those thoughts that wander through eternity,/ To perish, rather, swallowed up and lost/ In the wide womb of uncreated night/ Devoid of sense and motion?'"

Marlowe shrugged him off, took one step back; his handsome face drained pale. "A cure sad indeed, to suck all hope from whomsoever's lived and wakened here. If this be a joke, treacherous friend, I'll gut you like a rabbit, pull the hide off you from neck to toes."

"If 'twere a joke, would I not have told the bard as well, and let him share its humor? There's the cure. I told you true. Do you as you like, who once said that hell was 'just a frame of mind.'"

"The devil never forgives. Wait now, Will comes . . . I know that tread."

Milton reached out, took Marlowe by the hand, and the deed was done. "Kit, tell none or tell the world, your choice."

In that touch of hands, Milton thought he felt a spark ignite. Yet no maw then opened in infernity to drag Marlowe down; no demons came to carry him away; no disintegration turned his flesh to dust; the air itself did not smother and unmake him—*nothing* happened that Milton could discern.

Marlowe pulled his hand away, peered at it, then raked Milton with that penetrating stare and shook his head. Meanwhile, down the stairs clattered Will Shakespeare in a flurry, carrying bread and wine and toothsome treats that graced their table by the Archfiend's largess.

Shakespeare looked from Milton to Marlowe and back. "You two, what's this? Raised hackles? Bristled fur? What befell whilst I gathered our dinner? Tell all; while we sup and together pen some crafty lines. . . ."

Marlowe neither spoke nor moved but kept watch on Milton, who'd never seen such violence in a look.

"You, Kit," prompted Shakespeare, his joviality forced, "you're as pale as any ghost in 'ell. What's wrong? Surely the devil didn't appoint Milton as Master of the Revels? No less should cause that face I love to fall so far."

Love. So that was what the Adversary wanted here: to get between lover and beloved—win one from the other and take all. Silence boxed their ears and stretched as if to snap the world apart.

"Will, entertain our lord Milton. I have no appetite," said Marlowe, retreating toward the stairwell.

"How now, Kit? John Milton, prince of poets, is our esteemed guest, who'll turn his talent toward our goal once we've supped. We have a scene to write, all three of us," insisted Shakespeare.

"Not me, Will. I have no hunger, nor the zeal tonight for smithing words. By your leave, gentlemen, I take mine." And up the staircase clambered Marlowe until he disappeared out of sight.

So something *had* happened, when he'd spoke those words to Marlowe and flesh met flesh as demanded by the Prince of Darkness.

But what?

*

"He's gone, Kit."

"Is he?"

"Long gone; you've slept Paradise to rest and back again. What ails thee, that thou cannot write a lick with him and me?"

"Milton. His soul's embalmed, his heart too black." Marlowe swung his legs over the bedstead and sat up, wearing only his kirtle. "What did he tell you?"

"Beelzebub's fool? Nothing. What did he tell you, Kit?"

"Naught worth a memory."

"No scheme afoot betwixt you two? No bloody gambits 'midst a hundred hellish battlefields? No assassination or assignation planned? Then why this loathsome brooding? Are you ill? You neither eat nor drink. Bestir yourself, unless you're poisoned."

"No scheme, no murder. No poison, but what's native to my soul. Today I rewrite Faustus, lest I become him: 'Then swords and knives,/ Poison, guns, halters, and envenomed steel/ Are laid before me to dispatch myself/ Had not sweet pleasure conquered deep despair.'" *With a quote make light of this, these words, this cement around my mind.* "That stays the same, but this next I herewith emend to read: 'Have not I made great Shakespeare sing to me/ Of Juliet's love and Romeo's death?'"

"Kit, what's this? I think that pizzle Milton did poison you some way, or make you mad."

"No poison. No madness." *Coldest comfort: obliteration.* "Worse."

"What's worse?"

"Truth. Truth about myself. I've said all that can be said, done all that can be done—and what's come of it? Misery and calumny and death after death, all fault my own. Forgive me, Will, lest I brand myself coward, for I cannot face this damnation all alone—without joy, without words to thrill a heart—without you."

"Christopher Marlowe, I forgive you—for all your sins I know and those I don't. If you're not dying, get you up from that bed. I must work; to be with me, so must you. Work conquers all, puts calluses over outrage. Whatever

Milton wanted, he'll not get from us. Nor do us harm. This I promise and will make good: his devilish master does owe me favors."

With that, Shakespeare turned away, then stomped out and down the stairs, grumbling.

Alone once more, Marlowe rose and found his muscles sore and lax; dizziness overswept him and raced away. For a moment he dearly wished to follow, find obliteration, take the cure. "Never again do I deserve to touch another soul by word or deed," he told the empty room. "Not yours, Will, so freely given, since I've ravaged more hearts than my guilt can hold. But work I can, and must. For Will's truth is greater than deviltry's conjurations: I can conquer what's within me, and damn what waits without."

Easier said than done, now that Satan's battle horn resounds in his head and hell hounds scent his soul. But he had Will, a good nurse for any riven heart, to think of, and husband, and protect.

Grim

Andrew P Weston

I skulked back into the shadows and settled in for a long wait.

Not that I minded. It was rare, exceedingly rare, to get a *Topside* assignment, so the longer it took, the better. The pass inside my pocket burned like hot coals, and its heat was keeping me all warm and toasty. Just as well. It was past midnight, and the drizzle fell in billowing swathes, glazing everything in a fine sheen of moisture. The road was deserted, and the streetlights cast a somber pall over their own tiny bit of sidewalk. I had the place all to myself. Almost.

Behind me, the railway arches looped off into the distance like a giant Slinky made of greasy bricks, mortar, and lurking danger. The occasional coughing fit and bouts of drunken cursing echoing out of the darkness reminded me to be careful. It wouldn't do for one of the homeless sheltering under the spans to see me about my work. Well, not for them, anyway. Not that anyone would care. What's another dead hobo in the great scheme of things?

I didn't like to take a life off contract, but sometimes circumstances forced my hand. No witnesses. No trace. No links back to the Boss. That's exactly how he liked things, and so far I had a one hundred percent record.

A beat-up Ford rumbled its way toward me, its dingy lights and wipers working overtime. At this distance, the interior was a diamond encrusted mirror of deep mystery.

Pulling my hood forward a little, I dropped my gaze and ignored it until it passed. Stepping out at the last second, I caught my reflection in the windows and grinned. I certainly looked the part in my black trench coat and cowl. Likewise with the boots, gloves, and sunglasses. Dark as a grave, I reeked of potency and violence. Good thing I wasn't going to be here long. Discreet as I am, it wouldn't take the hookers and other undesirables working the area long to figure out what I was here for.

Beware! Contract killer.

The truck kept going, so I faded back into the gloom like a specter and resumed my vigil. Adjusting my weapon to keep it concealed beneath my coat, I marveled at its balance and beauty. I like working up close and personal, and this blade had served me well over the years. Ever sharp, it cuts through anything and is the trademark of my particular calling.

Tonight, someone else will feel the fire of its bite.

I shivered. The freshness of the rain made it appear as if a clean, tangy vibrancy was making a valiant attempt to wash the filth from the air. But the undercurrent of death and corruption lingered. I took a deep breath, reveling in that echo. It reminded me of my true nature. Content, I leaned into the slick stonework, and contemplated the work ahead of me.

Not long now.

I peered up at the attic window on the opposite side of the street. It was the only apartment with its light still on, and the occupant was blissfully unaware I was here to collect.

That's the thing about walking on the wrong side of the line for too long. Even for a denizen of hell. One day, you'll push things too far. Be privy to knowledge that subsequently becomes a loose end to be tied off. Piss off the wrong person or entity. Or you could just be in the wrong place at the wrong time. News of your misdemeanors will filter back, especially if those backstabbing Sibitti enforcers have anything to do with it, and the Boss will order your reassignment . . . or worse.

I snorted.

Why do some people seem to think they're exempt from having to settle up?

Tonight's target was a prime example. In life, Dr. Thomas Neill Cream possessed all the qualities we looked for in a model citizen. A backstreet abortionist among the dregs of society, he had a penchant for poisoning his victims and prolonging the misery of their slow and painful deaths. Self-centered, arrogant, and totally unrepentant, he was a perfect candidate for hell. Following his death by hanging in 1892, we welcomed him with open arms and thought he'd fit in nicely. Even the Boss seemed unusually pleased, as Cream's skill with potions and contagions was something he hoped to exploit.

But illusions of grandeur gradually sowed the seeds of discontent. Once Cream realized his reputation paled against the likes of Hitler, Vlad Tepes, and Genghis Khan, he became more and more determined to do something about it. But how to boost his standing with more human deaths? Those consigned to hell *stay* in hell.

Or they're supposed to.

To help pass the time, I retrieved Cream's rap-sheet and scanned its contents.

Sneaky bugger! Instead of using his talents in His Satanic Majesty's service, he deliberately chose to work against him. On the pretense of having discovered a more potent strain of Victor's Vaccine, he got the Boss and Victor together, hazed their sensibilities, and did a number on them.

I shook my head in disbelief.

How in Cursed Hell's name did he learn about the Pass of Passes? Or know where to look? The Get Out Of Hell Free card is supposed to be a myth. A carrot to test the unfaithful.

Once I collected, I'd have the Inquisitors do a number on him. Find out who the leak was. After all, we couldn't have the rabble thinking an escape clause actually existed.

Reading further, my eyes bulged in astonishment.

The Boss wanted the vaccine to serve as a purging laxative to clear the bowels of hell of all the dross we'd accumulated over the centuries. But if Cream got his way, and used it as a rave drug, it would not only be capable of killing thousands, but would completely undo all of the Master's plans.

We're trying to empty the damned place. Not fill it up again!

He was a fool if he didn't realize that messing with Victor Frankenstein in this matter was the same as messing with His Infernal Majesty.

I glanced up at the studio.

Well, you'll soon see the truth. I'm getting sick and tired of having to clean up other people's messes. I spat in disgust. *Damned Erra and his plagues! Why hasn't the Boss ever let me have* his *contract? Him* and *his bloody auditors? It would end debacles like this once and for all.*

Suddenly, I realized I wasn't alone. A young couple, high on chemicals and hormones, exited an alley near the apartment block. Goths from the look of them, and dressed to the nines in photonegative chic. Even with mundane sight I couldn't miss them. Dripping with metal, they chimed and rattled with every step, and had obviously decided to end their festivities early. From the way they gnawed each other's faces and necks, they were oblivious to my presence as well as the rain, and were clearly intent on taking their personal party home.

Nice one, kids. A part of me—just a tiny part—responded to their lust. *Enjoy yourselves while you can. You never know when death will come calling.*

Passing close by, they spotted me at the last moment. You'd have thought there'd be some form of camaraderie with the way I was dressed. But oh no! Recoiling as if my mere proximity would guarantee their demise, they quickly crossed the road, all thoughts of passion forgotten. Glancing repeatedly back to see if I was following, they didn't regain a measure of their former exuberance until they were almost to the end of the street.

I didn't take it personally, and let them go. I have that affect on others, which is why I live a life of self-inflicted solitude and cold-hearted service. Whenever I get lonely, I pay Strawberry Fields a visit. She's always accommodating, and so far she's the only one who seems to appreciate my *distinctive* tastes.

The shower became much heavier. Drumming a relentless staccato across the asphalt and parked cars, it seemed every drop was desperate to tell me its story. I found the beat hypnotic, one that would easily soothe me to sleep if it went on for too long.

Fortunately, the light flicked out in the window opposite.

At last.

As if on cue, a mystery sedan materialized from out of nowhere. Purring sedately, it glided to a halt right outside the apartment block. The engine was so quiet I could barely hear it above the tympanic greeting of the downpour.

I heard a brief hum as an electric window edged down.

Moments later, both front doors opened. Two hoods adorned in tan cashmere overcoats emerged from the climate-controlled interior. Their stony expressions creased slightly under the assault of the weather. From the way they ducked their heads and muttered, you'd think they were being stung by hornets. Their not-so-tough-guy reaction to a bit of water didn't earn any sympathy from me.

The driver carried a long black umbrella. But it wasn't for him. Shaking it loose, he quickly walked to the other side of the car. Opening the rear door, he held the umbrella high and waited for the main attraction to emerge. When she did, I could appreciate why she wouldn't want to get drenched.

A goddess uncurled herself from the seat. Even from the shadows, I could see the luster of her raven-blue hair. It cascaded down her back, a shimmering satin waterfall of purest silk. Like me, she was dressed from head to toe in black, only *her* ensemble was embellished by bright red nails and full scarlet lips. She had green eyes, like a cat. Piercing and predatory.

Tucking a clasp bag under her arm, she nodded her consent, and the entourage began to move slowly toward the main door. As they approached the lobby, her escorts scanned the street for any signs of unwanted scrutiny. Their hands hovered within the opening of their jackets, telltale bulges signifying what they carried there. The woman's heels clicked sharply. Echoing down the street like a metronome, each measured step was designed to navigate her safely across the slickness of the sidewalk.

She was beautiful, but like me, she was deadly. A black widow of unholy appetites. Within moments, the spider had ushered her lackeys into the building where I had no doubt she'd begin weaving her web.

That must be Cream's contact. I'd better follow them up.

Moving swiftly, I entered the hushed interior. The absence of both wind and rain was deafening, and it took me a moment to register the rhythmic *ting-ting* of the elevator as it coasted toward the top floor. Wet footprints trailed across highly polished tiles, and the black and white color scheme made it appear a fatal game of chess was underway.

It was. A pair of legs protruded from behind the reception desk. Glancing over the top of the counter, I saw the night porter had worked his last shift. His vacant eyes stared blindly toward the ceiling. His face was relaxed, all his worries now redundant. The small hole in the center of his forehead spoke volumes. As did the halo of ruby finality pooling beneath him. Poignantly, the small lamp to one side of his desk stuttered for a moment before giving up the ghost.

In the darkness, I sighed. "One more innocent lost. Yet another debt to add to the list."

The lingering scent of sweet perfume reminded me of the urgency of my assignment. I noticed the indicator arrow had reached the number six. A final *ting* announced the car had arrived at its destination. Using the emergency stairs, I flowed upward like the wind and prepared to act. Death is the only certainty in life, and I had to ensure the right people met that destiny tonight.

I arrived at the top floor just as the finale was about to begin.

The woman didn't want to attract too much attention now that she was inside the building. As I exited the stairwell, I noted she avoided touching the buzzer, and instead used the tips of her crimson nails. They rapped against the door like a woodpecker on steroids. Her voice was soft and deep. Like bourbon, it poured from her in liquid waves, both intoxicating and inviting.

"C'mon, Cream," she crooned. "You know the risks involved in an arrangement like this. Especially for me. If what you've said is true, we don't have much time before someone comes calling. One way or another, the exchange has to go down tonight or the offer will be off the table."

What's he been saying? Has this idiot opened his mouth and put others in jeopardy?

The bulbs lining the hallway started to fizzle and dim as my anger flared. Using the shadows, I glided forward unseen.

"Cream?" she moaned huskily. "Be a good boy. We don't want this getting more hazardous than it already is."

A muffled reply from within the apartment made her smile. There was no warmth in that gesture. She lifted her purse and casually unclipped the clasp. Her thugs removed their pistols from within their jackets. Each weapon had a silencer fitted. Both men were wary and glanced repeatedly up and down the corridor. I couldn't help but wonder which one of them had murdered the attendant down in the foyer.

My anger peaked, and the lights went out.

I heard a chain rapping against wood, then a latch being drawn back. An expectant hush descended, adding emphasis to that final *click*. The door began to edge open and a sliver of light intruded into the hallway. As the crack widened, I drew my own weapon and glided forward like a wraith.

A timid voice, quaking with fright, whispered, "Please . . . please don't go. I'm . . . I'm so sorry I kept you waiting. There's so much riding on this. Just give me a chance to show you how good this deal will be for the both of us."

Cream appeared, clutching a vial of phosphorous liquid in his hand, his face a desperate mixture of hope and fear. I could see he'd realized the enormity of his actions. His hand shook so badly the glass was in danger of breaking.

Good. I should be able to contain this mess quite nicely.

Sweeping my coat to one side, I freed my weapon and closed the distance.

The black widow removed her hand from her purse. So smooth, so natural was the movement that Cream didn't realize she was holding a gun until he caught his breath in pained surprise.

Phutt!

He glanced down in wide-eyed bewilderment at the stain spreading across his shirt. His head snapped up, and the accusation in his voice was pitiful to hear.

"But you said . . ."

Phutt!

He jumped again as she unloaded another one into him. This time between the eyes.

Like a statue, she remained still, the epitome of stark serenity. Smoke curled in lazy ribbons from the end of her silencer, and Cream folded to the floor. As he hit the stained carpeting, she sighed and reveled in obvious pleasure. For a trice, the ice chips of her gaze flashed with satisfaction. And then the moment passed. Quickly, she stooped to retrieve her prize and commenced to pat her victim down.

Part of me acknowledged her professionalism.

The assassin has completed her task. Oh, she loves her work, does this one.

Fortunately, so did I.

The lights snapped back on as I reached them. My blade flashed twice, left and right. The bodyguards fell, unaware I was even there. And at last, I stood before her.

She didn't move a muscle. Those cold eyes latched onto me and her gaze roved across my body, taking in my height, my stature, my clothing. All of it. It wasn't until her scrutiny fell upon the weapon held tightly in my hand that she responded.

Keeping her gun trained on me, she slunk closer and raised a manicured eyebrow in disbelief. "Seriously?" she purred, waving directions toward me at the same time with the muzzle.

For now, I obeyed her instructions. Gradually, I crouched down and laid my blade on the floor between us. Then I stepped back. Casually, I began to pull off my gloves by the fingertips, one by one.

Sliding forward, the black widow murmured, "What's wrong, baby? Lost your tongue?"

"Not really. It's just that I don't normally speak unless I've got something meaningful to say." Moving my hand slowly, I peeled back one side of my trench coat to reveal the inside pocket. An official-looking document, sealed in blood-red wax, peeked out. Despite her best efforts, I could see she was intrigued.

"Do you mind?" I whispered gently.

Using my other hand to reach for it with infinite care, I used just the tip of my finger and thumb to remove the deed. Extending it toward her, I added, "Here, this is for you."

She glanced at the title of the recipient written in glowing manuscript across the outer page. When she saw Cream's name, her eyes widened in shock. "How do you know him?" she snarled, a steely edge ruining the velvet texture of her voice. The hardness in her eyes never changed. Nor did she make any move to accept the certificate from me.

"It's my business to know the name of every person I'm sent to collect from. Including those who learn too much about . . . otherworldly dealings that don't concern them."

The tiniest dilation of her pupils indicated I had guessed right.

Without warning, the air shimmered. The impression of the name of a doomed soul became emblazoned across the outer veneer of my mind. Aloud, I continued, "Josephine Abigail Reed. You have trespassed into affairs no human has the right to know. I am authorized by His Satanic Majesty to carry out your execution. Sentence is—"

Phutt!

I wasn't surprised she shot me. To tell the truth, I'd expected her to do it sooner. Fixing her with the coldest stare I could muster, I shook my head and resumed my Hellegal Declaration. "—Sentence is to be carried out immediately. Are there any last words you'd like to say?"

Phutt!

The look she flashed toward me was incredulous. The fire returned and an ugly leer lifted the corner of her sensual lips. "So you're wearing a bulletproof vest. Is that supposed to impress me? Scare me? Is that why you're carrying a scythe? Are you honestly trying to personify the grim reaper?"

Phutt! Phutt!

My head rocked as the slugs impacted my skull, and I was forced to take a step back to regain my balance. When I peered forward again, I gazed directly into the void that was Josephine's soul. They say the eyes are a window into that most personal of places. Hers were like bottomless pits, but I saw the truth was finally registering.

"No!" I replied, stepping toward her so suddenly she had no time to react. "I *am* the grim reaper."

I slapped the gun from her grasp. It clattered noisily to the floor and bounced into the door belonging to Cream's neighbor. Within moments, I could hear faint complaints issuing from within, the occupant obviously disturbed by the ruckus.

No witnesses.

Fear now radiated from her in waves. My maneuver had caused a strand of immaculately fashioned hair to fall out of place. Smiling sadly, I tenderly reached out. Using the back of one of my bare fingers to brush it back into position, I whispered, "But I think you already knew that."

As I touched her, Josephine inhaled sharply and gasped. Stiffening for a second, her body went slack and she started to fall. Catching her, I enfolded her in my arms as if we were lovers bidding each other goodbye. Solemnly, I laid Josephine to rest on the floor, and her hair settled to form a nimbus of midnight blue around her perfect porcelain features.

This one's a surefire candidate for Slab A, or my name's not Daemon Grim.

I glanced up.

Without the need for further pretence, Dr. Thomas Cream, fugitive from hell, lifted his head and stared in wide-eyed horror toward me.

"No!" he gasped, panic stricken. "Please don't send me back for reassignment. Not yet. I've got—"

"You've got no say in this whatsoever," I hissed. Retrieving my scythe, I brandished it to good effect. "Not after what you've done. Did you seriously think you'd get away with this charade?"

Cream's neck pivoted rapidly from side to side in his desperate search for the nearest accessible exit. As he was unable to die or heal on this plane, his head wound sprayed fresh blood across the carpet.

I stepped closer and lowered the blade toward him. "Oh, you're not going anywhere, sunshine. Anywhere but *back down* that is."

"I, I just wanted—"

"Save it," I snarled. Bending to one knee, I recovered the vial from Josephine's purse. "I've heard every excuse under the sun, and I'm not interested." Holding the container out toward him, I snapped, "Is this it or have you got more stashed away?"

"No, no. That's it," he whined, scrambling backward across the floor. "It's extremely concentrated and that's all I had time to make. There's enough there for at least two thousand people."

I could see he was too petrified to lie. Pocketing the evidence, I closed on him and crouched down. Taking out his Writ of Banishment, I casually tossed it into his lap. "I'm not going to waste time with you, Cream. But before you go, the Boss asked me to ensure I retrieved his *Executive Card*, if you know what I mean."

Raising one eyebrow in expectation, I stared into Cream's eyes without blinking. His neck and cheeks immediately colored and he couldn't prevent a quick peek toward his right side. Automatically, his fingers started to worm their way into his pocket. Opening my senses fully, I confirmed the presence of my Master's most precious and mysterious enigma.

Thank Purgatory for that!

The heat it radiated through Cream's trousers was simply delicious.

I placed my hand on his arm to restrain him, and growled, "No need to take it out. Just keep the evidence on you where the Inquisitors will find it. It'll make their day."

Standing over him once more, I concluded, "How foolish. You *do* realize the suffering you've condemned yourself to by working against His Satanic Majesty like this?" I couldn't help but chuckle. "They'll hear your screams of anguish throughout the length and breadth of all realms of hell for centuries to come. Who knows? Perhaps he'll let Victor practice on certain bits of you before he sends you back to the Undertaker."

Cream's countenance fell and the remaining blood drained from his face.

Grinning cruelly, I chose that moment to stab down with the point of my weapon, and impaled the elusive card to his thigh.

He squeaked in pain, but a cautionary finger to my lips prevented any further protestations. He knew they'd serve no purpose.

Directing my strength along the shaft, I used the energy contained within the arcane pass to open a portal. An express elevator to hell—going down. Within an instant, Cream's limbs crisped and blackened. Then he began to twitch. Seconds later, his skin cracked open, revealing bright veins of lurid pulsing flame, like congealed magma. Abruptly, his entire body flared before disappearing amid a cloud of acrid sulfurous smoke. Transfixed, I watched as swirling flecks of glowing ash were sucked inward by the vortex created by his passing. The delightful odor of putrefaction and decay filled my nostrils.

I sighed deeply.

My reverie was disturbed by the sound of security bolts snapping back along the hall.

The neighbor!

In the blink of an eye, I was gone.

Outside on the street, I heard an elderly woman's cry of alarm, followed by piercing screams that split the night.

Poor old thing. I hope she doesn't have a coronary opening her door to all that death.

Pausing for a moment, I took the time to heal my wounds before securing my scythe within the folds of my trench coat. It wouldn't do for me to attract unnecessary attention now, especially with my payout so close.

I gave myself a once over in the reflection of a car window. Satisfied, I strolled off into the night. Soon, I was swallowed by the dark, and the only sign of my existence on this plane were the streetlamps that flickered off, one by one, in the distance.

The Right Man for the Job

Deborah Koren

New Bodie's streets rang with music, none of it melodious, tuneful, or in any way pleasing to the ear. That didn't prevent the damned from striking up a tune on guitars, fiddles, harmonicas; creating bands and orchestras; or simply opening their mouths and belting out a refrain. Bat Masterson, old West lawman, could not fault their eternal enthusiasm. Mankind, even in hell, needed music.

Like the blond fellow plunking away on the yellowed keys of the piano inside the adobe-walled cantina. Bat watched him from the doorway. There was skill in the player's hands, in the way his fingers neatly curled, in the way his hands rose off the keys so gracefully. But each key sounded a note that had nothing to do with its position on the piano, and the effect was a dissonant jangle. Rhythm alone told Bat the piece was probably a waltz, but that was as far as his guess extended. The player seemed oblivious to the discord, his hands moving precisely, lovingly. Bat wondered how the man could even stand to play when the result so clearly failed to match his intent.

Bat wondered this even more because the piano player had not been a musician in life. Not if George Armstrong Custer was telling the truth and the piano player was Dr. Henry Rinaldo Porter, only surviving surgeon from the Battle of the Little Big Horn. Porter's piano playing skills apparently had been acquired solely in hell, on instruments that never would offer the satisfaction of a real melody. How did one learn to play under those circumstances?

Bat shook his head and walked into the cantina. He knew of Dr. Porter, of course. Their earthly lives had run almost concurrently, and the Little Big Horn was a military disaster no one in the country had failed to read or hear about. Porter's skill and quick actions in the field had saved many of the wounded soldiers in his care.

The hot and stuffy air smelled of burning tortillas and beans frying in rancid fat. Bat waited until Porter finished the song before approaching.

Porter said, "I don't do requests," then launched into a new, livelier song.

Bat looked over the cantina's few patrons. Each sat alone at scattered tables, nursing drinks or eating, none paying the slightest attention to the house musician. "I'm not here for a song," Bat said. "Custer sent me."

Porter's fingers tripped on the keys, not that the caterwaul coming from the piano suffered for the lapse. "And what does the Lieutenant Colonel want?"

"Nothing. He merely recommended you as a fine surgeon and physician."

Porter laughed bitterly. "And what would he know? I was with Major Reno during the battle." Porter had an unusual way of cutting short his words when he spoke that Bat found slightly disconcerting.

Bat said, "It's not like you can hide history down here. The dead talk and tell stories. You know what he told me?"

"Do I care?"

"He said it was a damned good thing you rode with Major Reno that day, and not him. If you'd gone with him, you'd have been killed, your skills wasted, and all those wounded you cared for wouldn't have made it."

Porter paused in his playing, raised a hand to tug at one side of his handlebar mustache. Bat couldn't tell if it was a self-conscious gesture or an expression of irritation. Whatever the reason, the piano's silence was a golden thing. He could even hear the cooks arguing in Spanish in the kitchen.

"He said that?" Porter asked.

"Yes."

The doctor-turned-piano player regarded him with more interest. "So, then, who are you?"

"I'm Bat Masterson."

Porter's blue eyes widened slightly, and his gaze shifted to the pistol holstered at Bat's side. "I've heard of you, Mister Masterson. What do you want?"

"I'm looking for a medical man."

"Then apparently Custer hasn't kept up on news down here," Porter said, with an emphatic shake of his head. "I don't practice medicine nowadays."

"Sorry, I didn't use the right wording. I'm really looking for a man of science. It's a long shot, but I've exhausted all my other resources."

Porter swiveled on the piano stool, curiosity piqued, to face Bat. That would last all of five seconds, Bat thought, until he told the doctor his area of interest, and then Porter would either laugh or run him out of the cantina. Bat hesitated, delaying the inevitable, but found no better way of stating his needs than doing it outright. "I'm trying to find someone who knows something about curses down here."

Porter stared at him. Predictably, mistrust and skepticism replaced curiosity. Porter sighed and said, "Why would you want to ask *me*? We're all cursed. I know as much about it as you or Joe there, or Miguel in the back room. You don't want a surgeon. It's not something I can cut out of you, and you wouldn't want me near you with a scalpel anyway."

"Why not?"

"Because this is hell, Mister Masterson. Because of those curses you were just talking about. Because my torment is that if I try to help someone sick or wounded, they die."

"All right, fair enough," Bat said. "But like you said, I don't need surgery. What I need is someone who might have a scientific rationale for what happened to me and my friend, and a way to undo it."

"A curse isn't scientific!"

"I said it was a long shot —"

"Go try a witch doctor, or a medicine man, or someone."

"I did."

"No luck?"

"The medicine man just shook his head, and this old gal from New Orleans wanted a fortune I don't have for results she pretty much guaranteed would fail."

Porter raised an eyebrow. "This surprised you?"

"No, but she also recommended I see a man of science."

"A man of science." Porter laughed. He crossed his arms and said, "Before I realized the true extent of my own torment, I sought out any surgeon or medical man who had arrived down here after I did. The things I learned from them! The advances in knowledge, techniques, equipment! But after a while, when I realized I could not apply anything I learned . . . knowledge simply for the sake of knowledge, age after age, eventually becomes burdensome. I wanted to *use* this new learning." Porter struck an off-key chord on the piano and held it. The lingering tones vibrated painfully in Bat's ears. "None of it matters, Mister Masterson! I cannot use this knowledge to aid anyone. My hands are the hands of death now." He released the keys and looked up at Bat again. "You think if I had learned something about undoing hell's torments I wouldn't have tried it on myself?"

"Well, this curse is a little different: it's not the torment I started out with. Has to do with a demon —"

"*Doc!*" The shout interrupted Bat.

A tall, one-legged man in a cavalry uniform thrust through the cantina's doors. Worn wooden crutches punctuated his approach. He tugged off his forage cap before addressing Porter. "Doc, there's some wounded needing your help." An Irish brogue softened his words.

Porter dropped his head into his hands and rubbed at his temples. "Two useless cries for help in one day. This hasn't happened in ages." He took a deep breath, straightened again, and told the tall man, "I'm sorry, Mike, you know I'm of no use down here for doctoring."

"But Doc, it's a wagonload of women. Five or six of □em. They somehow made it across No Man's Land, but they're shot up something fierce."

"Who shot them?"

The tall Irishman shrugged sheepishly. "New Bodie citizens."

"What? Why?"

"Them women, they come down from Helldorado. They were shouting about escaping the plague." Mike reached down to touch Porter's shoulder. "Doc, you're the closest doctor. If someone don't declare them healthy, the townspeople are gonna shoot ☐em or burn ☐em, just to be safe. There's a mob gathered outside the storehouse they're hiding in, not more than a block from here."

Through gritted teeth, Porter said, "So what? How many times do I have to say it? I am not a surgeon anymore. I'm a piano player."

"Doc, you've got to. There's no one else close enough to help."

Before Porter could protest again, Bat interrupted gently, "They're gonna die or be killed anyway, Doc. Perhaps your ministrations will be a blessing."

Porter looked up at him sharply, but Bat regarded him steadily, letting the logic sink in. "This is a bad idea," Porter muttered. "A very bad idea." Nonetheless, he squared his shoulders and stood. "All right. Fine. I'll take a look at them. But you're coming too, Mister Masterson."

"Me?" Bat shook his head and held up his hands. "I'm no doctor."

"You heard Mike, here. There's a mob, Mister Masterson."

"That there be, sir," Mike agreed. "It's going to get ugly if nothing's done."

"I'd rather not be shot or lynched along with those women," Porter said. He pointed at Bat's holstered gun. "You were a lawman, and I'll wager you're as good with that as I was with a scalpel. You come with me and keep that mob from doing something rash, and I'll examine those women. Deal?"

"You don't have a scattergun hid under that piano, do you?" Bat asked. "Better for crowd control."

"No."

"That's a shame." Bat blew out a breath. The doctor was right; this was a bad idea. On the other hand, Bat thought, maybe a little action would be a welcome break from searching for answers that did not exist. He finally shrugged. "All right, what the hell, Doc. Let's go."

*

Henry Porter felt the tension as soon as they stepped out of the cantina. Porter had been a contract surgeon with the army several times, seen action in Arizona and, of course, on Montana's infamous battlefield. He'd been afraid more times than he could count. Fear in hell, however, was a more palpable thing than it had been when he'd been alive. In hell, fear was a mist-like miasma that seeped through the air, infecting others with terror, anger, or other mob-generated emotions. It lured more damned to the mob, like flames drawing moths, and just as destructive. Breathing that foul air made him curl his fingers into fists and tighten his gut with apprehension. It made him want to lash out at those around him. He clutched his black bag closer to him and fought the feeling.

Mike's eyes glittered, but Porter knew the ex-soldier was a good and brave man. Private Michael Madden had been one of the soldiers with Porter at the Little Big Horn. The private had been shot trying to fetch much-needed water for the trapped men, and Porter ultimately had to amputate his leg to save his life. He was a good man, and Mike had proved that again now, fighting the mob's fear-compulsion to come fetch Porter. Not that Porter's presence would do anyone any good.

Masterson, Porter observed, seemed oblivious to the miasma, at least on the surface, though his fingers tapped lightly against the hilt of his gun, ready to draw.

"Make way! Make way!" Mike shouted, his words cutting through the mob's overlapping voices. "The doctor's here."

A big, soft-bellied man pushed out of the rabble to block their approach. A dirty hat topped long gray hair, and a gray beard hung over his stained shirt. Suspenders barely kept his britches up. A heavy brow furrowed over hooded eyes. "We don't need no doctor," he growled.

"And how would you know?" Porter said coldly. "Did you examine them?"

"Don't need to. They somehow made it down here from Helldorado, and they were screaming about plague."

"That doesn't mean they're infected, you idiot. Do you think they could have made it across No Man's Land if they were ill?"

"Well . . ." The man scratched at his beard and glanced left and right at his nearest companions for support, but they had fallen silent.

Masterson spoke up. "All right, here's what's going to happen, Mister . . . ?"

"Pearce." The man eyed Masterson, noticing the lawman for the first time. "My name's Pearce."

"Mister Pearce," Masterson said. "Here's what's going to happen: Before you go arbitrarily shooting and burning innocent people, the doctor here is going to take a look at those women."

Outraged shouts rose from the crowd. Porter shifted uneasily. These people wanted blood, regardless of who the women were or what they suffered from, and the sudden fear that they might be denied murderous satisfaction set them surging forward like snarling wolves. Let them do what they want, Porter wanted to tell Masterson. He couldn't help those women anyway, if only someone would realize that.

But Masterson hadn't budged and, under his unruffled gaze, Pearce took a step back and the crowd stopped behind him, like a tide caught by an invisible dam. Masterson still hadn't raised his voice. "If the doctor says they're a danger, then you can shoot and burn away."

A bloodthirsty cheer rumbled through the crowd.

Masterson's voice turned steely. "But not until the doctor says."

Pearce's gaze darted to Masterson's still-holstered gun before he held up his hands, palms out. "All right," he said. "All right."

Masterson gestured to Porter. "Get moving, Doc."

As they passed him, Pearce grabbed Masterson's arm. Bat turned his blue-gray eyes on him, and Pearce's fingers snapped open, releasing Bat. The mob leader swallowed, then poked a finger at Masterson's chest instead. "But just you lookee here, Mister. If it is plague, doctor or no, gunfighter or no, you ain't coming out of that storehouse any more than those whores are. You understand?"

Masterson stared at him a moment longer. "You back this rabble away from the storehouse right now. The way you fellas are talking about plague, I'm surprised you're willing to stand that close."

His words worked like magic. A path opened up, the crowd scrambling away from the storehouse. The wagon the women had arrived in had crashed into the corner of the building. No one had attempted to move it, and two hell-horses stamped and snorted in their traces.

Porter walked toward the storehouse, conscious of the glares and hard looks, the stink of unwashed bodies, and the threats whispered at his back. This wasn't a bad idea, it was a terrible idea, he told himself, but he was committed, like it or not. Madden and Masterson followed a couple steps behind him, and Porter was surprised at how reassuring the lawman's presence was.

"Mike?" Porter said. "Please stay outside the door. Give us warning if things get worse out here."

"Yes sir, Doctor Porter."

"Good man," Porter said, clapping him on the shoulder. "Mister Masterson, come with me, please."

Masterson caught up to Porter just before the door. Softly, he asked, "You have a plan if those women are infected?"

"Sure. Find out how fast you are with that gun." He grinned suddenly at the lawman.

"Comforting," Bat said. "Real comforting."

Hinges squealed as Porter opened the storehouse's door. The interior of the building lay dark and full of shadowy shapes. His nose wrinkled at the reek of blood. One uncurtained back window let in enough light to make out flour sacks piled high against one wall and wooden crates in banked tiers against another. Dry straw littered the floor, crunching underfoot. It should have given the storehouse a pleasant, barnlike smell, but the odor was thick and cloying, like decaying leaves and swampy earth. A crooked table with an oil lamp sat near the entrance. Porter struck a match and turned the wick up to gain maximum light. Dust motes spun in the amber light.

Masterson gestured. "Over there, Doc."

Porter saw the women. Four of them. Three seemed to have collapsed in the process of dragging themselves across the open floor. The fourth was propped against the wall of flour sacks. None were conscious. They were probably close to death. Half of him was relieved at the prospect, half flared in anger that he was too late to help them.

While Porter hesitated, Masterson prowled the storehouse, checking the corners, the back door, and the window, before returning to Porter's side. Porter was well aware that he had made no move toward the women yet.

"The longer we dally, the more bloodthirsty that mob is going to get, Doc," Masterson warned.

Sound advice, but that didn't make it any easier to do his job. But what was he here for, then? Porter asked himself. Who else was going to help? He forced himself forward, holding the lamp aloft.

The two closest women were young, clad in cotton calico dresses. Porter leaned over them, inspecting them without getting too close. "Multiple gunshot wounds on these two. But they're still breathing."

"Any signs of the plague?"

Porter studied their skin, seeking signs of boils, pustules, lesions, even a rash or discoloration. There was nothing obvious that he could spot, and he shook his head. "Looks like bullets are all they're infected with."

Masterson leaned against the wall nearby. "What if you don't touch them? What if I be your hands instead, and you tell me what to do?"

"You think I haven't tried that already? It's still me providing the help, and my patients still die. I can't even remove a splinter from someone's finger without losing them." Porter stepped toward the third woman. This one wore a red silk dress in a fancy cut. Her matching hat was askew, but still pinned to her auburn hair. She appeared to have only one bullet wound, in the left thigh. It didn't appear the bullet had touched the bone; it should have been treatable, even in hell.

"Doc?"

Masterson's voice jogged Porter out of his reverie, and he turned angrily on the lawman. "What do you want me to do, Mister Masterson? If I take that bullet out and bandage her . . . she'll die. From a wound that shouldn't be fatal. And there's nothing I can do about it except not touch her at all." Porter's hands trembled, and he set the lamp down on the floor beside the woman. "And each one that dies is on my conscience. I can't do it."

"Doc, if you don't help her, she'll bleed to death."

"Lose-lose." Porter laughed, heard the edge of hysteria tinging his words, and gritted his teeth until he could breathe around the tightness in his chest. "All right," he murmured. "All right." He knelt beside the woman and opened his bag. "Just keep talking to me, Mister Masterson."

"Bat. Call me Bat."

Porter nodded and began examining the woman's wound for real. "All right," he said. "Bat."

"What do you want me to talk to you about?" Masterson asked.

The bullet had missed both bone and artery, passing through her leg. He turned the woman to inspect the exit wound. Clean and bandage it, that's all he could do. "Different how?" Porter asked.

Bat blinked. "What now?"

Porter said, "Back at the saloon, you said your curse was different. Different how?"

"Well, Wyatt and I —"

"Wyatt Earp?"

"Yeah. Long story short, we riled up some local underground demons. They punished us with a curse so that we can't get near each other without trying to kill each other."

Porter cleansed the woman's wound with a carbolic acid solution, letting Bat's voice and words distract him, keeping him from focusing too much on the woman. "That sounds fun. Is it a physical or mental compulsion?"

"Physical."

"Interesting."

"Does that mean anything to you?"

"No, it's just interesting." Porter pressed a bandage against the front and exit wounds in the woman's leg, bound them in place. Blood stained his hands, and he reached for a cloth to wipe them. "So, what if Wyatt shows up here?"

"Better hope he doesn't, Doc. Otherwise, he and I will be compelled to shoot each other, and Wyatt doesn't miss."

"Good," Porter said. "At least then I won't have to try to treat you and have your death on my conscience too, will I?"

Bat laughed. "That you won't." His laugh stopped abruptly.

Porter glanced up and saw the lawman staring at the woman Porter had just bandaged. He didn't want to look, but his gaze followed Masterson's back to his patient. Her eyes opened, and she moaned. "It hurts! I need a doctor. A doctor . . ." She trailed off and, just as suddenly, her eyes closed and her breath rasped out a final time. A moment later, her body vanished, returned to the Undertaker's slab.

Porter gave a strangled cry and pushed himself to his feet. He staggered for the door.

Masterson got there ahead of him and grabbed him by both arms to keep him from rushing outside.

Porter tried to pull away, but Bat's grip held him immobile. "You see?" Porter's voice cracked. "You see what happens? I *kill* them! She asked for a doctor, and she got a murderer!"

"Stop it!" Bat shouted. "Just stop!"

The woman against the flour sacks coughed, interrupting both men. "You sound like just the man I need, Doc."

Porter started laughing, but Bat squeezed his arms until the pain made him stop.

"I'm being perfectly serious," the woman said.

Porter met Masterson's eyes, then nodded once. Bat released him, and Porter approached the woman.

"That was Stella you just released back to the Undertaker. The other two are Lucy and Carmen. I'm Mary." She was older than the others, still handsome. Strawberry blonde hair framed a well-proportioned face with full lips. She sat propped against the flour sacks, legs stretched out straight in front of her like a child's abandoned doll sitting stiff-limbed and broken.

"I'm sorry for your friend —"

"Don't be," Mary said. Her gaze, appraising and hungry, made him turn away. "So, you treat people and they die?"

Porter couldn't bring himself to answer that.

She smiled at his silence. "Good," she said firmly, and coughed again. "You're the doc I want. I *want* to die."

Her hands were folded over her stomach, and Porter could see the bloody wound there. Gutshot.

Her voice lowered, almost conspiratorially, and she looked around as if fearing eavesdroppers. "Do you have any?" she asked.

Porter exchanged a glance with Masterson. "Have what?"

She licked her lips. "The vaccine, of course."

"What vaccine?" Porter asked.

"For the plague."

"No. The plague hasn't hit here yet. I wasn't even aware there was a vaccine."

"The vaccine is what I want."

"You're gunshot, ma'am, not ill. You don't need —"

"I don't care what I need, I want to *die*!"

"What the hell vaccine are you talking about?" Masterson asked.

"You haven't heard? This vaccine . . ." She pulled herself up straighter, grimacing, beckoning them closer. "Sometimes it works, sometimes it don't. And when it don't . . . you don't come to, not on the Undertaker's table."

"Where *do* you come back?"

"You don't." A crooked smile crossed her lips.

It took a moment for that to sink in. Porter and Masterson exchanged another glance.

Porter said, "You . . . Oblivion? *Nothingness*?"

"You are gone, sirs, permanently. That's what they say. It's not heaven, but it's a way out. An escape. No more hell. No more anything."

"I'll be damned," Porter murmured.

"We already are," Mary said, then sighed. "No vaccine?"

Porter shook his head.

"Then you're the next best thing. Help me."

"No."

Her hand shot out, talonlike, and gripped his wrist. "Please! Please, Doc. I don't want to live. My life . . . you don't know what it's like, you don't know how miserable . . . Speed me on my way. Maybe I'll get lucky and won't come back to the Undertaker's table. Maybe you're as good as the vaccine."

Porter gaped at her, appalled at the thought.

Her grip did not slacken. "Doc, bandage me up. I'm going to die anyway, we both know it. Do me a favor and hurry up the dying."

"Let go of me."

"Not until you promise."

"I need the lamp and my bag."

"Promise me!"

"I promise!" The words jerked out of him, more to get away from her than anything, and he regretted them seconds later. But he had always been a man of his word; he had to honor his promise.

Mary let him go, and he stumbled away from her. He brought back the lamp and his black bag, avoiding the bloodstained floor where Stella had died, not looking at Masterson. "It's peace, you give, Doc," she said. "Not murder. Peace. You gotta know that. I'm ready to go."

He ignored her and did his duty as a doctor. The woman groaned and whimpered as he worked on her. Her fingers balled in the material of the flour sacks, and she closed her eyes.

He finished extracting the bullet and sewing the wound shut, then carefully cleaned and bandaged her before he sat back on his heels and stared at her.

Sweat dripped off her brow. "Thanks, Doc. I mean it. Thanks." She closed her eyes again.

Porter waited, watching for the moment her breath stopped and her body relaxed.

The moment didn't come.

Her eyes flew open suddenly, and she looked down at her stomach. "What in blue blazes? I don't feel the pain no more." She tugged at the bandages, ripping them off. The wound had already knit shut.

Porter blinked and reached out to touch the fresh pink skin. He stared at his hands, then at her, then started laughing. "Mary, you're going to *live*."

Her slap across his cheek sent him reeling. "You said . . . you promised. . . . Why am I not *dead*?" She spluttered with rage, and Porter just laughed at the irony of it. Somehow, he had saved her life.

"Doc," Bat cut in. He pointed to the other two gunshot victims. "We got a problem."

Porter raised the lamp for a better view. The skin on their faces, neck, and exposed arms had broken out in blisters. His laughter died, and cold dread spidered up his spine.

Mary chortled gleefully. "That's the plague, boys! We was overrun with it up in Helldorado."

"Shit," Bat said. He grabbed Porter's arm and yanked him to his feet. "You touch either of those two?"

"No."

"Out. Out the back and get out of here. Run, man, run!"

Mary was still cackling. "Just try running! See how far you get! Serves you right, *Doctor*!"

Bat snatched the lamp from Porter's hand and threw it at a wall where it exploded in a gout of flames. He shoved Porter, and the doctor sprinted for the back door. Porter yanked it open, then turned, waiting for Masterson. One of the plague victims got to her feet and lunged at Bat.

"Behind you!" Porter shouted.

Masterson pivoted, drawing his gun. He shot her down and dashed for the back door, only to pull up sharply.

"Bat, what are you waiting for?" Porter called. The fire was spreading rapidly up the wall, already consuming the rafters with a terrible roaring sound. Smoke spread through the room. The acrid smell of burning wood and creosote choked Porter, and he coughed. He waved a hand in front of his face, trying to clear the smoke for a better view.

Bat had reversed direction and headed toward the front door. His gun was in his hand, aimed ahead of him.

"What are you doing?" Porter yelled.

Calmly, Bat said, "Wyatt must be outside. I can't stop myself."

Porter ran forward, dodging a portion of the roof that fell. The heat from the fiery beam burned at his legs. He grabbed Bat's arm, half-spinning him, and slugged him hard in the jaw. He caught the lawman as Bat slumped and snatched the pistol from his limp hand. He shoved the gun in his own belt, then bent and shouldered Bat in a soldier's carry.

The sound of the fire had finally drowned out Mary's laughter. He could see her through the smoke, sitting just where she had been, making no attempt to escape the blaze. He heard a hiss and saw the second plague victim on her feet and coming for him. He kicked the smoldering beam along the floor in her direction.

Stepping forward, her foot rammed into it, and she fell. Her fingernails dragged across the floorboards as she clawed toward him.

Porter didn't wait around. He ran out the back door into the hot, clear air of the back alley. A few gulps of smoke-free air steadied him as he hurried down the empty alley, grunting under Masterson's dead weight across his shoulders.

The storehouse burned behind them.

*

Bat groaned. He blinked, waiting for the world to swim back into clarity. Tattered lace curtains wavered in the window's breeze. He could hear the clatter of wagons passing on the street outside, and the distant strains of a fiddle sawing out a melancholy melody. A sagging mattress cushioned his body. His jaw ached, and he touched it tenderly.

"Easy," Porter said.

The doctor caught hold of Bat's arm to help him sit up and swing his legs off the bed.

"Didn't think you could hit that hard," Bat muttered.

"You're welcome."

Bat surveyed the small, tidy bedroom. "Where are we?"

"As far away from your friend Wyatt as I could get you. Which was just to my room here, but looks like it was far enough to escape the compulsion."

"Thanks, Doc." Bat winced and asked, "The plague victims?"

Porter tugged at his mustache uncomfortably. He took a seat on a chair facing the bed. "The fire you started took out the whole block. None of those women got out of there."

"I'm sorry."

"Don't be. I saved that woman, Mister Masterson. I actually *saved* her."

Bat could hear the wonder in the doctor's voice, and he decided mentioning the woman's ungrateful attitude would be of no benefit.

Porter went on, "I never thought that could happen."

"Your torment must also be tied to the wounded you work on," Bat guessed. "Everyone wants to live. Even here in the afterlife. Survival at any cost. So their desire to live, plus your desire to heal them. . . ."

"Equals death." Porter nodded. "But for someone who genuinely wants to die . . ."

"Then your curse does the opposite." Bat swallowed. His throat felt more parched than normal, and he gestured at the pitcher of water on the side table. "What are you going to do now? Go back into doctoring?"

"No!" Porter said, standing. "I can't. . . . But today," he hesitated, staring off into the distance, searching for words. "Today was . . ."

"I know," Bat said. He was surprised how envious he felt of the doctor. Moments like that were so rare. "Just hang onto that. It's not likely to happen again anytime soon."

"Besides, I'm a damned good piano player. And I like it."

Bat raised an eyebrow. "Really?"

Porter shrugged sheepishly. "No. But it fills the days, and it's harmless." He poured water into a glass and pushed it into Bat's hand.

"Nobody's shot you for playing the wrong tune?"

Porter blinked in surprise. "Good Lord, would they do that?"

Bat grinned at him. "I've seen it happen."

"You must hang out in a rougher part of town than me. Remind me not to visit your preferred watering holes," the doctor said, smiling back. "What about you? What are you going to do?"

Bat drank the glass dry before replying: "Keep looking for answers. There's got to be a way to break this compulsion."

"You try leaving?" the doctor asked.

"Run away? I've been running from Wyatt since this happened. Just like we ran today."

"No," Porter said. "I mean leave New Bodie entirely. Get away from here, *with* Wyatt."

Bat cocked his head. "How, exactly, would two people compelled to kill each other leave *together*?"

"Get help. Your brothers? Wyatt's brothers?"

Bat rubbed at his jaw, not sure he wanted to invite deliberately getting knocked unconscious on a more regular basis. Particularly as he knew his brothers, at least, would agree to such a plan with far more enthusiasm than Bat felt was necessary. "What are you getting at, Doc?"

Porter leaned forward intently. "Those underground demons who put this curse on you: they're local. Indigenous to this region. Which means their powers are probably localized too. So," he spread his hands, "get out of their range."

"I . . ." Bat trailed off, a thoughtful look on his face. Then he shook his head. "No, that can't possibly work."

"How do you know? Besides, what do you have to lose? Do you and Wyatt really want to spend eternity gunning for each other? If it doesn't work, nothing's changed. But if their power *is* local . . ."

"Damn," Bat said. "You might be on to something." The skepticism in his eyes was replaced by a twinkle of hope. "But how would we leave New Bodie?"

"I didn't say it would be easy."

Bat laughed and clapped him on the shoulder. "Then how about it, Doc? You done playing piano in that run-down cantina? Want to see some place new?"

"What, *me*?"

"Come on, Doc. Custer told me about your past. You signed up repeatedly as a contract surgeon with the army, and you can't tell me it was the army pay and good food that kept you coming back. Piano playing might be safe, but I doubt it's very satisfying to someone like yourself who thrived on excitement. So, what do you say? Ready for a little adventure?"

Porter's grin told Bat all he needed to know.

Memory

Nancy Asire

Hell was infested with vermin, and that included humans.

Even those with privileged status suffered those in-
festations. The residents of Hellview Estates had dealt
with toads, bats and other unwelcome invaders in the past.
Crowned Row, its mansions and palaces across Decentral
Park, had not escaped either.

But now, a new torment arrived: rats.

Not the familiar gray-furred rodents people recognized
from their lives on earth. Oh, no. These rats were huge, nearly the size of hellcats, scaled and glaring from baleful red
eyes. They seemed to be everywhere, having appeared from
out of nothing between one day and the next. It didn't matter how clean and clutter-free the dwellings, yards, bushes,
streets and sidewalks, the rats proliferated.

Of course, it was worse in New Hell City itself: the
slums and the back alleyways, the rundown apartments, the
storefronts. Not to be excluded, residents of government
buildings fought against the rats. Tales made it all the way to

Hellview Estates and Crowned Row of the overabundance of the skittering menace.

One more torture to be experienced. Life in hell was one attempt after another to deal with whatever Satan chose to inflict upon his subjects.

Still bivouacked in Louis XIV's opulent palace by orders from Satan, Napoleon, once Emperor of France, saw more than his share of rats. At first, it posed a problem easily dispensed with by liberally depositing rat poison around the grounds. That at least appeared to keep the vermin out of the palace itself.

Wellington, celebrated Iron Duke of Britain (also reactivated by Satan from retirement along with Napoleon), kept careful watch over the houses in Hellview Estates. Poison, similar to that employed by the residents of Crowned Row, maintained a fairly rodent-free environment.

And then, naturally, another problem arose from that solution. What to do with the dead and decomposing rats killed off by poison? Leave it up to hell: there existed a multitude of other beings that crawled, oozed or flittered across damnation, happy to consume the deceased. No rejuvenated rats issued forth from the Undertaker. No, once the rats were dead, they apparently stayed dead.

So, on this morning, Napoleon walked the perimeter of Louis' palace, a daily routine to ascertain the efficacy of rat poison. Marie Walewska, Polish countess and his lover in life and afterlife, accompanied him.

"They are so many," she said, brushing her long blond hair over her shoulders. "Where did they all come from?"

Napoleon shrugged. "The same place, I imagine, that spawns the bats, toads and other creatures we must endure. Satan is, if nothing else, inventive."

"You'd think the hellcats would keep the rats in check."

"They're fairly outnumbered, I suppose."

"Ugh." Marie made a face. "I hate rats. Not that I was overjoyed by the toads. *That* was an experience I don't want to repeat. Have you heard from Wellington?"

"No. Not yet. I'm afraid, barring new orders from Satan, he's stationed in Hellview Estates for a while." A slight grin. "You know he can't stay far away from Queen Victoria for very long."

Marie smiled back. "That woman. I don't think there's much that intimidates her. He shouldn't worry about her so much. She's more than capable. What about Attila? We haven't seen him in weeks now."

"Something really disturbed him," Napoleon said, pausing to look down the curved drive leading from Louis' palace grounds to Decentral Park. "Wellington was present when Attila killed some kind of relative in a sword duel, and a Hun god appeared to snatch that opponent back to Hun hell. At least, that's what I got from Wellington. He was concerned about Attila. He said he'd never seen him so subdued. And we all know how much Attila likes a good fight."

"Maybe his goats will take care of the rats."

"Satan knows they eat everything else."

Marie lifted her head and stared up at what served as hell's sky. "How much longer do we have to stay here? I hate this place."

"No more than I do. With our changed orders, you and I are stuck here until Satan relieves Wellington and me from our duties to keep *both* sides of the Park calm. Louis is still incarcerated in his private quarters, so he doesn't pose too obnoxious a problem. Sulla and his Romans are keeping the idle curious of New Hell City from wandering around

Crowned Row. Attila's Huns and Mongols are posted at the entrance of Hellview Estates, doing the same. So, as far as that's concerned, I think we have the situation under control."

"Oh, look!" Marie pointed to the boulevard that ran along Decentral Park.

A large rat was staggering toward the Park, seeming unable to keep upright. A few more lurching steps and the rodent collapsed in the middle of the boulevard.

"Well," Napoleon said, "there's another one down. But at the rate we're going, we'll run out of poison." He shook his head. "Another wonderful day in hell, Marie: the torments just keep on coming. All we can do is try to deal with whatever Satan throws at us."

*

Wellington grew frustrated by inactivity, insulted at being underutilized. Once a noted general and governor, he now was charged merely with keeping Hellview Estates calm and, recently, as rodent-free as poison could ensure. Beyond that, his days were, in a word, empty. It became dispiriting.

At least when he and Napoleon were neighbors, he had constant interaction with someone who understood where Wellington came from, his earthly accomplishments, his military talents. Now, on Satan's orders, when the two of them would periodically switch sides of the Park (a situation Wellington truly disliked, preferring to be over on Crowned Row and close to Victoria), communication continued to occur via leeches. That still unnerved him to a certain degree, yet it kept him in contact with what happened on the other side of the Park.

Strangely enough, the Vietcong had gone comparatively silent. Wellington supposed this stemmed from the rats and the Cong's war against them, for the Park offered a haven for the rodents with all its bushes and undergrowth. His knowledge of rats came from his life on earth and was, to a certain extent, limited. People of his exalted station would have been horrified to find even the hint of such filthy creatures on their estates or in their mansions. But what were these rats of his afterlife eating? That question was one he couldn't easily answer. Garbage, most likely. He remembered rats scurrying around trash set out by Londoners, lurking in alleyways close to dining establishments. None of that here. Even the country club had taken to incinerating their garbage rather than disposing of it as they had always done.

Today he walked down the sidewalk, examining the houses to make certain nothing seemed out of the ordinary. His neighbor, the Homeowners Association president, was not at home. Not that this bothered Wellington. The man was a nuisance, but his lawyerly profession kept him at the Hall of Injustice most of the time, an occupation for which Wellington thanked Satan and all the multitudinous lawsuits that kept the wheels of injustice turning.

A momentary pause. Had he actually thought his day-to-day existence dull? Had he become so jaded by his sentence to eternity in hell that an infestation of rats, of all things, proved merely annoying? He rubbed his long nose, stared again into the depths of Decentral Park, and shook his head. For at least the millionth time, he questioned why he, of all people, was consigned to such an afterlife. Damn! No matter how he contemplated what could have placed him in hell, it still rankled.

Rats! One more torment visited on the condemned. He knew far more horrible manifestations could arise at any time, so rats, at least, were somewhat tolerable.

"Hoi! Wellington!"

He turned. Attila sat on the steps of his front porch, waving a hand in greeting. From what Wellington could see, the king of the Huns appeared changed from the last time he'd seen him. After the duel in his front yard, Attila all but disappeared. Only a few times had Wellington noticed him out feeding his goats (as if they needed help), but aside from that, Attila remained a recluse.

"So," Wellington said as Attila joined him on the sidewalk. "Are you winning against the rats?"

Attila frowned, pulled at his mustache, and growled something in Hunnish. "Damned things! Even my goats don't like them, if you can believe that. I'm running low on poison, but I've found a use for my bow. Target practice. An arrow through the fuckers' heads kills faster than poison."

"One imagines." Wellington tried to assess what changes he could see in Attila's demeanor. The nearly stunned expression he'd witnessed on Attila's face after the duel was gone, replaced by what could be termed weary resignation. He tried a gentle probe.

"What about your wives? How are they dealing with the rats?"

A flash of something odd lit Attila's eyes for an instant. "Don't ask." He fell silent, then spread his hands in exasperation. "You were there, Wellington. You witnessed the duel and the death that followed. I think I can talk about it now, but it's not easy. The man you saw fighting me was my brother."

A cold chill swept over Wellington. A brother? As far as he knew, Attila's family only consisted of his wives and his juvenile delinquent sons. Where had a brother come from? And how?

"Don't interrupt," Attila said when Wellington tried to speak. "You're no Hun but you witnessed what happened. Because of that, I owe you an explanation. If I don't tell you all of it, I probably won't be able to talk about it for a long time. Bleda, my brother, somehow escaped from Erlik Khan's domain and managed to find me. He sought my death because he was certain I'd killed him to take over rulership of the Huns all those centuries ago." He drew a deep breath. "He slaughtered my wives, killed my sons, and came close to killing me."

As Attila paused, Wellington got out only "Oh," unsure of an appropriate response. He'd seldom heard Attila so exacting in his speech. "I don't know what to say."

"There's not much *to* say." A glint lit the Hun king's eyes. "I thought them gone forever. When Satan pulled me out of Hun hell, I came alone. But somehow, later, Satan snatched my wives and sons from under Erlik Khan's nose. My wives turned into raving shrews, not that they had ever been sweetness and light when we walked the earth. My sons, my strong adult sons, transformed into troublesome children. It's my personal torment, you see." A bitter smile touched Attila's mouth. "Well, they're back. All of them. Returned from the death of the dead and driving me crazy! I don't know how Satan managed *that* one. Maybe he and Erlik Khan came to some sort of agreement, and that makes me fucking nervous."

"Oh," Wellington said again. "Well, I've been worried about you. So has Napoleon. You know we're here if you need anything." As soon as the words left his lips, Welling-ton knew how hollow they sounded. What could anyone say in the face of such a tale? Brother killing brother? Again, perhaps?

Attila shrugged. "You can tell Napoleon what hap-pened, but don't let word of it get out. The less said about it, the better. I don't have any idea what Satan has in store for me, and I'd rather not know." He glanced over at the Park and back. "I suppose the rats are just another torment inflict-ed on us. No matter how we keep after them, those fucking things are everywhere."

Relieved by the change in subject, Wellington nodded. "What I don't understand is that they don't seem to act like any rats I encountered in my earthly life. Garbage was their sustenance, and we've been assiduous in keeping every-thing here as clean as possible. No garbage, no trash of any sort. They seem to exist on nothing."

"Well, aside from my wives giving me more trouble than usual, at least I'm getting practice with my bow. For-tunately, I'm not running out of arrows. Once they're shot, those rats stay dead, so I can always get all my arrows back." A touch of mirth narrowed Attila's eyes. "If you want, I could always go after the little shits at your house, or Napoleon's. Our supply of rat poison must be running low by now."

The vision of Attila lurking by the hedge separating Wellington's backyard from Napoleon's flashed through the Iron Duke's mind.

"If we need your help, we'll jolly well let you know. And you might enlist some of your Huns and Mongols. Practice makes perfect, or so they say."

*

"Napoleon?"

Duroc, once High Lord Steward of the Empire and Marshal of France, remained Napoleon's closest friend and the one person he trusted to keep things running without serious trouble at Louis' palace. The man who had stood proxy for Napoleon on Crowned Row waited at their front steps as Napoleon and Marie returned from inspecting the lawns and drive.

The expression on Duroc's face hinted at trouble. Not a look Napoleon welcomed at any time, and events lately were unsettled enough to elicit increased wariness.

"What now, Géraud?"

Duroc glanced around, as if to make certain no one was close enough to hear. "A message from Sulla," he said. "Quintus brought it. New Hell City has reported incidents of what appears to be the plague."

Napoleon drew a long breath. "Plague?"

There. He'd said the word, a word he'd said before, what with Erra and the Seven running rampant through the hells. A word that brought back memories he'd hoped were buried deep enough to ignore.

"What's the origin?" he asked, noticing Marie going a bit pale at the news.

"No one knows. Any number of plagues could be caused by that Babylonian inflictor of death and destruction, although this one doesn't seem to bear his mark. It could be another of Satan's torments unleashed in his hell. It's anyone's guess."

Napoleon rubbed his forehead. "What type of plague? Hell has a long history of numerous plagues. There have been so many."

"From what Quintus said, its symptoms manifest similar to bubonic plague."

"Oh, damn!" Napoleon's mind was overwhelmed by what he knew could cause an outbreak of plague and what to do about it. "The only thing that strikes me now is—"

"Rats!" Marie got out. "Rats, Napoleon. We're inundated with rats!"

"I know," he said. "And we've been battling rodents for weeks now. Rats, *and* fleas. Rats are supreme flea carriers."

"I can understand, to a certain extent, New Hell City experiencing the plague. Areas of town are festering with slums and rundown apartments." Duroc waved a hand at the grounds around Louis' palace. "We've kept the rats at bay, and I don't think there's a place around Crowned Row that isn't kept clean. No trash, no garbage. From what Wellington says, the same is true in Hellview Estates."

"Doesn't matter." Napoleon briefly shut his eyes. "All it takes is one rat carrying the plague that's infested with fleas. The plague-carrying fleas jump from rat to rat, and so on and so on. Then the disease multiplies exponentially. Oh, shit! Now we have to go after fleas?"

"I suppose," Duroc ventured, "there's something we can get our hands on that passes for flea poison. We could spread it everywhere. If we can keep the rats away, we might be able to avoid the fleas."

"Easier said than done. One thing's certain: no one—and I mean *no one* from this moment on—should be out on the grounds without being fully clad, boots to the knee, heavy breeches, so they avoid being bitten. No one goes into bushes, long grass, anywhere that can harbor fleas. And before any soul enters the palace, each must be thoroughly examined. Has this news spread throughout Crowned Row?"

"I'll make certain everyone is alerted, if they haven't already heard the news."

"Do so. And Géraud . . . I want every corner of this palace spotless. I don't care how long it takes. Additionally, make sure all our soldiers, servants, whoever else is in residence here, know about this. We can't take the chance of someone, in ignorance, bringing an infected flea into contact with anyone else."

"Consider it done." Duroc's expression softened. "You can trust me to do everything I can to prevent disaster."

Napoleon put a hand on Duroc's shoulder. "Trust, with you, my friend, has never been a question in my mind. Do your best. I can't ask any more than that."

*

Marie found Napoleon sitting silent in what served as his office, and Wellington's whenever the Iron Duke was present. Napoleon's head was bowed, his eyes half closed. She knew from years of watching him when he was sunk deep in thought. And he was today. What was passing through his mind was hard to tell. So many day-to-day problems to deal with, and now this plague.

From past experience she was keenly aware of the horrors that could be unleashed on the condemned in New Hell: Satan was past master at tormenting his subjects. He had so many ways to make existence a living nightmare. Was he the architect of this new harassment? Or someone else? "Napoleon," she said quietly, taking a chair beside him. "Have you let Wellington know?"

He lifted his head and nodded. "I just got through talking with him. He's alerting Attila and all the residents of Hellview Estates about the outbreak in New Hell City. The same protocols we're instituting on this side of the Park will go into effect over there immediately. Oh, Marie. You have no idea how this haunts me. Plague. Damn, damn, damn! We've been so fortunate to be spared the horrible torments most of those in Satan's hell experience. He deems certain of us condemned valuable to him in some way, and grants us existence far better than the terrors suffered by the rest of New Hell. But now this. I've got to come up with some solution, and there seems nothing I can do short of what I've set into motion now."

"We'll get through this," she said. "We've weathered troubles before."

"But you . . . you shouldn't need to endure these things." He reached out and took her hand in his. "You shouldn't even *be* here. You had your chance to return to purgatory, with its eventual hope of heaven."

"I made my choice to stay here, and I haven't regretted it. Do you honestly think I could stand eternity without you?"

A rueful smile. "Time after time, I've questioned that. Am I truly worth it? Worth you throwing away your chance for heaven itself?"

"I think so." She smiled back and squeezed his hand. "All the more reason for me being here, in hell. I can't change my love for you, and that's what doomed me to be sent from purgatory to hell—to be purified of my illicit love of you when we were alive. So I guess I'm in hell because of that choice, and I don't think I'll ever repent of it."

His expression was difficult to read. She saw a distance come to his gray-blue eyes that told her he was falling back into his silent meditative state. Some kind of memory, she was certain, but of what she had no idea.

Recognizing he needed time to be alone, to wrestle with whatever dark thoughts assailed him, she squeezed his hand again, rose and left the room.

*

Jaffa. Syrian town, bleached bone-white by the unrelenting sun. A bloody victory. French soldiers rampaging through the city, slaughtering enemy Turks and Jaffa's residents. The killing of around two thousand Turkish troops who had surrendered. And later, by order, the execution of an additional three thousand Turks, fearing they would melt into the desert to fight again, although they considered themselves prisoners of war. The vicious killings ending three days later, but worse yet to come.

Upon first arriving in Egypt, becoming aware that the desert, the burning sun and its reflection from the sand and rocky soil, caused disease and injury to eyesight. Orders issued to keep the surroundings of the French army as clean and sanitary as possible. Dehydration and scorpion stings testing the bravery of the soldiers. So many ways a man could die besides death in battle.

And now, in Jaffa, French soldiers falling ill, delirious with painful headaches, high fevers and gross swellings under their arms.

Plague.

Plague already surfacing in localized areas: the outposts of Abukir, Damietta, Rosetta and Alexandria. But now threatening the entire French army.

"Get me Doctor Desgenettes!"

"Yes, General Bonaparte."

"Immediately! And find Doctor Larrey!"

"He's with the wounded, General."

A brief wait: Desgenettes appearing at the door.

"Yes, General. How may I be of service?"

"Two days after taking Jaffa, our soldiers contracted the plague. All the doctors assured the sickened it wasn't the plague, but some other illness. I've done the same myself, trying to keep up morale."

Spreading both hands in acknowledgment. "That is your privilege, General."

"Today, we're going to visit the hospital. I want the men to see I'm not afraid, that they don't need to be incapacitated by fear."

"I would strongly advise against it, General. The plague is highly contagious."

"I know that. But I must do something to reassure the men. If they see me walking among them, unafraid, this will lift their spirits. Now, accompany me. And that's an order."

The hospital in Jaffa. Full of wounded and plague-stricken men. The stench, the moans and cries of the suffering soldiers. A backward glance at the general staff, cloths held over noses and mouths; then walking through the hospital and the annex, pausing to touch and speak with whomever was conscious enough to carry on a conversation. Orders given, details of administration. Reaching a crowded ward, himself helping lift and carry off the plague-ravaged corpse of a dead soldier, his torn uniform dampened by the bursting of a huge abscess.

And all the while, the looming specter of the French army dying piecemeal.

Issuing orders to Adjutant-General Grezieu to hold Jaffa. Haifa and Acre attacked next. The news arriving that General Grezieu had himself contracted the plague and died a hideous death. And the plague, like a demon of death, following to Haifa and Acre. Abandoning the siege of Acre, the march back to Egypt. Doctors Desgenettes and Larrey trying everything they could to stop the spread of the plague. Changing camp positions, isolating plague victims and ordering everyone to keep as clean as possible.

The return march to Cairo, leaving behind the dead on the desert sands. Reaching Jaffa, beset by the ominous fear that the Turks would catch up with the beleaguered French army. And now, another consultation with Desgenettes:

"If I were in your place, Doctor, I'd end the suffering of the plague victims and prevent the disease from killing more of us."

"What are you asking, General?"

"You know what I'm asking. Give overdoses of opium to the dying."

Desgenettes lifting both hands in denial. "I can't do that, General. My duty is to preserve life, not end it."

"What kind of life are you offering my soldiers? Agonizing death? Better a quick, clean escape from terminal agony. If it were my son, I'd do the same. Whether you approve or not, I'm giving that order."

"And, General, with all due respect, I refuse."

"So. If you won't assist in this, have Rouyer do it. He's chief pharmacist. He'll know the quickest and least painful way to put these suffering men out of their misery."

Watching Desgenettes turn away, face darkened with disapproval.

Now, the burden of knowing he'd participated in, and witnessed, so much death. The knowledge weighing down like an inescapable heaviness of the spirit. Such was war. You tossed the dice and lived with the outcome, no matter how terrible.

So it was. The ravages of plague. The beginning of the end of a glorious attempt to seize the Orient.

Death laughing in the darkness, a laughter that would never go away.

*

Attila stood at the edge of his front lawn, his bow strung and an arrow nocked. So far, he'd killed over five rats up and down the street but hadn't seen more. He spat to one side. Fucking vermin! Even Huns had known better than to allow rodents close to campsites. When the tribes had been on the move, keeping rats and other scavengers away had been easier than when they'd settled into a more sedentary life.

Days had passed since Wellington told of the outbreak of plague in New Hell City. Plague was something everyone, even in the distant past, understood and feared. Not that hell had ever been free of such sicknesses; periodically, Satan unleashed all manner of illness to beset his subjects. From what Wellington said, this plague raged virulent. People were dying in great numbers all across New Hell City. As of yet, the plague hadn't spread to Crowned Row or Hellview Estates, but Attila didn't for a moment believe that such luck would hold out.

Satan or Erra? It didn't matter who was responsible. People died all the same.

Attila scratched an armpit and frowned. Not a flea bite, he was certain of that. However, a cleansing bath when he returned home was definitely in order. He snorted. A bath? Taboo for the tribes: do not wash in running water. Well, on the grassy plains, streams were often in short supply. He remembered being hostage to the Romans in his youth and their predilection for sumptuous baths. How he had hated being forced to bathe, although after a while he grudgingly admitted enjoying the custom.

The Vietcong were still mostly silent. For weeks, they hadn't appeared to demand their delivery of ribs. That, in itself, was puzzling. Odd, also, that they hadn't shelled the neighborhood, their usual response to a refused tribute.

Not that anyone with half a brain would brave Decentral Park now, what with rats lurking beneath every bush and in the high grass. Travel across the Park was now not an option. So, despite Wellington's wish to trade places with Napoleon on Crowned Row, the Iron Duke was for all practical purposes exiled to Hellview Estates.

Attila grinned. Poor Queen Victoria. She'd have to carry on without her Iron Duke. As if she needed his help, what with all the military types surrounding her.

Sudden movement down the street drew Attila's attention. A man had entered the gateway leading to Hellview Estates. Attila squinted: he didn't recognize the newcomer and he knew nearly all their neighbors. As he watched the man, Attila tightened his grip on his bow. There was something wrong with the way the man was walking. Walking? Nearly stumbling.

Attila ran toward Napoleon's house, his breath coming quicker. Diving behind a large bush on the opposite side, he watched the newcomer, his mouth gone dry. Could it be? Could someone who'd contracted the plague actually have found their way into Hellview Estates?

Wait. Make absolutely certain. He didn't dare do any-thing rash until he got a closer look at the newcomer.

And . . . *yes!* Now he could see the ravages of plague on the man.

No time to hesitate. This didn't call for use of his bow. He drew his pistol and, taking careful aim, shot the man in the head.

As the corpse fell to the street, Attila looked around for Wellington. A brief glimpse of red in Wellington's yard. Hol-stering his gun, Attila raced toward the Iron Duke's home.

"Wellington!" He skidded to a stop on Wellington's driveway. "Get over here!"

Hedge clippers in one hand, a puzzled expression on his face, the Iron Duke joined him. Hell would come to an end before that damned man stopped keeping up appear-ances.

"What?"

Attila pointed down the street. "Plague victim. I shot him dead."

Wellington paled. "How? How did he get here?"

"He fucking walked!" Attila spat. "Now we've got to get rid of the body."

He waited, willing Wellington to respond, but the Iron Duke stood mute, momentarily robbed of speech.

"Bloody hell!" Wellington finally growled. "Just what we need! I'm certainly not going close to the chap, dead or not."

Attila couldn't have agreed more. "He's still there. What's wrong with Reassignments? He should have disap-peared by now."

"Maybe they're overwhelmed," Wellington offered. "So many deaths. Even the Undertaker must be up to his malformed eyebrows in bodies."

Attila snorted. "Keep watch," he said, gesturing toward the entrance to Hellview Estates. "And get your sidearm. That sword you're wearing won't help you much if more victims arrive. I've got fuel for my Armed Personnel Carrier. If that fucker isn't gone by the time I return, I'll set him on fire."

Wellington turned toward his front door.

"And let Napoleon know what we're dealing with here."

The Iron Duke pulled a face, no doubt unhappy at the prospect of using a leech.

Attila ran to his house, tossed first his bow, then his quiver on his front porch. Jerking open the door to his garage, he grabbed a full canister of fuel. Where the hell were his wives?

"Damn women!" he yelled, finding a box of matches. "Keep your pretty little asses inside! And don't let the boys out!"

Although the canister was heavy, Attila rushed down the sidewalk. As he passed Wellington's house, he saw the Iron Duke on his front porch, one hand held over his left ear, leech obviously in place, and his pistol in his right hand.

The body was still there. Reassignments was falling down on the job or, as Wellington pointed out, the numbers of dead were beginning to stack up. Whatever the reason, that plague victim had to be disposed of.

Cautiously, he approached the dead man. Now he could see the oozing pustules under the man's arms, staining his shirt. Unscrewing the lid to the fuel container, Attila doused the body liberally until a puddle formed on the street. Retreating a good distance away, he deposited the canister in a nearby driveway.

The plague victim still hadn't disappeared. Spitting to one side, Attila struck a match and threw it on the fuel-drenched body, followed by another to ensure ignition. The roaring eruption of flames drove him back, but he didn't leave until he was certain the dead man's body itself had actually caught fire.

Coughing at the stench of burning flesh, Attila stepped away from the pall of greasy smoke. Damn! He needed more fuel to complete his task. Another trip to his garage for a second canister full of fuel. Cautiously, fearful of back-flash, he quickly doused the burning body a second time and jumped away. For a long while he stood vigil, until he was satisfied that nothing remained but charred bones.

No one could convince him now that an increased watch wasn't necessary to keep other plague victims away.

The country club and the rest of the neighbors had to be alerted.

A looming nightmare, that's what it was. And, knowing hell, Attila was certain the terror would return.

*

Several days had passed since Wellington's communication regarding the plague victim in Hellview Estates. Such news heightened the vigilance on Crowned Row. Queen Victoria and the Austrian Empress Maria-Theresa placed their households on full alert. Soldiers and retainers from all the palaces and mansions kept watch on the boulevard separating them from Decentral Park. Sulla and his Romans tightened their lines, fearing confrontation with anyone carrying the plague.

Napoleon's orders to keep Louis' palace spotless (and hopefully flea-free) were followed to the greatest extent possible. No one was allowed on the grounds without protective clothing, and everyone had to divest themselves of any outerwear before entering the palace. Consequently, the grass surrounding the palaces and mansions grew unabated. This, of course, only further unnerved the residents: more breeding grounds for rats and fleas.

Now, attention focused on the unkempt reaches of Decentral Park. Napoleon stood on the roof of Louis' palace, spyglass in hand, scanning the Park. He feared Vietcong plague victims could easily emerge, cross the boulevard, and make for Crowned Row.

Satisfied, seeing nothing untoward, he descended to the first floor and found Quintus waiting. The young Roman had eschewed his usual khaki uniform and was clad in heavy layers, booted to the knees. Not taking any chances, this Roman.

"Quintus," Napoleon said in greeting, extending his hand and gripping the messenger's arm in a Roman handshake. "What news?"

"*Imperator.*" Quintus had lost some of the formality he'd employed in the past, a welcome change encouraged by Napoleon. "We haven't seen anyone coming in this direction from New Hell City. Sulla assures you we're on high alert. He's given orders to shoot first and ask questions later."

"Probably a wise decision. No residents are leaving here now, so we can't trust outsiders coming in. Do you have enough firepower to take care of any concerted effort to enter Crowned Row?"

"I think so. Sulla wonders, if we run low, can we take additional weapons and ammunition from the Armory?"

"I doubt Caesar would mind, nor would anyone attached to the Infernal National Guard." For the thousandth time, Napoleon asked himself where Caesar could be, especially since his villa had been blown to bits by someone or something. Not a word from the Roman dictator, no hint as to his whereabouts. Yet another mystery: hell was replete with them.

"You're an asset to all of us, Quintus. I think I can speak for nearly everyone: we appreciate your vigilance. If there's any aid I can supply, ask."

Quintus nodded, his youthful face breaking into a grin. "I'll let Sulla know, and I'll continue to bring you any information you need. *Salve, Imperator*!"

As he turned to leave, Napoleon called: "Be careful. I don't want to lose any of you."

*

Something rotten was burning. Wellington paused in his tour of the neighborhood, his pistol ready in hand. The blackened smear and bone shards of the plague victim immolated by Attila still marred the street, a reminder of the danger that could manifest at any moment.

The Iron Duke sniffed again and sneezed. Wiping his nose, he looked across to the Park. Several black plumes of smoke rose from the trees. What the devil was going on? What in Satan's name was burning with such a stench?

He quickly approached Attila's house. The king of the Huns sat on his front porch, no doubt driven outside by the insistent demands of his wives. No one had seen the brats; they stayed homebound, the ever present danger of plague something even they understood.

"Attila. What do you think is burning?"

Attila shrugged, pausing in cleaning his collection of sidearms. Shooting rats with bow and arrow was one thing; downing any invading plague victims entirely another.

"Don't know. I have my suspicions. If the wind's right, you can smell it."

"Smell what?"

"The Cong. They're burning bodies. That's my guess. Bodies stink when they burn."

Wellington frowned. If what had *not* happened to the body Attila had finally set on fire was true, and plague corpses didn't return to the Undertaker, a surfeit of dead and possibly decomposing bodies must be everywhere.

"Bloody hell. Believe it or not, I can actually feel the tiniest bit of pity for the Undertaker and his assistants. With any kind of luck, the carrion-eaters that populate hell should dine well."

That still didn't answer the question as to why plague bodies weren't returning to Reassignments. What happened to these poor souls who died of the plague, whose bodies never disappeared to reappear at the Undertaker's? An unanswered question to be sure, and one he carefully avoiding thinking about.

Oh, well. Satan ruled; he'd rectify the situation. Those souls were still his. It was only a matter of time (which hell possessed in abundance) before the bodiless dead were reanimated, fresh fodder for more eternal punishment.

"See anything on your tour?" Attila asked.

"Not a bloody thing. Quiet, so far."

"Have you talked to Napoleon today?"

After moving aside several high-powered handguns, Wellington took a seat next to Attila on his porch. "Earlier. It's quiet over there, too." He stared across the Park at the smoke rising from the trees. "I wonder how many Cong have died."

"They'll be back," Attila said, "eventually. Satan won't be cheated of his prey."

"My thoughts exactly. Damn! I wish I weren't trapped here!"

Attila snorted, reaching for another supposedly dirty sidearm. "So you don't appreciate my company, hey?"

"Oh, no." Wellington glanced sideways. "Never that. I miss being close to Her Majesty, that's all."

"I'm sure Victoria is surviving without your presence."

Wellington felt his ears go hot. "That's hardly the point."

Attila reached out and laid a hand on Wellington's shoulder. "We know how much you long to be of service to your queen, but she's a damned fine warhorse and she'll take care of herself and all her household."

"Bloody right she will."

"Yanush, with our best Huns and Mongols, is on patrol. They're armed to the teeth. Nobody's going to get past them."

Yanush, Attila's second in command, was more than capable, as were the men that rode with him. Still, the black smoke rising above Decentral Park didn't lend optimism to the future.

*

Left mostly to her own devices now that Napoleon and all the residents of Louis' palace were on continual alert, Marie wandered from room to room, leaving Napoleon and Duroc to deal with the possible arrival of plague victims. In addition to keeping everyone on Crowned Row safe, he didn't need her lingering by his side, distracting him.

She paused by one of the windows overlooking the Park. For several days now, columns of smoke kept rising over the trees. Napoleon thought the Cong were burning bodies; in one of Wellington's communications, the Duke had explained that this was what he and Attila suspected. The tale of what Attila did to the plague victim who found his way into Hellview Estates unsettled residents.

There was nothing she could do about that. What bothered everyone most was the supposition that the Undertaker might be overwhelmed by the incoming flood of dead to be reanimated. If true, how many corpses could New Hell City tolerate before Reassignments caught up with the backlog? She rubbed at her forehead; the annoying headache would not go away. She prided herself on being healthy; since choosing to remain in hell to be with Napoleon, she had never been seriously sick.

Turning from the window, she sought the bedroom and possibly the only comfortable couch Louis had installed in his over-the-top palace. She had to admit to feeling a bit tired, but that could easily be explained away considering the tension that permeated the household. Stretching out, she pulled the light covering up even though the room wasn't chill, and nestled in for a short nap. With luck, a little rest would chase her headache away.

*

"Have you seen Marie?"

Duroc shook his head. "Not since earlier this morning."

"It's not like her to disappear," Napoleon said. "I'll see if I can find her."

Up the sweeping staircase, down a wide hall, and to the bedroom the two of them shared. He stopped at the doorway, smiling as he saw Marie curled up on her favorite couch. Everyone was operating on too little sleep and too much anxiety.

Should he let her sleep? She probably needed it. He turned to go but halted, wanting to at least pull the coverlet up around her chin. Why she sought warmth puzzled him: the temperature inside and outside the palace verged on what for hell felt balmy.

Certain he made no noise, he bent over her and gently pulled the cover up close to her chin. A lock of her hair fell on one cheek, so he reached out a finger and pushed it back over her forehead.

His heart jumped in his chest. She was more than warm to the touch. A fever? Exhaustion?

"Damn!" He stepped back, hands clenching at his sides. Could it be? Oh, for the love of everything he held dear. . . .

Sprinting down the stairway, he nearly collided with Duroc.

"Géraud! Do we have a doctor in residence?"

Duroc's eyes widened. "No."

"What about Victoria? Maria-Theresa?"

"I don't think so, but I'll check." Duroc drew a quick breath. "Marie?"

Napoleon stood rooted, unable to think for a moment. "Do that. I don't know, I just don't know. She's running a fever and has mentioned she feels tired." Anger fueled by fear suffused him. He swung about, looking for something to punch his fist into. Drawing a calming breath, he faced Duroc. "If you can't find a doctor, we'll have to put out a call for one."

"I'll do my best," Duroc said. He gripped Napoleon by the shoulders. "Don't jump to conclusions, Napoleon. She's been under the same stress as everyone here, though she doesn't complain about it. I'll find a doctor, somewhere."

Napoleon nodded. "Go!"

Find a doctor? Where? With the plague sweeping through New Hell City, every doctor was hard at work treating those who might survive.

He threw his head back and stared at the ornate ceiling. Not Marie!

No matter what, he had to get help for her. If anyone could find a doctor, it would be Duroc.

He bowed his head. Prayer was useless in hell, except when offered to Satan and his powerful cohorts. One never mentioned Satan's arch enemy who dwelt in heaven. Nevertheless, he voiced an inward plea that Marie had merely caught a cold.

And not the plague.

*

Wellington's leeches did everything but handstands in their water-filled bag. He growled a curse, opened the bag, and selected what he thought to be the least offensive of the slimy things. Attaching it to his ear, he waited for contact. The agitation of his leeches could mean only that an urgent communication was pending.

No surprise there. The caller was Napoleon, and the emotions Wellington sensed were stunning.

Remind me. Do we have a doctor living in Hellview Estates?

Puzzled, Wellington shook his head. This was unlike Napoleon, who knew the identities of every resident in Hellview Estates. *Not that I know of. Why?*

Marie's fallen ill. I need to find a doctor for her.

Bloody hell! I can't think of a doctor living anywhere close by. How long has she been ill?

I think just today. She seemed well yesterday. We're running in circles over here, so I could have missed signs she wasn't feeling well.

Wellington chewed on his lower lip. *I'll see what I can find but, Napoleon, you realize that every doctor in New Hell City is already treating hordes of plague victims. We'll be damned lucky to find a doctor at this stage.*

We've got to try. I've sent Duroc on the search. If it is the plague . . . I can't lose her, Arthur, I can't.

Arthur? Wellington couldn't remember the last time Napoleon had called him by his given name.

I'll do my best. Maybe Attila knows someone.

Be quick about it. Keep me posted.

The communication went dead. Wellington squared his shoulders, returned the leech to its bag, and headed over to Attila's house. Where the devil could they find a doctor and, having found one on this side of the Park, how could they rush him over to Crowned Row?

First things first. He hoped Attila knew something.

It was a slim hope. In hell, hope and good luck were strangers.

*

"Marie's sick?" Attila waited for Wellington to reply.

The Iron Duke seemed momentarily bereft of speech. "I communicated with Napoleon not five minutes ago. You're a damned hard chap to find."

Attila looked across the Park. "So are you. Sometimes."

"Do you know of a doctor living in the neighborhood?"

"No. We've got one overbearing lawyer, a number of Satan's governmental favorites who stay in New Hell City a lot, and us. That's about it. We're not overcrowded here."

"And so far, we've managed to keep whoever's still here housebound, now that the plague is afoot. Damn!"

Attila pulled on his mustache. "One of my Huns had some training with a shaman. We depended on them as both healers and contacts with the spirit world."

"Do you think this fellow knows how to treat the plague, if that's what has sickened Marie?"

"I don't know. I'll find him and ask." He met and held Wellington's eyes. "How's Napoleon?"

"Understandably upset. He and Marie. . . ."

"I know. Keep watch for anyone trying to enter the neighborhood. I'll find Tokhash and question him."

He set off down the street at a trot; Tokhash wouldn't be hard to locate. He and several Huns under Yanush's command rode up and down the streets, ever alert for anyone leaving the Park and heading for Hellview Estates. A quick glance to his right, at black smoke drifting up from the trees, confirmed that the Cong wouldn't be letting anyone wander around without killing them at first sight.

*

Where was she? Marie opened her eyes to a view of the ornate ceiling above her. Her headache had worsened, and she felt chilled. She pulled the blanket up around her neck, the movement telling her she no longer lay on the couch. Somehow, someone had moved her to the bed. She dimly remembered Napoleon sitting beside her, cursing softly in every language he knew.

She was alone now. It was quiet, too quiet. She turned her head and looked out the opened door to the hallway. She'd never been the sickly sort, even when she lived on earth. Purgatory was a distant memory: death tended to jumble things together. Her punitive arrival in hell gave her a body identical to the body she'd had when alive. And since then she'd never suffered more than a passing cold.

She counted herself fortunate to have so far avoided the various afflictions that sometimes preyed on the residents of New Hell City and, eventually, Hellview Estates. Worse torments existed than a passing sickness.

What was wrong with her now? She couldn't think clearly. Whatever she'd contracted was far worse than a cold.

Yes, too difficult to think. She closed her eyes, attempting to will the headache away. She was tired enough that she didn't want to move.

Yesterday . . . only yesterday, she felt fine. Just this morning she began chilling and attempting to wish her headache away.

Maybe more sleep would help. She closed her eyes and sought slumber.

*

By now, Napoleon was certain he'd worn a groove in the floor with his pacing. He left Marie sleeping, but she didn't look restful. He rubbed the bridge of his nose, making a conscious attempt to keep breathing normally.

Whatever had sickened her had all the symptoms of the onset of plague. Time after time, he reviewed every possible chance encounter she might have had with an infected flea. No one else in the palace had come down with similar maladies. Where the devil could she have gone that might have left her vulnerable to a plague carrier? He simply could not guess.

The temptation to grab a leech and talk to either Wellington or Attila tugged at him. He knew the two of them were trying their best to locate a doctor, as was Duroc. But Wellington was correct: finding a doctor now with New Hell City full to bursting with plague victims was a long shot. An incredibly long shot.

And one that he hoped might bear fruit.

Here he was—Emperor of France, King of Italy, once ruler of a vast empire—rendered helpless by circumstances he couldn't control.

"Napoleon?"

Having arrived unnoticed, Duroc stood a mere few paces away.

"Any luck?"

His friend shook his head. "I've mobilized everyone up and down Crowned Row, but no one's heard of a doctor taking up residence. Of course, I didn't bother checking with Tiberius. I wouldn't trust anything or anyone associated with that idiot."

"Keep looking." Napoleon drew a long breath. "I can't believe it, Géraud. We've been so vigilant in keeping the place free of any kind of vermin. If it *is* the plague, how the devil did Marie come down with it? What did we miss?"

"Nothing. Don't torture yourself with trying to figure out what happened."

Napoleon clenched his teeth. "Easy for you to say," he ground out. "Do you truly understand? Marie's not even supposed to *be* here. She had the chance to return to purgatory and refused, choosing to stay in hell with me. And, dammit, I still don't understand why she thinks I'm worth it."

"Love is strange," Duroc said. "Strange and unaccountable to logic."

"What happens if she dies?" Napoleon began pacing again. "If either you or I die, or anyone else in Satan's hell dies, we go to Reassignments. She doesn't belong here. No trip to the Undertaker for her. Will she just disappear? Fade away like some pleasant dream?"

Duroc reached out and touched Napoleon's arm. "No one knows. I don't know; you don't know. We have no history to provide us with answers."

Napoleon bowed his head. "You're right, Duroc. There's nothing we can do unless and until we find someone who can cure her." He straightened. "Keep looking, my friend, keep looking. That's all we can do now."

*

"Attila!" Wellington stood in the middle of the street at the entrance to Hellview Estates. "Hold your fire! Don't shoot!"

The king of the Huns lowered his pistol. "Who is it?"

Wellington looked down the street leading into the neighborhood. "I don't have a clue, but this chap doesn't seem to be ill. And he's waving an arm as if to tell us he's no threat."

It was true: the man approaching appeared healthy. Dressed modestly, he carried a black bag in one hand. More importantly, he was unarmed. Wellington waited until the man drew close. There was something about him that triggered a memory from the past.

"Greetings," the man said with a slight bow. "Please don't think I'm a danger. I've been looking for the Emperor Napoleon and was told to come here. Is this where he lives?"

Wellington exchanged a quick look with Attila. "Usually," he replied. "Who are you?"

"Dominique-Jean Larrey, at your service," the man said, bowing again.

He couldn't be. Wellington stared, his mouth falling open, only now recognizing the fellow.

"*Doctor* Larrey? What . . . how did you get here?"

"It wasn't easy. I had a vehicle, but it ran out of fuel about a mile away."

Wellington shook his head, not believing his eyes. Memory took him back to the battlefield of Waterloo. Larrey was so highly regarded as a physician that even Napoleon's enemies held him in high esteem. During the shelling of the French lines, Wellington had recognized the doctor giving aid to the wounded under fire and directing that they be carried off the field. Seeing this through his spyglass, Wellington ordered his soldiers not to aim in the doctor's direction. Doffing his hat in salutation, someone, he didn't remember who now, had asked whom he was saluting. He'd lifted his sword and, pointing at Larrey, responded that he saluted the courage and devotion of an age that had passed.

After the battle was over, the doctor was captured by the Prussians and given a death sentence. His life was saved by the intervention of a German physician who'd previously been his student and by orders of the Prussian commander, Blücher, whose wounded son had once been taken prisoner by the French. Enemy or not, Larrey had saved the son's life.

So highly regarded was this physician that, after the battle, Blücher had returned him to France with a Prussian escort.

"You know this man?" Attila asked, holstering his weapon.

"Not personally, no. His reputation is beyond compare." Wellington extended a hand. "Doctor Larrey, you couldn't have arrived at a more fortuitous time. Napoleon isn't here. He's on the opposite side of Decentral Park, but he needs you more than I can say."

Larrey's eyes widened. "He's not contracted the plague, has he?"

"No. He's worried about Marie Walewska."

"She's here? That stuns me. Such a wonderful lady and so utterly devoted to him."

"Oh, she's here in hell but it's a long story, and we don't have time for that. Somehow, we've got to get you across the Park to treat her. Napoleon thinks she might have the plague."

"How many days has she shown symptoms?"

"From what Napoleon told me, just this morning. She seemed quite fine yesterday."

"That's welcome news. If it *is* the plague, we may be in time."

"And *if*," Attila inserted, "we can manage to get you to Crowned Row. Why are you here, Doctor?"

Larrey set his bag down and spread his hands. "I wanted to offer my services to my emperor during this terrible time. He was always a good friend and I couldn't stand the thought of him being unprotected from this illness."

Wellington turned to Attila. "You've still got the APC, don't you?"

"Yes. Fueled and ready."

"Can we get Doctor Larrey to Crowned Row?"

"Damned chancy. The Cong are running scared and will be shitting bricks if anyone tries to cross the Park."

"We'll have to take the risk." Wellington laid a hand on Larrey's shoulder. "We'll get you there, Doctor, somehow, even if we have to kill every Vietcong between here and there. Go, Attila. Bring every man you can fit into the APC. And make certain each of them is heavily armed. We've got a mercy mission to execute, and I won't take no for an answer."

*

Napoleon's pacing only added to his unsettled state of mind; he forced himself to stop and sit. Seated at his desk, he stared at the wall, his mind gone quiet. He recognized his own state of denial, his disbelief that anything could take Marie from his side. After a chance meeting at the License Bureau, he'd taken her home and held her close to his heart ever after. Of all the women he'd known, including both his former wives, she was the one who would never desert him. The past had proven that, time after time.

And now, out of her love for him, she had chosen to stay in hell, a decision he sometimes found difficult to understand. However, as Duroc said, love was unfazed by logic.

The sudden vibration of the leeches on his desk brought him out of his musings. He grabbed for the water-filled bag, snatched out the first leech he touched, and slapped it on his ear.

Napoleon! We've got Doctor Larrey! Attila's going to try making it across the Park!

For a long moment, stunned, he didn't reply. Larrey? What the devil was *that* man doing in hell? It was the last place he should be. That doctor was as close to a saint as anyone Napoleon had ever known.

When? he sent. *When did you find him?*

Minutes ago. He found us. He was looking for you. Wellington paused briefly. *Attila's getting the APC. He's going to attempt the crossing.*

Is he coming armed, besides what the APC carries? The Cong will surely try to stop him.

He's bringing several Huns with him, all armed to the teeth.

I can't believe this. Such luck is sorely lacking in hell.

Believe it. A Hun who, Attila said, had some training as a shaman denied he could do anything to cure the plague. I'm staying behind. Until we're told otherwise, one of us must stay here and keep watch over Hellview Estates.

Napoleon fell silent, the sudden misting of his eyes betraying him. *Think good thoughts, Wellington, if that might help. You have no notion how much this means to me. Keep me advised. I'll have the leeches with me so you can contact me at any time.*

Of course. Here comes Attila now. I'll be back in touch.

Still astounded by the news, Napoleon returned the leech to its bag. Jumping to his feet, he hurried out of the office.

"Duroc! Where are you? I need you!"

*

Attila started the APC, belting the doctor into the front seat and issuing commands in Hunnish to the three men in back, whom Yanush had chosen for the mission. They were heavily armed, those Huns, each more than competent with modern weapons. Slamming the passenger door, he ran to his side of the vehicle and quickly attached a strip of white cloth to an antenna. Even the Cong should recognize the universal sign of truce.

He hoped.

Putting the vehicle in gear, he drove to a roadway that cut across Decentral Park in the direction of Louis' palace. Now, if he could make it across the Park without incident, he would consider the trip a victory.

"It's going to be a rough ride," he said to Larrey. "We'll be traveling as fast as possible."

The doctor nodded. "I understand. You're Attila?"

"I am."

"I've heard of you."

Attila grinned. "So has just about everybody else. All of them giving such glowing reports of what a decent, up-standing man I am."

The doctor's mouth twitched slightly, evidence of a smile. "If Wellington trusts you, far be it from me to do otherwise."

Attila turned down the road and gunned the APC into high gear. "If I tell you to duck, duck. I don't know what the fucking Cong will do. They've been burning bodies for days now, since the Undertaker got overwhelmed with incoming victims. I'm sure you've noticed that bodies haven't been disappearing as usual."

"I have. That only adds to the problem."

As he entered the Park, Attila hoped he wouldn't need the armaments the APC boasted. He hoped the three Huns would be protection enough to repulse any attack from the Vietcong. Hope be damned! He fervently *wished* the trip was over, and he'd already reached Crowned Row with his precious cargo.

*

Napoleon stood at the top of the steps to the palace, face expressionless. He didn't dare let anyone, save Duroc, witness his anxiety. Surety is a requisite of command: never let the men who serve you sense any uncertainty.

"Attila's on his way," he said to Duroc. "He's bringing Doctor Larrey. Don't ask me how he wound up in Hellview Estates today; I don't know."

"Coincidence?"

"In hell?"

Duroc shrugged. "Coincidence or not, fortunately for us he was searching for you. If anyone can cross the Park now, it's going to be Attila. With luck, the Cong will be so disorganized they won't prove an insurmountable problem."

"From your lips to Satan's ear. That would be best." He nodded toward the group of soldiers gathered at the foot of the steps, armed with modern weapons. "I want these men to take up positions just inside the Park; don't let them go farther than that. Even though we haven't seen any Cong, we don't know how close they might be to Crowned Row."

He met and held Duroc's eyes. "I'd rather you didn't go with them."

Duroc smiled. "In your place, I'm their commanding officer. We can't risk you. Besides, you'll want to be at Marie's side when the doctor arrives."

"Then be careful, my friend. Be very careful. Don't take any chances. I don't want any of you harmed."

"We'll be as timid as rabbits," Duroc said. "Rabid rabbits with poisonous fangs."

*

The road ahead appeared free of Vietcong; although a welcome sight, Attila was keenly aware that their situation could change in an instant. He glanced sidelong at the doctor, who had remained silent since leaving Hellview Estates. Apparently, Wellington was familiar with Larrey and held him in the highest esteem. This was enough for Attila. At times, he dismissed the Iron Duke as being overly officious and somewhat of a dandy, but he could never deny the man's military knowledge or his courage. There was steel in Wellington when called for, a determination that underscored his actions. An unlikely friendship had blossomed between him and Napoleon, a relationship that belied what the two had experienced in their earthly lives. That, in itself, was odd. Old enemies often remained adversaries after death.

Unbidden, the memory of his brother Bleda's attempt on his life rustled in Attila's mind.

Well, stranger things happened every day in hell. Who was he to question?

Over halfway there. Attila kept the APC speeding along, his eyes scanning the road ahead and the trees and bushes on his left and right. Periodically, the smell of burning bodies drifted across the road. What the shit was going on in Reassignments? Sooner or later, Satan would have to do something—anything to bring this chaos to an end. Unless, of course, this chaos was part and parcel of Erra's devising.

Erra. Attila still couldn't understand where the Babylonian god of disaster had come from, but he knew Erra was a plague god. Who released him and his Seven to decimate the hells, to have power over the gods of the damned who held sway in their own domains? Another unanswered question: life in hell was one shitty mystery after another.

Damn! A round of ammunition fire sounded, but no bullets strafed the armored sides of the APC. The three Huns riding in back readied their weapons, rolling down the windows to allow unfettered aim if needed. The stench of burning flesh filled the vehicle.

"Keep your head down," Attila snapped at Larrey. "We're protected as we can be, but I can't guarantee anything. Those fucking Cong can be anywhere."

The doctor nodded, placing his bag between his feet and leaning forward as far as possible.

"How soon will we arrive?" he asked, his voice muffled.

"We're getting closer. If we can keep up speed, we—"

In an instant, before Attila could react, a man stumbled into the road directly in front of the APC.

The collision between an APC and a damned soul left no doubt as to the outcome. The man rolled up on the hood and slammed into the windshield. A brief glimpse at the dead man's face told Attila this was a Vietcong, and an obvious victim of the plague.

Gripping the steering wheel, Attila swerved to the right, throwing the body onto the side of the road. He glanced in the rearview mirror to see the Cong lying crumpled, partially hidden by the shrubs he'd rolled among. Straightening the APC, Attila accelerated to an even faster speed.

"Another plague victim," he growled. "At least, it looked like that."

"I couldn't see," Larrey replied. "You told me to keep my head down."

"So I did." Attila licked at one side of his mustache, caught himself showing his nervousness. "Whatever made him walk in front of us makes no difference now. He's dead. Another body for the Cong to burn."

"We're almost there?" one of the Huns in the back asked.

"Close. Very close," Attila replied, then switching to English: "If we don't hit anyone else and the Cong don't come after us, we should make it."

Ahead he could see the edge of Decentral Park and the welcoming sight of the boulevard that ran by Crowned Row. *Almost there.*

Incoming rounds hit the panels of the APC from both sides of the road. One of the rear windows took a hit but didn't shatter. Attila's Huns returned fire in the direction they thought the Vietcong hid. And then other shots rang out from closer to the boulevard.

Damn, damn, damn! Who was attacking the Cong?

Who the shit cared? Leaning forward over the steering wheel, Attila burst out of the Park, took his bearings, and aimed directly toward the drive leading to Louis' palace.

"We made it," he said as Larrey lifted his head. "Now, let's hope you're in time to help Marie."

*

A leech to his ear, Napoleon bolted down the steps, hearing the exchange of gunfire coming from the Park. It could only be Duroc's soldiers confronting the Cong. Moments later, Attila's APC pulled onto Crowned Row.

Wellington! Napoleon sent. *Attila's made it!*

Oh, excellent news! came the response. *I was hoping he would. If there's anyone who can help Marie, it's Doctor Larrey. He's the best!*

Believe me, I know. Here they are! I'll let you know what happens. He started to detach the leech and paused. *I can't thank you enough, Wellington. You must know that.*

I do. Go greet Larrey and get him to Marie's side as quickly as possible.

Removing the leech, Napoleon rushed over to the APC and opened the passenger door. The doctor looked a little shaken, but gathered his bag and exited the vehicle.

"Jean," Napoleon said, taking the doctor by the shoulders. "Old friend. I need your help."

Larrey blinked several times and smiled. "That's why I'm here. I couldn't let you face whatever has sickened Marie without some medical assistance. Where is she?"

Napoleon gestured up the steps. "In our bedroom. I'll lead the way."

As he and the doctor started toward the front doors, he heard Attila call out:

"You owe me big time, Napoleon. And don't think I won't remember, hey!"

*

Time felt odd. Sleeping and waking, the hours passed in a jumble. Marie changed positions in bed, still exhausted. Her headache pounded no worse, but it seemed every part of her ached.

Footsteps. She turned her head, opened her eyes, and saw Napoleon and a man she didn't recognize approaching the bed. At a nod from Napoleon, the man pulled a chair to the side of the bed and leaned closer.

"I'm Doctor Larrey, Marie," he said. "Please let me examine you."

A doctor? Here? She licked her lips and tried to smile. "If you can make me feel better," she said, her voice sounding somewhat hoarse, "you can look at any part of me you wish."

The man smiled and pulled back the bedclothes. His light touch aroused no alarm in her. First he ran his fingers over her forehead, then looked into her eyes, felt the line of her jaw, and finally placed a hand under each arm, gently probing.

"How long have you been feeling like this?" he asked.

"This morning, I think. It came on suddenly. Yesterday, I didn't feel bad at all. I was tired, but so was everyone else around here. Now I ache all over."

"That's good, very good." The doctor opened his bag and rummaged around. "I'm going to give you some medicine. It won't taste good, but it's what you need right now."

"Even if it tastes horrible, I'll take every bit of it."

The doctor turned to Napoleon. "I'll need a glass of water."

As Napoleon went in search of a water glass, the doctor removed a jar filled with some kind of powder. "This will help, I promise."

"Napoleon knows you?" she asked, eyeing the medicine.

"We're old friends. Ah," he said, as Napoleon returned. "Thank you."

Larrey retrieved a spoon from the depths of his bag and carefully shook out a portion of powder. Pouring it in with the water, he stirred the two together until satisfied. Nodding to Napoleon, he slid a hand under Marie's head and lifted it so she could sip from the glass.

She met his eyes, saw only concern there, and took a tentative drink. She grimaced; the doctor hadn't lied, the taste *was* bitter. Another sip. She heard him murmur encouragement and, bracing herself for the vile taste, she emptied the glass.

"That's good, that's very good," the doctor said, setting the glass on the table beside the bed. "Now I want you to sleep, even though you've probably slept more lately than you ever have before. Rest and this medicine will help you feel better. I promise."

She looked from him to Napoleon. The tightness had disappeared from her beloved's face; all that was left was a combination of relief and tenderness.

"Jean?" Napoleon asked. "What is it?"

"What it *isn't* is the plague," Larrey responded. "It's a bad case of what moderns call the flu. That illness can strike without warning, leaving the patient very, very sick."

Marie reached out from under the covers, seeking Napoleon's hand.

"If you can stand it," she said, trying to smile, "I think I'll sleep some more."

He smiled back and took her hand. "Sleep all you wish, Marie. What's important is that you recover."

*

Wellington stood on his front porch, gazing up and down the street, his sidearm ready at hand. No one stirred. With Attila gone across Decentral Park, he was left to defend Hellview Estates. Attila's Huns and Mongols would respond to his commands, since Attila had made it known that Wellington would be in charge of them in his absence.

A feeling of utter amazement stole over him: how entirely unlooked-for was the appearance of Doctor Larrey. How that coincidence happened, he didn't question. Only a bit of empathy was needed to understand the terrible and utter helplessness Napoleon must have suffered when Marie fell ill. With the plague erupting everywhere, she'd seemed to evince preliminary symptoms of that deadly disease.

Now everything depended on Larrey's skill. Wellington didn't question whether, even as a last resort, the doctor might be able to stop the progression of what Napoleon feared was the plague. A brilliant field doctor, specializing in caring for the wounded, Larrey was nonetheless a highly-trained medical doctor, well equipped to deal with civilian illnesses.

The leeches stirred in their bag. Sighing, he removed one and settled it onto his ear.

Wellington, Napoleon sent. *Doctor Larrey has treated Marie. It's not the plague! He says it's a bad case of the flu. She should recover in about a week of rest and medication.*

Not the plague? Even so, considering the risk of plague, with a doctor found and treatment given, the gamble of Attila crossing Decentral Park had paid off.

Marvelous news! Wellington responded. *Be sure you reward Attila. That must have been an edgy ride.*

Oh, trust me, he won't let me forget it. And Wellington . . . thank you again.

Wellington chuckled. *What are friends for?*

*

Hell was hell. Hell, as far as anyone could postulate, would remain hell for eternity. And, hell being hell, continual torments were meted out daily to the condemned. However, once in a very great while, something occurred so extraordinary that those imprisoned in Satan's realm could hardly believe their good fortune.

Napoleon sat on the edge of the bed, holding Marie's pale hand while she drifted off to sleep. Doctor Larrey closed his medical bag and leaned back in his chair, a satisfied expression on his face.

"Jean," Napoleon said, keeping his voice low so as to not disturb Marie, "for what you've done I have no way of repaying you."

The doctor smiled. "You know I'd do anything for you. Our past links us together and all the good you did for me when we were alive makes us even closer friends."

"I can't believe you're here in hell. You're one of the worthiest men I've ever known. Dammit, Jean . . . of all people *you* should be in heaven. I simply don't understand what happened that I find you here."

"I don't understand, either. I have no idea what I could have done that sent me to hell after I died. Believe me, I've questioned why I'm here over and over again."

"As do most of us. Where have you been? It's rather common knowledge around here that I live in Hellview Estates." Napoleon shook his head, baffled. "Why haven't we met before?"

"To tell the truth, I don't know *where* I've been. I remember dying and then a long period of darkness. Only recently did I awaken to find myself in New Hell City. Perhaps I was held outside the passage of time and reanimated recently. I've been trying to find you for weeks now."

"The plague. Maybe that's what happened. I can't guess as to Satan's mind, but there's a chance he decided to grant me a favor. For some reason, he considers Wellington and me necessary to advance a hidden agenda of his. We don't question; you'll find out that questions aren't always the healthiest path to take." Napoleon glanced down at Marie who, for the first time since morning, appeared peaceful. "I know our neighborhood and who lives in it. There's an empty house several doors down from mine. If I can get permission and unless you have a place to stay, I'd be honored if you would consider living there."

Larrey's eyes widened. "Of course. But I have nothing save the bag I carry."

"That's not a problem. A number of houses in Hellview Estates come fully furnished."

Napoleon looked up at the sound of a knock at the door to find Duroc standing half in and half out of the bedroom.

"Géraud, please meet Doctor Larrey."

Duroc stepped forward and shook the doctor's hand. "Your reputation precedes you, sir." Glancing at Marie, he lifted an eyebrow.

"The flu," Larrey said, a slight smile touching his lips. "Not the plague."

"Thank all the powers that be! And all our thanks to you, Doctor." Duroc grinned and motioned in the direction of Decentral Park. "You were right, Napoleon. The Cong were waiting along the road, but totally unprepared to be attacked by us. We didn't lose a man."

Bowing, Duroc left the room.

"So," Napoleon said, a feeling of unexpected joy filling his heart, "in the meantime, you'll be staying here, Jean. I'll fill you in on all the details. One thing's for certain, every neighborhood should have its resident physician. In my case, it's doubly wonderful that the physician is a friend."

Yes, hell was hell. And despite that fact, rarely, extremely rarely, an ever-so-fleeting glimpse of light penetrated even Satan's darkness.

What Price Oblivion?

R.E. Hinkle

"Thou art a soul in bliss, but I am bound
Upon a wheel of fire that mine own tears
Do scald like molten lead."

—Shakespeare, *King Lear*

He held only a piece of old rust-barnacled metal, an impromptu weapon at best. But that was enough. An improvised weapon suited a spontaneous kill.

Charles Baggs clenched his teeth in horror as the metal penetrated flesh, sending an impact shock up his arm. In life he'd been the grifter who invented the fake gold brick swindle, but never a killer. That shock reflected in the tall man's widening eyes as the makeshift blade sank seven inches into his belly. Blood, slick and steaming, belched out onto Baggs' hand.

The tall man fell back against the filthy alley wall. A slow breath gurgled over his lips and teeth. He tried wrapping his own hands around the metal searing into his violated guts, but pain and surprise worked a wicked one-two punch that left him impotent to save himself. He could only clutch feebly at the blade.

Sorrow and remorse bubbled up inside Baggs. "I'm sorry," he said.

The tall man blinked at him, uncomprehending.

"I'm sorry," repeated Baggs. "It's not me. It's hell. I'm so, so sorry." Then he brought his other hand up for better purchase on his weapon and dragged it sideways with all his strength. The sounds of torn fabric and rent flesh ripped into the rancid alley air. The tall man drew in an inverted scream. His fingers scrabbled at Baggs' cheeks, leaving bloody commas behind. Baggs closed his nose to the stink of blood and intestines and looked away, his own guts heaving.

"Be still," pleaded Baggs, looking out of the alley mouth onto empty streets. "Be still, be still, be still." With shaking hands he cut again, this time back down and to the left, completing his butcher's cut.

The tall man's dying throat clicked and bubbled.

Baggs yanked the metal free and let it clatter to the ground. Just as his hands had been spurred first to take up and then to use the weapon, so now his eyes were drawn back down to witness the last moments of his latest victim. He was as helpless to resist this as he had been to avoid the murder in the first place. This was the nature of his hell: to act, to witness, and then to agonize. It wasn't fair. Hell was supposed to hold each soul's just punishment. But *this*? How was this just? This was only evil compounding evil.

The tall man remained upright, helpless as a pinned insect against the alley bricks. He began to gasp his last. He slid slowly downward until his backside bumped concrete. Then he simply sat there, eyes wide, legs akimbo, crimson-smeared hands trying to hold back the guts tumbling out of him in gray coils.

Before anyone could stumble by and identify Charles as the Tally Man, Baggs ran.

*

Once, literally a lifetime ago, he had been known to some as Doc. They had called him that, some said, because his skill at 'skinning suckers' was as sharp as any surgeon's. That had been in Denver, and in Omaha, and in Deadwood, and a dozen other places whose names lurked in the fog of his memory. When Oscar Wilde journeyed to Colorado in 1882, the *Rocky Mountain News* had weighed up his gifts against those of Baggs and decided that, by comparison, the great writer looked like "thirty cents."

No one called him Doc here. That was as much mercy as he could hope for in this cellar of the forsaken. Instead, on the streets of Incendianapolis, those few who knew him at all knew him simply as Charles. To the rest, his true name meant nothing; they knew only the reputation of the Tally Man, and this they feared. His victims never remembered enough after his attack to connect his two identities. He was the anonymous bogeyman of lost souls, striking without warning, spurred on in the moment by irresistible impulse. So many deaths could be strung back to a common source solely by the fact that each of Baggs' kills woke in the Mortuary while being subjected to the Undertaker's perverse modifications—small in these cases, but crucial and consistent.

In life, Baggs had deplored his fellow confidence men when they resorted to violence. Here, he had become the very thing he loathed. If death could provide an escape, he would take it. Without reservation. But a man was allotted only one death. After that came only a brief pause in darkness and, thereafter, the resumption of a hell worse than life.

*

He moved quickly along gloom-shrouded sidewalks, head down. He encountered no one. Were such things as blessings possible in hell, solitude would be one. And was, today. Normally the streets of Incendianapolis would be choked with the day-to-day crush of lost souls. Now they stretched empty and haunted by silence.

The plagues had brought this silence, born of fear and quailing before the wrath of Erra and the Seven . . . or Satan himself, some believed, although few gave voice to it. Diseases so fiendish and terrible no human mind could have conjured them. Baggs himself had once seen a woman—or rather, the putrid remains of one—attacking randomly on the street until at last she swelled up and burst into a shower of maggots. These days, folks remained indoors. There were worse things than disease. There were worse things even than the Tally Man.

He cut across the broad empty lane and rounded a corner, head down, ears pricked up for the sound of approaching plague-gangs, and collided with another form so hard that his breath caught in his lungs.

"Charles!" said the man he had bumped. "I've been looking all over for you. What in hell's name are you doing out here? It's not safe!"

Relief flooded into Baggs. "Gnaeus," he said, and put his hand to his pounding heart. "Thank God it's you."

The man called Gnaeus, or Pompey the Great, clapped a hand over Baggs' mouth. "Don't blaspheme," he said as the ruddy vault above them grumbled like thunder and his dark eyes shifted.

Baggs knocked the hand away. "Don't touch me."

Gnaeus' face twisted with shock, and then mustered a sly grin and a peal of low laughter. "Ah, Charles, my good friend, it's a shame you weren't born in Rome during the days of her full glory. You would have fit right in." Gnaeus himself, a talented general, had married Caesar's daughter Julia to join the First Triumvirate, and knew the workings of Rome's glory firsthand.

"Never mind Rome," said Baggs. "If it's not safe for me to be out here, it's equally dangerous for you."

"Just so," said Gnaeus. "But the difference between us is that I am quite capable of taking care of my rather prodigious self." *Prodigious* was a good word for him: underneath a threadbare yellow suit, Gneaus bore a conspicuous resemblance to a globe belted at the equator. "You, on the other hand . . . surely you agree that some men are naturally suited to the subtle art of dispensing violence—when necessary, of course—while others are not."

Baggs was tempted to say, *You'd be surprised*. Instead, his gaze fixed on the scar on Gnaeus' cheek, in the shape of the number *19*. Soon, courtesy of the Undertaker, the tall man Baggs had left ripped open in the alley would be sporting a similar mark of his own. Only his would be *65*: the Tally Man's running score.

Gnaeus lost his good humor. His fingers came up and lightly touched the old wound. "I know," he said. "The thrice-damned bastard took me by surprise. I only wish I could remember his face. Still, sooner or later someone will catch him in the act, and then a great number of us are going to spend some pleasurable weeks paying the Tally Man back in kind."

"There's no pleasure in hell," said Baggs.

That made Gnaeus grin again. "Not for *him*," he said, and then took Baggs by the arm. "But come! We're late! Or rather, *you* are. What you asked of me proved difficult to arrange, even for me. And the man who has what you want isn't the type you keep waiting."

*

Before the advent of the pestilences, this place had housed a tavern called the *Thorn and Crown*. Recently, a plague-gang had cornered the infected owner inside and set the barroom alight, watching while he screamed and the building burned around his infected self. Now it was a jackstraw monument to the ravages of combustion, all melted glass and charcoal timbers, as black and empty as a diseased tooth.

Gnaeus led Baggs to the doorway and stopped. "This is as far as I go," he said, and extended his meaty hand.

Baggs considered the ringed fingers a moment, then shook the Roman's hand. "You're not coming?"

"Not I," said Gnaeus. "For once, I'm the facilitator and not the negotiator."

Baggs nodded and withdrew his hand. "If this works, I won't be seeing you again."

"That's true."

Baggs narrowed his eyes. "You sound skeptical."

Gnaeus chuckled. "I am eternally skeptical," he said. "Remember, Charles, this *is* hell. The only thing you can count on is that you can't count on anything." He turned and disappeared back up the street with surprising speed for one so fat.

Baggs steadied himself and went inside.

A man stood in burnt shadows near the remains of the bar, his back to the doorway. Long, pale hair spilled over the upturned collar of his black leather overcoat, his hands thrust deep into its pockets.

"Mister Baggs," said the man, not turning. His voice was low and smoothly confident.

"That's right."

After a short pause, the man in the shadows said, "You're late."

"I know," said Baggs. "I was—" He swallowed, feeling stupid. His words had dried up on his tongue. Irritating. Words were his gift, the tools with which he prised fools from their fortunes. Words had never failed him before.

"Unavoidably detained?" asked the man in the shadows.

"Something like that, yes." Baggs had a strange urge to fidget.

"Understandable," said the man in the shadows, and then he turned around.

He was surprisingly young and handsome, smooth-skinned and bright-eyed, with high cheekbones and a pale, errant lock of hair drooping down his forehead. Maybe in contrast to all the shadows, Baggs guessed.

Something about him was . . . familiar.

"Have we met before?"

"No," said the man in the shadows. He smiled oddly. "I don't believe we have."

Baggs frowned. "I feel I know you."

The man shook his head. "No, I would remember. My name is Legea Cojocaru."

"Cojocaru," said Baggs, trying out the name like a pair of new shoes.

"That's close enough," said Cojocaru. "For business, anyway. Speaking of which . . . shall we get down to it?"

"If you like," said Baggs.

"Oh, I do," said Cojocaru. "These days, I find myself in high demand. Yes, yes. In times like these, there's always a great deal of business for a man who . . . well, let's just say for a man who knows how to get hold of the things other men need. Things like *this*, for instance." He pulled his hands from his pockets; in one of them was a flat case, not very different from the one Baggs once used to hold his spectacles at night.

"Is that . . . ?"

"That's right," said Cojocaru, and opened the lid. Nestled on a bed of what appeared to be red felt were a hypodermic needle and a small vial of clear liquid. "Nepenthe."

Baggs licked his lips. "Where did you get it?"

Cojocaru laughed softly. "Through many hands," he said. "I'm surprised Gnaeus didn't tell you. My specialty is the hard-to-find."

"Actually, he did," said Baggs, eyes drawn to that small miracle on red felt. "But I didn't expect it to actually happen."

"Hell," said Cojocaru contemptuously as he snapped the case closed. "It's bad enough that earthly life is plagued with doubts. This place only magnifies them and turns them back on us." He sighed. "Still, I suppose we must resign ourselves to that. What cannot be cured must be endured, as the poet once said."

Baggs pointed to the case. "That's the cure."

"Indeed it is," said Cojocaru and slipped the case back in his pocket. "The best cure of them all."

"Oblivion."

"Oblivion," said Cojocaru, nodding. "Oblivion can now be had." He turned and stepped a few paces toward the bar. "So what remains, then, if not negotiating the price?"

"First I'll need to know it's the real thing," said Baggs. "I'll have to know that it works."

Cojocaru turned back toward him. "A demonstration? I don't see how that's possible. Aside from the problem of finding someone to test it on—it obviously couldn't be either of us—what you crave requires a full dose, and then I'd need a replacement supply. But then, I suppose you'd want that one tested, too. Which would require me to find yet another. And then another. And then another." He spread his hands. "You see the vicious circle we'd be caught in?"

Baggs did. "Still, you don't expect me to just take you word for it."

"As a matter of fact," said Cojocaru, "I do."

Baggs folded his arms.

Cojocaru sighed. "Suit yourself." He started for the hole where a door had once been. "A prize like this can easily find itself another buyer."

Baggs put his hands up. "Wait!"

Cojocaru stopped, and studied the silent Baggs patiently.

"It's just—how am I supposed to just trust you? Like you said, this *is* hell."

"And hell is for liars and thieves."

"I'm no thief," said Baggs.

"As I'm no liar." Cojocaru sighed. "But I suppose one of us will have to concede, and I'm feeling unusually generous. So here's what we'll do. . . ." Cojocaru came forward, drawing the case out of his pocket again. He took Baggs by the hand and placed the case into it. "It's yours," he said and raised one finger. "But I expect you to meet my price before you use it."

Baggs looked down at the case on his upturned palm. It weighed almost nothing. "How much?"

"*Money?*" said Cojocaru. "I *have* money. What I want in return from you is a favor. Nothing substantial." He closed Baggs' fingers around the case.

"What do you want me to do?"

Cojocaru smiled. "I want you to kill someone for me."

*

Fifteen minutes later, Baggs was striding with head down and shoulders hunched along the streets that led to Mauldine Square, Cojocaru's answer to the question Baggs had asked echoing in his skull.

Because I loathe *her. Because that sound she produces makes me cringe. Because I want you to, and because for what you've asked it's a small price to pay.*

But was it? *Was* it? Baggs had agreed to the terms. He had done so without thinking twice. Who and what was this Cojocaru? In hell, most people were at least notorious, yet he'd never heard of Cojocaru. But now, as his boot steps trailed along in his wake like curses, now that he had nothing but empty time in which to consider his decision, he had to ask himself the one question he most feared, because the answer might freeze his nerve. *The chance to* Not Be—*was that worth the price of one more death on his conscience, however impermanent that death might prove in this infernal place?*

Baggs thought about the case in his pocket, about the needle, about the vial with its cargo of clear liquid touted as the ultimate panacea. He decided that it *must* be worth it. After all, what vengeance could he fear from a conscience that would become extinct along with him? Let it rail at him. When he plunged the serum into his veins, remorse would be silenced at last.

As he rounded the corner and began walking along the last block to his destination, Baggs stopped in his tracks, arrested by the sound that flooded his ears.

Singing.

Never before had he heard anything like it. The sound was—

"Beautiful," he whispered. And made even more so by the sad, terrible anguish that saturated its one lamenting ululation. A song, yes; but wordless. With its perfect indecipherability, the grief and misery cut through and rent his heart. That wail brought scalding tears to the rims of his eyes. It was the sound of a soul in hideous, ongoing pain, yet still beautiful. Baggs was aghast that hell could contain such a paean. It hurt him more to suspect that infernity might have inspired it.

Cojocaru's words resounded in his ears: *You'll know her when you see her. And when you see he*—trike!

Baggs curled his fingers around the switchblade Cojocaru had given him. His palm sweated against its handle. His pulse thumped against the sides of his neck and his temples. *Do it*, he told himself. *Do it now, and do it quick. Last time pays for all.*

He drew the switchblade from his pocket and thumbed the release button. Six inches of polished steel flicked out. Gripping the handle tight, he ran the final distance into the Square.

If Cojocaru had not used the word *she*, Baggs would never have known that his target was a woman. The thing on the sidewalk with its back against brickwork survived beyond such distinctions as male and female, barely recognizable as once being human. This was a broken, twisted, malformed mass of flesh and bone, more lump than person. What sins could have provoked such punishment? It seemed monstrous even by hell's own pitiless standards. Now Baggs understood the source of that beautifully terrible song. The pain that produced such sounds was beyond his ability to imagine. Never before in his miserable posthumous incarceration had the depths of hell's black Deep seemed so bottomless.

The thing on the sidewalk stopped singing, and Baggs forbore his fascination with its disfigurements.

The horror was looking at him. One good eye, a perfect shade of eggshell blue, regarded him with unreadable emotion. Somewhere in the back of its broken throat, this thing formed a chain of desperate clicks and gutturals.

Baggs hesitated, his fingers first loosening and then tightening on the switchblade. He hovered on the sharp edge of . . . uncertainty. Action eluded him; indecision smothered his thoughts. On one side shouted the urge to complete his part of the bargain with Cojocaru: to strike, to kill, and then to be free.

But on the other side wept pity.

Pity? In hell? This was as laughable an idea as a Saharan snowstorm. But the emotion nearly overwhelmed him, nevertheless.

Pity.

Baggs knew he was a monster, yes. No argument on that score. Hell had made him so. But if anything in this underworldly existence had a more terrible fate than himself, it would be this thing squatting on the sidewalk, this thing watching him warily through that single blue eye.

Baggs gnawed his lip while the thing examined him. He looked down at the weapon in his hand and considered the needle in his pocket. He tottered between decisions and then realized, all at once, that he *could* decide. This once, he could make a *choice*.

Perhaps, he thought, the damned weren't entirely powerless. Was there free will, even in hell? Could he put that theory to the test, here and now? Could he *prove* it thus and, so proving, liberate himself from the shroud of monstrosity sewn tight around him?

He looked at the thing on the sidewalk again.

It made another sound, desperately mewling.

Baggs felt his doubts congeal into certainty. "I'm not going to hurt you," he said, drawing closer.

The thing on the sidewalk repeated its last sound, more intense now, more imperative.

"I'm not going to hurt you," Baggs repeated. And then, to prove it, he folded the blade up again and slipped it back into his pocket. "I'm not going to hurt anyone anymore. And I'm going to set you free."

Baggs took the case from his other pocket. Opened it. Emptied it. He speared the small rubber seal in the vial's top and loaded the barrel of the syringe. The vial fell away from his fingers and broke into bright glass crumbs at his feet. The thing on the sidewalk uttered a high, panicked shriek.

Once, they'd called him Doc. Now he would live up to that name.

"Sssssh," Baggs whispered, closing the remaining distance between them. He hunkered down beside that travesty of disfigured flesh and bone, so close he could smell the stench of rot. He selected a spot on what might have been its left arm and dimpled the thing's flesh with the point of the needle.

The wretch made another terrible sound.

Baggs looked directly into that single eye. "It's going to be all right," he said. "Whatever you did to incur this punishment, it doesn't matter now. *Ego te absolvo*."

He pressed the plunger home, into that rotted flesh.

The thing on the sidewalk screamed as the serum hit its veins.

It jerked, seeking escape, but Baggs clenched his teeth and, determined, drove the plunger the rest of the way down. Then something came up quickly on the fringe of his vision and struck him in the side of the head. Hard.

He bounced off the wall, head striking the bricks with enough force to ignite lightning-spots before his eyes; his ears rang. The crunch attending the collision reverberated in his skull, and for a moment he reeled, then simply slumped down onto the sidewalk.

At the fringes of his shaken awareness, someone was screaming.

He looked up. His vision blurred, doubled, then righted itself. Warm wetness trickled down the stinging side of his face. He blinked twice and decided he must be hallucinating.

A woman stood on the sidewalk where the thing had been sitting: naked, slender, beautiful, and screaming at the sky with her fists balled white in rage.

Baggs croaked, "Who—?" Then once more his words failed in his throat.

The woman stopped screaming and looked down at him, torn between heartbroken anguish and a lunatic fury that burned in her eyes like devil's coals.

Baggs saw seven numbers on her face, carved deep into her flesh in haphazard arrangement:

12.

7.

17.

22.

Baggs shuddered, felt sick, nearly gagged.

The woman screamed into his face: "*Why do you keep doing this to me?*"

Before Baggs could answer, she reached down and grabbed the sides of his head. Long nails dug into his skin for purchase.

He had only enough time to think, *What?*

Then she slammed his head back against the wall. She did it again and again and again, screaming and shrieking with each impact, until finally the brains were beaten out of his skull.

Somewhere in the midst of agony, darkness swallowed him whole.

He fell into nothingness, relieved.

*

Eventually, the darkness passed.

Somewhere in its wake, Baggs realized that he was staggering down unfamiliar streets, lurching from curbs to broken storefronts and back again. Something foul roiled and curled in his guts. Something worse lingered in his nostrils like a haunting, a stench beyond foul—a stink that the word *foul* whiffed once and then went running for safety. And it was familiar. It was—

The word *Undertaker* bubbled up from the pits of his consciousness like ghoulish laughter, freezing his heart.

Dead. Returned. Reassigned.

"No," he whispered. But his denial was feeble at best. He moaned the word again, but repetition brought no comfort. Someone had killed him. Someone had—

No, not *someone*. That woman. That *thing*.

All came back to him in a rush: Gnaeus and Cojocaru; the needle; the thing that sang. *Te absolvo.*

Baggs noticed a large plate glass storefront window beside him and turned slowly toward it, almost in tears. The Undertaker's perverse sense of anatomical humor was legendary for good reason, and rightly feared. What damage had the Undertaker done him? With a furious burst of resolve, Baggs looked at his reflection.

It was perfect, just the way it should have been, except

. . .

Oh—*except* . . .

Tears flooded out of him now, lava over the caldera of his soul. Comprehension forced them out, and they burned him. They blurred the reflection staring back at him, but he could see through them to truth. Those truths were there, carved into his cheeks and his forehead and his chin and his neck, and peeking out from his collar:

6.

19.

23.

31.

50.

And more. He could feel them under his clothes, crawling over his skin like grave beetles.

"No! Oh, Lord, no! Have mercy!"

Those numbers mocked him as he sank to his knees, broken, and curled up on the empty sidewalk. How many numbers; how many times? What kind of merciful God could allow this? He blanked out any answers, terrified of what they might reveal. He ran from them. He hid in the collapse of his own misery and ruin, and within it found nothing for him but further torment.

*

Soon the tears exhausted themselves. Then, to his surprise, Charles Baggs found himself curled up on an unfamiliar sidewalk. He lay empty, wept out.

He sat up, muscles stiff and argumentative from lying too long on concrete. What had he been weeping about? The tall man, he decided: his latest victim. That word haunted him, but he could find no grounds to argue with it. Victims they were, victims they would always be. *His* victims. Victims of an impulse beyond his ability to control. This was the nature of his hell: to act, to witness, and to agonize. It wasn't fair. Hell was supposed to hold each soul's just punishment. But *this*? How was this just? This was only evil compounding evil.

Charles Baggs (who once, a lifetime ago, had been known by the admiring cognomen of Doc) got to his feet and caught a glimpse of his reflection in the big window.

Something about his own face snagged and held him. He stared at himself for a long time.

His face. Something about his face. He rubbed a hand over his stubbled cheeks, puzzled by his fascination. After all, it was only his face. It looked no different now than any of the million other times he had seen it. No different. No different at all.

"Guilt," he told himself. Somehow, that seemed right.

Charles Baggs pulled himself away from his reflection, put his head down, and continued on.

In The Shadowlands

Richard Groller

"Time is not composed of indivisible nows
any more than any other magnitude is
composed of indivisibles."

—Aristotle, *Physics* 6.9

The crumpled body of the demon that pulled Harry Houdini the escapologist back to perdition lay before him, a knife rammed into its skull. The night-black, bat-winged creature with horns and a long spiked tail had brought him back to this place of desolation, but with a passenger. He examined it—not quite a Fury, but close. This was a faceless demon, some variety of Tartarosian perhaps, well muscled with smooth skin glistening like fresh tar. Nevertheless, cold steel to the brain pan will do the trick every time. That knife had been his only choice, having no other weapon available to him, unless you included the wand he absconded with. Thinking better of it, he retrieved the knife, wiping its gloss of black ichor from the demon's skull on his pant leg. As he bent down, he realized that his shoulders burned and bled profusely where he had been pierced by demon talons.

The lawyer who had clung to his waist for dear life now sat on the banks of the river Acheron, bemused, perplexed and incredulous. He bore a nasty cut on his head from when he'd hit the ground after Houdini felled the demon. He kept chanting under his breath, "I'm hallucinating, or maybe delirious, or dreaming."

Then Houdini heard him say, "If this is a nightmare, all I have to do is wake up."

Houdini offered him his hand. "What's your name?"

"Peter Kallinikos, J.D." was the reply. "And yours?"

"Erik Weisz," the short muscular man replied, "but you might know me better by my stage name, Harry Houdini."

"And now I *know* this is a dream. That, or I am dead," came Peter's reply.

"Wrong on both counts, Counselor. And though you are not yet dead, you might soon be if you are not careful. For you are in hell. I will tell you what I can."

*

When Houdini vaulted through the so-called demon gate on Onogoroshima, he had no idea where he would materialize. He had hoped to escape from hell—and did for a brief moment, only to be untimely sucked back into it with an unforeseen passenger: a living, breathing human who had not yet earned damnation. Now he found himself and his charge on the hellish side of the shadowland frontier between earth and hell, one of the many historical entry points into the underworld related by the seers and mystic historians of legend and lore. The Vikings had Hekla, the Japanese Chinoike Jigoku, and the Turks had Ploutonion.

Before him was the storied river Acheron, where Charon the Ferryman plied his trade. The entrance at Ephyra was hopefully on the other side. No dead could cross this watery chasm to the world of the living . . . but the living? The mythos tells of many heroes who entered hell and returned to live another day: Theseus, Odysseus, Heracles, Orpheus, Psyche. This poor soul's inadvertent *katabasis* must now be made right, with *anabasis* back to the world of light. He may not be a hero, but he did not deserve this (even if he was a lawyer) or, more to the point, a Juris Doctor. His pro bono work for the Committee for the Scientific Investigation of Claims of the Paranormal (CSICOP) proved his undoing. No good deed goes unpunished. Q.E.D.

"Why?" Houdini mused to himself. "Under *whose* aegis did I return to earth on Halloween night, at the exact moment when a delegation from the Society of American Magicians was holding their yearly ritual of keeping vigil at my grave?" The meeting exceeded the bounds of coincidence. A karmic joke? A demonic prank? Divine intervention? Or maybe there was truly an affinity between the sensible world and the afterlife, where things *could* be influenced—such as the Catholic tradition of having Masses said for the dead to lessen their time in purgatory. He did not know. He knew for sure he did not direct himself there. So maybe the will and hope of the magicians pulled him there.

"And how and why was I directed here? Does some higher intelligence intend this man to return to the land of the living before any harm can come to him? No matter. The best I can do is *try* to do what's right by this innocent."

Although Houdini now had a good question to ask Pythagoras, if he ever saw him again.

*

Zeno of Elea called the Colloquium on Time Dilation to order from his refuge at the Infernal Observatory Department of Apparent Time at Mount Sinai. All attendees were 'plagued' by drops and distortions on their closed-circuit networks, but these annoyances were infinitely preferable to the real plagues raging around them, making traveling outdoors a dangerous proposition. He was glad to have made it back to the remote observatory before the plague hit. His special assignment in New Hell City following the "accident" (which the Department of Infernal Energy (DIE) scientists theorized was a hole ripped in the fabric of space-time by Nikolai Tesla's power source as it created a vortex, consuming a large chunk of the city by dragging it into the virtual substructure of the universe) had left him in a unique position:

The recoil experienced in the time field left everyone in the city disoriented, and it took many weeks to ensure that all time-dependent mechanisms were resynchronized. Zeno was pulled from his duties at Mount Sinai by Satan himself to oversee these efforts personally. He frankly welcomed the opportunity as a vacation from the intractable task at hand, finding out the source of the time dilation phenomena that was adversely affecting Michael, Satan's familiar.

Now that Zeno was back home, he must concentrate on solving the time dilation problem or risk Satan's wrath. Luckily, he'd come back with ideas. Nichols, Dick Welch's right hand man in the Devil's Children, arranged for him to communicate with Tesla while the theorist remained under house arrest and before he was broken out of prison to assist in the failed assault on heaven.

Tesla's power system gave Zeno the idea to build a detector sensitive to perturbations of the time field. This would basically be a series of devices including wideband antennas and oscilloscopes to monitor and pinpoint the location of spatio-temporal perturbations in virtual space. These would need to be dispersed among the planes of all the hells and their outputs measured and correlated so that they would act like an interferometer, pointing to the source of the disturbance.

Zeno's plan required two components. One part was the hardware. But the software (or more to the point, the "wetware") was equally vital. If Zeno was correct, Michael became the key piece to solving the problem. Michael's behavior, the philosopher believed, was the canary in the coal mine, a tripwire or alert system registering whenever hellish ley lines were being perturbed. Michael, in fact, was *the* wetware.

The vision Zeno had seen when Satan first entrusted him with the task of solving this problem was burned forever into his psyche: a great serpent and winged clocks with spearlike arms; chariots with wheels of flame and mushroom clouds upon which they rode; the sun swallowing up the sky and the earth charred to a cinder, deep within the corona of that sun; a huge cloud of gas with thousands of angels, brushing wings as they worked. And around all these images, surrounded by the serpent, shimmered Satan in his full and terrible panoply, wrapped in the coil of the serpent. In that devil's arms Michael was cradled, and within the jaws of Michael whirled the entire universe. He visibly shuddered at the recollection.

Zeno believed that when Michael felt the terrible effects of time perturbations, the equipment could pinpoint the source and, hopefully, provide clues to the mystery. All he needed was buy-in from Welch and Nichols on monitoring Michael, and their consent to providing immediate alert status should Satan's familiar succumb to another disturbance such as the one that affected him when Satan visited the Infernal Observatory. Zeno had given Michael a bowl of milk. The familiar moved as if caught in a tape loop, making equal and opposite movements toward and away from the bowl. The poor creature yowled in an intermittent, tortured way as it did its uncontrollable dance, backwards, then forwards. Satan had been absolutely beside himself: he truly *cared* for Michael, that creature part cat, part bat, part excrescence from the bowels of the deepest hells.

Since Michael was Satan's sole familiar, Zeno knew this plan called for delicate handling. He requested a meeting with Welch and Nichols to discuss the matter in detail. For Zeno, having seen Satan in his full dark majesty, was afraid. The Elean could not muster the courage to talk to Satan directly, so he would ask Welch to be his emissary. Nichols could vouch for the fact that he was acting on Satan's behalf, with no ulterior motives other than to do as Satan commanded and in so doing save his own skin.

Zeno would deal on an inter-agency basis in his official capacity at the Infernal Observatory with the assistance of the DIE in building and monitoring the dilation detectors.

Edison was still running the DIE, and had sent some Greek 'time' experts (Anaximander, Parmenides, and Plotinus) to the colloquium to placate him with a long winded theoretical discussion about risk and DIE policy to cover for their delays while they attempted to get their collective shit together building the Tesla-designed equipment.

After many hours of fruitless discourse, matters finally reached a breaking point when Anaximander pounded his fist on the table, nearly shouting at Zeno: "I have said that whence things have their origin, thence also their destruction happens, according to necessity. For they give to each other justice and recompense for their injustice in conformity with the ordinance of Time. Now you are simply restating what you have long maintained about the world of the living: that Time in hell is an endless series of infinitely divided instants."

In frustration, Zeno screamed, "I invented dialectic! Do not try to use my own words against me! Tell Edison he has a week to work through the risk analysis before the system goes online, or he will be answering to Satan himself."

*

When he heard the stealthy helicopter land outside the Infernal Observatory, Zeno hastened outside to greet his guests. There he noticed on the wall outside the main door graffiti, in red paint (or was it blood?) "$T = \infty$?" The sight sent a shiver down his spine. What happened next shook him even more. . . .

Welch and Nichols were flown there by Achilles, and when Zeno saw Achilles, he blanched. Achilles had a hard-on for him ever since he used his name as an exemplar in a now famous paradox. Achilles brought along a present for Zeno: a tortoise, which he proceeded to fling like a discus at Zeno's head. He missed on purpose, but his point was not lost. Never involve your friends in stories that besmirch their abilities, especially if they value their reputations. Now that the ice was broken, Welch wasted no time in cutting to the chase.

"My time is valuable, this had better be good."

Zeno assured Welch that indeed this was a matter of utmost delicacy that needed to be handled in person, and proceeded to ask for his intercession with His Satanic Majesty. Welch, being well versed in the fiasco of the moving island and the demon gates, agreed to help without further discussion. Welch knew this mission's importance, and he was intrigued by the thought that ley lines could exist in hell, which might explain a few things. If Zeno was right, and ley lines existed in the shadowlands where the borders are permeable—*that* could be problematic.

As a bonus, Welch volunteered the Devil's Children as the rapid response force to recon the source of any new perturbations. If you want the job done right, you gotta do it yourself. No more leaving this particular problem to chance or volunteers with vested interests. Next time, Welch himself would go.

*

Edison's minions at the DIE finally built the required number of units to make the direction-finding system operational. The prototype was based on a design Goethals and Tesla worked on prior to the blowup that vaporized a third of New Hell City—a computer-controlled pointing mechanism using spherical coordinate techniques in virtual space for precision detection, orientation and position fixing. This they modified for autonomous operation, so it needed no operator, only a power source. The system would track the ambient temporal state of the virtual substructure of infernity, using only a trickle charge to keep all the devices in synch. If any sort of spatio-temporal disturbance caused more than a one tenth of one percent perturbation from ambient, the master controller that maintained autonomous operations would engage at full power to position-fix the source. A minimum of five devices would be required in every region of every hell, to obtain the desired resolution. The irony was not lost on Edison that the vertices formed a pentagram.

Zeno was very explicit when they spoke via closed circuit: "Have your men do the installs in the remote locations I've outlined to limit collateral damage, in case we cause any side effects in the virtual sphere. We had enough trouble with the unforeseen the last time."

Edison laughed. "This is not a weapons system. There is no way for it to cause any kind of physical damage."

Zeno responded with, "The potential damage I am worried about is temporal. I do *not* want the time synchronization of hell to be affected by anything we do trying to detect any perturbations. Ever heard of the effect of the observer on the observed? I'll take no chances if I can help it." Then he added, "And ensure you only send healthy men out to do the installs. I don't need well meaning, honest mistakes brought about by workaholics with plague sickness. I need competency."

Edison gruffly responded, "Very well, as you wish," and hung up.

Zeno silently swore to himself, secure in the knowledge that there would literally be hell to pay if Edison could not be trusted to get the job done right. The last thing Zeno wanted was to risk the health of Michael, Satan's familiar, or for that matter to incur Satan's wrath.

As for the unforeseeable, Zeno could only hope.

*

Doctor Peter Kallinikos had a hard time wrapping his head around the concept that he had been sucked into some sort of psychic nexus that brought him bodily into hell—or into hells, since infernity was said to hold quite a few. Peter knew drugs could induce delusions, but everything around him *felt* real. The Tartarosian or whatever Houdini called it certainly was quite solid and quite dead, and had dragged them both through—what? The sensation was weightless, dreamlike, peaceful even, with no sense of time passing at all. Did that interval last seconds or eons? He did not know. All he knew was, he did not belong *here, now.*

Above him he could see the light of Paradise. He knew he was not on earth. But he also knew he must do something. He was a lawyer after all; he needed to plead his case. Maybe he could entreat the Heavenly Host to come to his aid. Surely, as a living human, he was entitled to divine intercession, if what Houdini said was true. And his patience was growing thin, waiting around for Charon the Ferryman to appear and return him to the land of the living.

His headache was getting worse. The gash on his forehead was a bleeder, and Houdini had offered him gauze from his medkit, still intact from his expedition to Onogoroshima. Houdini wrapped his forehead, then took some of the remaining gauze to wrap his own wounds where demonic talons had pierced his shoulders.

Houdini explained that he did not trust the water of the river to rinse in, so he just wrapped his open gouges. He still had Peter's blood on his hands.

What happened next was nothing short of a miracle:

Where that blood touched Houdini's wound it burned like fire—then the throbbing stopped. Houdini now rubbed Peter's blood into those wounds in earnest: "It burns!"

Then those demonic gouges healed—Houdini's flesh was unbroken. "The pain—gone!" Houdini was amazed, thankful.

Peter Kallinikos realized that this could be a good thing or a bad thing, but as long as Houdini was adamant about returning him home, he was not going to worry about it.

*

Zeno's time-perturbation detection network had been up and running for three days when the alarm sounded, indicating a massive temporal breach. When Michael "got funky" again, Nichols sent a flash override message to Zeno on the communications equipment provided by the Devil's Children.

The perturbation sensor levels spiked off the charts.

Zeno powered up the network to max, and the virtual lines of bearing converged through the manifold planes of hell to the vicinity of the *Necromanteion* of Ephyra, the confluence of the rivers Acheron, Pyriphlegethon, and Cocytus. Zeno relayed the coordinates to Nichols, and Welch and the rest of the team went into action.

*

Before too long, a gaunt, hooded, bearded figure with sunken eyes and a long pole in his right hand brought his shallow boat alongside the shore where Houdini and Kallinikos waited.

Houdini gravely handed Charon a double headed silver dollar he used for parlor tricks as the living man's *viaticum*, and given that Charon was accustomed to copper or bronze for his *obol*, with inflation, the silver was definitely appreciated. Charon said no word, merely extended his left hand to receive the passenger, bound for the living side of the river.

Houdini asked him, "What will you tell them?"

Kallinikos said, "I don't know, but I'll think of something. I certainly do not want to be locked up for being insane. I owe you one. Anyone I can speak to for you?"

Houdini answered, "You know where I am, so my odds of salvation are slim. But if you ever get the urge, light a candle for me. You never know, it may help," and with that waved him goodbye and said, "Godspeed."

Thunder rolled and the fundament shook as the gods of hell took offense at an invocation in the Almighty name.

*

The stealthy Huey Cobra touched down on the beach. Welch and Nichols jumped down and saw Houdini sitting on the banks of the Acheron, staring across the water at nothing in particular.

Nichols looked at Houdini and said, "I should have capped you in the cave back on the island. You have a lot of explaining to do. Where have you been all these months?"

Houdini looked up and laughed. "Months? Don't you mean hours?"

Nichols was about to slug Houdini for his impertinence when Welch stepped in.

"Okay, we'll need a full debrief. I need to hear this directly. Get in the chopper."

Houdini smiled, and with a twinkle in his eye said, "Anything you say, boss."

Let Us Kill the Spirit of Gravity

Matthew Kirshenblatt

"It was only illness that brought me to reason."
—Friedrich Nietzsche, *Ecce Homo*

Down through the Valley of the Shadow of Death, barren and dry, writhe the deathless.

Not even the eternally crimson light of Paradise bathes these unfortunate, these arrogant immortal souls . . . this legion made before Creation and doomed not long after. But there are exceptions.

One luminous being remains above the rocks and orange dust of the Valley ground, but it's a small consolation. Stones—like the unnatural fetters they are—pin his feet and hands into the gritty soil. The placement of his bindings forces him to bow, forever, to the Paradise in which he once had some regency.

His skin glitters as translucent and blue as his multifarious wings fluttering free and futile against the dry air. The angel almost envies his compatriots, buried underneath the dust. His very being aches from millennia without touch.

153

Exposed as he is, he—if his noticeably swollen celestial member and testicles indicate the sex to which his essence is perpetually bound—literally has blue balls.

Still, he has some other consolations. Sometimes, finding his mind drifting between the realities and hallucinations of Gehinnom's shimmering heat, he sees a mass of figures coming toward him. Misshapen in various ways and massive—almost rivaling the mountains of the Valley itself—they come, periodically, to visit him and the others.

And Samyaza, formerly caretaker of the throne of the Almighty, must admit that between watching the plague god Erra and his Seven living weapons wreak havoc on the Mediterranean Old Dead and the beautiful sight of pale, winged Lilitu hovering just out of his reach from their nearby home in Arali, these loud, boisterous, feuding visitors swearing in their patois of broken Enochian are one of his ever fewer joys in hell.

"Ah, my sons." Samyaza smiles with pride and malignity as he sees the growths on their flesh. "Whatever new torment has hell brought upon you now?"

Samyaza merely looks on as they approach, waiting patiently as their lengthening shadows almost blot out the infernal light of Paradise. Foremost even amongst his peers, if there is one thing Samyaza is known for, it's that he loves to watch.

*

"Give me one good reason why I shouldn't make you wish for the Undertaker."

Friedrich Nietzsche's mouth drops. It isn't because he finally mustered the courage to come to the Whore of Babylon's lair: although he had certainly been rather ill at ease as he'd found himself nearly lost in the spindly, hissing grey-green foliage—worse than the forest of suicides—of her Hanging Garden; nor because of the small, goat-horned, beige-furred creature with its disturbing gaze and its deep crackling voice that rumbles through his skull. Ever since Nietzsche's employers had procured the services of its mistress, the Whore, he'd known the creature to be far too intelligent for anyone's good. And he isn't gaping at the burning body of the Whore, igniting under melting gold as it's methodically dragged apart by vines near the fire pit just beyond him.

No. It's the *other* woman, whose name he fears to think, let alone speak.

Under the interplay of Paradise's distant light through tortured trees, Nietzsche can't discern whether her tall, voluptuous form is dark or pale in the bronze hue of fire and damnation, but he sees her red hair as a rosy halo around a smooth face with glittering blue eyes of glacial fury.

If Nietzsche didn't know any better, he'd have thought her to be one of His Satanic Majesty's fallen angels, or at least one of the Eumeneides, the Furies themselves; but he knows what he's truly looking at: a powerful, naked, and very angry woman. Her wrath makes him wish he'd remained lost amid the trees.

Terror freezes him between heartbeats and, frozen, Nietzsche's pain finally catches up with him. The low-grade ache he'd nurtured back at his room in Turin Towers, before he decided to look for Babylon, flares into two white pinpricks behind his eye sockets. At the same time, he feels distanced from his body, as though his mind is splitting away from his writhing soul. The philosopher falls to one knee in front of this effulgent harbinger, as the tenuous bridge between Nietzsche's thoughts and his sensory torment snap together viciously, while his agony propels him back to that place and time wherein he served as Dionysus' stand-in, when he held that whipped ass on the streets of Turin—his Turin—as he wept.

Now the face of the other woman looms, achingly familiar. A pang in Nietzsche's chest threatens to explode out of him like a dancing star; his mouth moves almost of its own volition. He almost says *her* name, almost . . . a name he's loath to remember. . . .

Somehow, he manages to stop himself. Even so, other words come out of him: "My apologies, *Sophia*." He blinks up at her. "I came here to find a Whore, but instead I find a goddess." He almost sees *her*, his Daphne, in the contempt on her face. "May you burn me in my laurel leaves."

Nietzsche knows, immediately, that this is the wrong response. Shame and despair fill him, a deep heaviness in the pit of his being. Then it too sloughs away, leaving resignation in its wake.

Yet, inexplicably, his mind clears. After all, there are worse ways to meet the Undertaker than at the hands of a beautiful woman.

*

Lilith, the immortal First Woman and erstwhile wife of Adam, needed one good excuse not to send the Undertaker on a scavenger hunt for the pieces of this wretched soul before her. The crackling, crystalline fury of an Enochian curse bristles on the tip of her tongue before she registers one word and the sentences that surround it.

Sophia . . .

She came to the Hanging Garden to pursue her plans, to get away from hell, from Atlantis, from . . .

Lilith already had made one too many compromises: using Eden's words to unleash her owl-name from her flesh; consorting with the foul Whore of Babylon to gain an audience with her master; even preparing to unveil the Beast's true nature . . . until the interruption of this strange little man whom she was about to send to the Mortuary in dumb, mustache-trembling silence.

But then he spoke that word.

That one word.

Sophia.

The First Woman had heard this word spoken many ways throughout her long lifetime—but always, its sound made tangible the feminine symbol at Western philosophy's heart. One philosopher, in particular, called her something similar once: his *daimon*, his Diotima—

For that reminder alone, Lilith should obliterate this one man from among all the leprous sinners in hell.

Still . . .

She *sees* . . . something. Seeing auras remains one passive ability that a Baal Shem such as she always possesses. If anything, it's more instinct than skill.

Lilith studies the man in front of her. "Perhaps I should. Burn you, that is." She spares a small glance back at the golden bones of the late and unlamented Whore. "Doing so certainly would be more of a mercy than coming here for Babylon's services."

"That is Nietzsche," the Beast growls, crawling up paw before paw until it crouched beside her. *"A plaything of my pet. You have a place to find. Complete our agreement and I will consume him and be done with it."*

Lilith turns and looks down at the squat, disgusting creature. Some things just cannot be countenanced. "Do not forget yourself, Beast. I am not your Whore."

Silence blooms as the Beast slowly ambles away from Lilith, undoubtedly not willing to risk its freedom.

"I long to be done with this," comes an aged voice.

Those words draw Lilith's attention back to the man in front of her. He's standing now, although his shoulders are sloped, his eyes downcast. Having banished the Beast, she finds much of her ire gone with it. She raises one eyebrow at Nietzsche.

The man starts, as if suddenly realizing he's spoken aloud. "That is to say . . . *this*." He waves his hands around him. "All of this."

"You and all infernity, philosopher." Lilith spits out the last word like the invective it is to her. But even so, her rebuke is half-hearted. She's fascinated by the nature of the aura around Nietzsche, shimmering naggingly at the edges of her vision.

"*Ja*, Fraulein." The man grimaces at his own words. "I must be out of this place. Out of hell. And I might know a way."

This remark startles Lilith out of her metaphysical examination. She keeps her face carefully composed as she stares at Nietzsche. "Oh?"

Nietzsche hesitates before nodding. "In my life . . . I was a Doctor of philology . . . that treasure trove of words, of origins and etymologies between literature and philosophy. But that wasn't enough. In my studies I had a few friends." He pauses for a moment. "Jewish peers. From both I heard about the Jewish afterlife, so different from what I'd been raised to believe. Perhaps it is different. Souls, *ja*. Souls weighed down by sin are sent into that place in Sheol—"

"Only shades of scholars and philosophers such as yourself dwell in Sheol." Lilith's tone barely registers her surprise that they both seek the same place. But she isn't quite willing to share. "A place where souls debate in tedium. Although, after Erra finishes with them, I'm not sure they are even that anymore."

Nietzsche's face falls briefly; he brushes his mustache; his brow furrows with thought. "I know of that place. But that is not it. Sheol is said to be a place where the spirit is purged of all evil. Where the soul can either reincarnate, ascend, or be destroyed. Perhaps it is just . . ." His foot taps nervously, as though he remembers something. "Perhaps it's not in Sheol, but somewhere in Gehenna?"

"Or somewhere near both," Lilith finally allows, seeing the resolve in this otherwise timid man's eyes. Whatever else the philosopher is, he has been determined enough to brave the advances of the Whore. She cautiously considers her options.

"*Ja.* The names had been used interchangeably by different texts." This time, Nietzsche meets her eyes. "You know of this place, Fraulein."

Interesting. During their entire exchange, so many emotions played across this philosopher's face; more than a simple mustache could hide. Nietzsche appears focused, his fear of Lilith forgotten. He knows, or thinks he knows, enough to save himself. She can read him; she can use him.

"The question is, philosopher, just what *else* do you know?"

Nietzsche squirms with discomfort. "Little beyond what I've said, I'm afraid."

"I see." Lilith spares a glance at the loitering Beast, only out of earshot, pushing at a patch of charred grass with one impatient hoof. "And do you know what place you seek? What it looks like?" she asks the philosopher.

"*Nein*, Fraulein." Nietzsche's eyes try not to look beyond her. "I came here to seek Babylon. To ask her where Sheol might lie. But she is . . . gone."

"Sheol, true Sheol, is a dark place: the border of the shades, and the heart of Inner Gehinnom." Lilith speaks quietly, her own thoughts far away in dark memories. "A chamber. A cavern. A tunnel. *A palace*. It travels back to the earth and up the branches of the Life Tree to the seven heavens, and down again through its roots into oblivion."

"Does Yggdrasil truly span both earth and hell?" Nietzsche jolts as if stung by some infernal insect, obviously surprised by his own words and boldness. This, more than anything, allows Lilith to make up her mind.

"So you know of Yggdrasil, hmm? I suppose that makes sense. It even has a serpent." A smirk threatens to twist one corner of Lilith's mouth. "Your philology truly does branch into poetry and myth."

"I . . ." Nietzsche glances down at the ground again. "It was through my passion that I knew of that world, Fraulein, not through my field of study."

"Myth travels far, philosopher. But we will need to travel farther. Yes. I think we have an arrangement."

Before Nietzsche can say anything, Lilith strides away, toward the Beast, and stands directly in front of it. The creature looks up at her and chuckles.

"Help me spread the Word, Mother of Demons."

Lilith scowls and points at the creature. She doesn't have to do so, but for some reason she desires to do so—for

emphasis. The word comes up through her throat: an undulating, thermal resonance between her feet and the infernal ground underneath her—a parody of the terrestrial paradise from which she has sprung. It is enough, more than
enough.

The Beast slowly begins to smile.

*

Mother of Demons. . . .

Nietzsche's dawning realization of just *whom* he is
dealing with is overshadowed by the word that comes out of
the woman's mouth. The logical parts of Nietzsche's mind,
or what's left of it, register the sound: deep and reverberat-
ing like thunder.

Where is the lightning?

Nietzsche shakes his head. No, this sound is definitely a word, from a language that speaks to the most integral
and primal parts of his being. Long had theories pointed to
a universal language that once existed, perhaps predating
Indo-European linguistics. Since Nietzsche came to hell,
he'd been exposed to many different tongues beyond what
he knew in life—some even considered mystical in nature—but deep in his bowels he *knows* that what he hears is
something else, perhaps a force that reaches out from man's
earliest days to hit too close to home. These sounds are from
no language of angels or demons.

Somehow, the sounds feel all too human.

Yet what occurs in front of Nietzsche is anything *but*
human.

The Beast before them is changing. Its smile almost
makes the philosopher forget about the woman. Not in all
his time with the Whore at Turin Towers had he seen the

Beast smile before. Nietzsche wishes, fervently, that he'd
never seen that gargoyle grin. Like a digestive movement in
hell, the woman's single word trembles through Nietzsche,
the solitary beginning of a terrible, organic process. Then he
notices the spot on the creature's forehead.

Strange. Nietzsche always thought that spot to be a
blemish, a birth mark or a tumor . . . one more deformity on
a hideous mutation.

But now Nietzsche understands.

He knows, now, just what she said, the importance of
the word she spoke. He watches as the mark spreads red and
chitinous across the creature's face like one of Erra's diseases. Its beige fur begins to fray around the site of that ex-
panding growth. Then its fur shreds and falls out in clumps
as its skull expands and its neck stretches out. Even its stub-
by yellow teeth elongate apace with its horns.

The horror unfolding in front of Nietzsche—a squat
form splitting and rising sinuously above his head, its growing feet and talons and bones knit with red matter from its
pulsating back—is almost an afterthought. Nietzsche recalls
what he saw on the creature's forehead, and what the woman
actually said. Even its long neck sprouting six other ten-
drils—blooming versions of its now beaklike head—only
serves to remind him of this terrible realization.

Finally—as the creature looms over them, raw, wet,
and bloody; the gnarled red bones on either side of its
spiny, scaly hide overflowing with a sickly yellowish mem-
brane—Nietzsche must accept the awful fact that the woman
didn't speak a word so much as a name: a *Name.*

And that name was made up of three ominous numbers.

Seven maws stretch out and roar into the sky, challen-
ging Paradise, hating it. Nietzsche thinks of Midgard, and

dwarves; of Yggdrasil, and the Serpent, and Hel. As the creature's wings fully develop, the philosopher knows this is no dragon from a Wagnerian opera or ancient Germanic saga. It's neither Fafnir nor Regin, but part of something far larger and more repugnant. Nietzsche wonders if Saint George ever encountered such a monster, but he already knows the answer to that question.

Enormous, rank, and utterly disgusting, this monster is born from the refuse of men, from earth and hell, where it has always dwelt and where it will one day return. This monster had masqueraded as the Whore's pet this entire time. Pet had been monster all along.

This is *the* Beast, the beast with seven heads, changed drastically from the Beast they'd met before.

"Come." The Beast lowers one head and one hand and allows the woman to climb up one neck.

Nietzsche watches her. He sees her pale skin splattered with drying blood as she sits on the Beast's back. What surprises him more is that he finds himself placing his own foot on the Beast's skull as well—one of seven skulls that suddenly lies on the ground before him like a stair.

Land and air seem to undulate as the Beast raises its seven necks. Nietzsche screams as he falls . . . only to yelp as his arm is almost wrenched from its socket. The woman holds his hand—she has a strong grip—and pulls him up. Nietzsche gasps as he finds himself behind her, but tries to find purchase on the Beast's scales.

"Hold onto me, philosopher!" the red-haired woman shouts over the Beast's flapping wings. "I'll need you to tell us where we're going!"

"Me?" Nietzsche cries, his arms circling around her back. "But Fraulein, you said you—"

Nietzsche barely registers that they are sitting on the Beast's central neck, as he feels gravity fall away. . . .

"Yes," the woman says. "Only a New Dead soul, an unaltered one, can find true Sheol. But we also need something else. Beast, you know *whom* I seek."

Seven heads roar as one, grinding through Nietzsche's mind. The woman's bare flesh is warm against his clothed body. She smells of lilacs and ashes.

"This is going to be a long ride, philosopher," the woman says. "You say you like words. Well, so do I. Perhaps you might teach me something I don't know, to pass the time."

Just one more intimidating prospect after another, Nietzsche tells himself. "I—if that is the case, Fraulein"—he oozes into the calm part of himself, a part he otherwise would not have dared to brave—"please call me Nietzsche."

"Yes," she says. "Nietzsche. As for me, you already know who and what I am."

Nietzsche nods, shutting his eyes, trying not to look down, or at his companion, or at anything.

"Good, Nietzsche." He feels her grow still. "Do you remember what you called me earlier? *Sophia.* . . ."

He opens his eyes and sees the perfect side profile of her face as she turns to regard him.

"Don't ever call me that again."

Nietzsche swallows, trying not to retch in terror.

"Yes," he says as they fly away into the amber vistas of damnation, "Frau Lilith."

Pavlovian Slip

Bill Snider

"Most people do not really want freedom,
because freedom involves responsibility,
and most people are frightened of responsibility."
—Sigmund Freud

The doorbell howled; its incessant clawing whine echoed dissonantly through the cavernous building and crawled down deep into the soul. It was Sinday, so the building was mostly deserted. A few shadowy souls occupied areas throughout, performing menial tasks, simple housecleaning chores. Most days, they went unnoticed, with little attention given to their unsavory appearance or the odors emanating from them.

"Someone is at the door? How odd, how peculiar. I wonder who it could be? Visitors are discouraged—this is highly irregular." Ivan Pavlov looked up from his notes. Dim incandescent bulbs lit the room, etching him eerily against the sparse environment. He stretched as he considered his options: Ignoring the summons might beg increased disturbance; answering it might entail excessive interaction with unsavory types; ignoring it might mean missing a useful opportunity; answering it could bring about unforeseeable possibilities.

Pavlov rose from his chair, which scraped against the concrete like fingernails on a blackboard.

"One, attend me!" This he directed sharply at the shuffling, hulking presence of a Grumble that lurked just past sight in the shadows, the corner of the room. It moved into the wan light with Ivan at a slow, sloppy pace, shadowing its master. Mottled and torn, blood splattered and heavily worn, its face indifferent to the things which people of intelligence made manifest in their lives: this was a Grumble, an un-hale thing, a creature of nightmare, a beast of brute strength and absolute dedication to purpose. Bone showed between stretches of gangrenous skin; blood and other viscous liquids seeped through, decorating its clothing.

Several minutes passed as the two, damned soul and damnable Grumble, wound their way through labyrinthine corridors. Ivan's lab nestled deep inside the building. Many stairs and hallways stood between it and the front door. From the outside, the building looked like a squat, three-story combination of office and warehouse; many windows, several doors, dock-level loading doors out back. The only signage on the front of the building said: "U.S.U.H.C." Those who knew what that meant—'UnSafety and UnHealth Commission'—knew to stay away.

The door buzzer screamed at least three more times, demonstrating the visitor's tenacity, impossible to ignore. The annoying sound grew louder as one approached the front entryway. Its main door was frosted glass, an opacity that prevented visual contact from within or without. A monitor mounted on the inside of the vestibule showed only a single individual outside, about to press the buzzer once again.

"Halt!" Ivan whispered as he opened the door. "I have spent countless years monitoring behavioral patterns of all manner of creatures and I am still perplexed as to why human beings fixate so intently on repeatedly pushing a button or ringing a bell." He glared at the soul who stood beneath the front lintel. "I give you fair warning: If you're trying to sell us something, my associate, One" —as he spoke, Ivan pointed to the hulking mass of decrepit flesh behind him— "is always hungry. Now, kindly state your business and then be on your way." Ivan gestured impatiently at the dapper older gentleman outside the door.

"Oh, well; my wants are very simple. I was in the neighborhood and thought I'd drop by to visit. I was hoping perchance to meet with Fionn. You may have heard of me, sir. My name is Sigmund Freud. I presume I am speaking with Ivan Pavlov? I have heard that you are an associate of Fionn's and a soul from a distinguished philosophical background."

"'In the neighborhood?' I'm sorry, but . . . being blunt: are you insane? Your wits addled? This is not the kind of neighborhood to merely drop by. I have no time for foolishness; I have many things currently underway that require my attention and must be about my business." Ivan waved at him with an irritated air.

"Oh? I am intrigued, sir. You may or may not know of my specialties. I, too, am a practitioner of philosophical sciences. Perhaps I could assist in some manner?"

"Yes, yes; I have heard your name. We both lived above around the same time; it's a shame we never met while alive.

Perhaps we could have engaged in more lively discourse then. However, your appearance here, now, as you are, is most unseemly and rather suspect."

"True, very true. However, I wish to spend time in discussion with your associate, Fionn mac Cumhaill, the Celtic hunter-warrior of yore. I have sent him a number of messages requesting a talk, but he doesn't respond. I thought maybe a more forthright and direct approach might yield better results." Freud shrugged, looking a bit more bedraggled than previously, as if his confidence was slipping away.

"Ah, on that matter I must disappoint. Fionn is off on some grand adventure at the moment, involving snakes and grass and thwarting enemies in the mist prior to their gaining too much root to be rooted out. He's never still for very long, nor inclined to discuss psychological matters, unless they are strategic, some way to best an enemy. It would be vexatious, if he were one of my subjects; but he is not." Ivan rubbed the bridge of his nose.

"I see you do know him; hence my desire to pursue a more direct route. Under normal circumstances, merely showing up unannounced would be the height of rudeness, nearly unthinkable. However, in hell, we do as hell is wont, yes?" Freud shrugged a second time in the diffuse light.

"Indeed. However, you have piqued my curiosity now. All right, come in and tell me what business could warrant such efforts as this? Why would Fionn be of interest to a soul such as yourself?"

"A fair question. And easily answered, if I may. Simply put, I believe my research would benefit greatly from a conversation with him. I believe that he, like others of the Old Dead, represent the true state in which the human mind resides: a combination of its *id,* bestial in nature but civilized in form and function, with its *superego,* somewhat civilized in nature but bestial in execution. I was greatly influenced recently, having met Fionn during the dedication ceremonies at the Hall of Injustice Library. Very intense individual he was."

"Hmm; that's a slippery slope you are choosing to climb. Fionn is not one to talk about himself. Ha, especially if you are trying to get him on the couch, as it were."

"Indeed, I am aware. I tried," Freud admitted, "and was met with extreme resistance. I do believe his spear actually threatened me, but I am unsure if the spear was making the gesture or the man was."

"Oh, most definitely the spear. That weapon is one of the most bloodthirsty things I've ever encountered; I could tell you some stories."

"And what is that thing that stands behind you?"

"That? That is One; he is a Grumble, a lethal killing machine with no moral ambiguity, no questions of right or wrong, just feed. They are the perfect expression of all of my theories on consumption and human nature.

"But that is not why you are here, now is it?"

Freud's eyes wavered up and left, evasively. "Herr Pavlov, you are a most learned man of philosophy and humanity's stare upon the world. Perchance I could discuss a few things with you? I find myself out of sorts down here in hell. Most people I meet are less than engaging. I am aware of the tenets of hell's purpose: suffering. It is possible that my punishment here is to be constantly without interesting discourse. For men such as ourselves, is it not pure torture to be unable to explore ideas, thoughts, philosophies?

"I have a so-called job in New Hell, Herr Pavlov. I tend and administer to souls who seek relief from the pain of their mental anguish. It is hell, how am I supposed to 'relieve' anguish when the whole purpose for being here is anguish! I might as well be babysitting. I can do nothing to provide surcease to people here in hell; for the very nature of hell is to make that anguish more manifest, to tighten the knots that bind their souls. There is no release from discomfort here. So instead I seek purpose. Most souls do not seek true reparations with their cognizant selves; they merely seek approval, release, abstinence from external suffering, but never seek true change within themselves—they seek absolution of the self, without reforming the self to achieve it.

"Ultimately, it boils down to the fact that I am unchallenged; so much so that I would approach an unknown organization, with unknown assets and agendas, merely for an opportunity to engage strong minds with conversation less banal than wondering, 'Why me?'"

"Is this where we whip out our memberships and see who's got the bigger one?" Pavlov asked dryly.

"Hah. Hah. Herr Pavlov, that is indeed a very good subversive subjective use of what I've since come to understand has been dubbed 'Freudian.' Touché."

Again, the doorbell shrieked; Freud jumped at the sound, frantically looking around for its source.

Pavlov waved his hand in annoyance. "It's the doorbell."

"That's horrible sounding."

"I know; why do you think I so dislike coming up here to answer it?"

"Why not have servants do it?"

"We don't have any, just the Grumbles. It's hard to find servants willing to put up with Grumbles. Besides, it's Sinday—most souls are off doing . . . who knows what? Pfagh!" Pavlov shooed Freud out of his way and reached for the controls to the view panel. Pushing a button to direct the camera's stare outside, he was met with an unlikely sight: A young man, chewing something akin to gum (possibly just the insides of his own mouth) waited with a thin but wide red and yellow box, about sixteen inches by sixteen inches, in hand. The youngster was of moderate height, average build, with a face pock marked and severely scarred.

Both his jacket and the box matched in design: garish and outlandish, boldly demanding attention, advertising slovenly dedication to gluttonous consumption. The motto on the box stated: 'Dead right: you'll never go wrong with Avernal Pizza—we'll burn you to a crisp with taste!'

The young man reached to ring the doorbell once more.

"*Do not do that again!*" Pavlov barked through the grill.

The young man jumped back a full two steps.

"Uh, pizza delivery, sir." The young soul's voice was high-pitched, disconcertingly inappropriate for his body.

Pavlov swung open the door and stepped onto the porch, One closely following behind in a parody of his approach.

"Let me be very clear. I did not order pizza. I do not, nor will I ever, order pizza. Is this some kind of joke? Who sent you here with this, this, this noxious concoction?" Pavlov leaned in menacingly; more so as One, the Grumble, followed very close in kind behind him.

This Grumble seemed to pant, tensing, preparing to lunge at the poor fool, awaiting only Pavlov's word to do so. A small sliver of desiccated flesh peeled off One's face and fell to the ground as the pizza delivery guy watched in horrified fascination.

"I don't know, sir; I just deliver them. I don't even like pizza myself; my ma and pa used to own a shop, and I could never get rid of the smell. They make me do it down here; over and over and over again. Get the pizza, deliver the pizza, get abused by customers, no tips, no rest, no joy. The delivery slip says to deliver to here; if I don't get paid, they'll whip me again!" cried the high-pitched voice, plaintive and whining.

"Well then, I guess you're going to get whipped. I did not order it, nor do I want it. Begone; or else One, here, will eat you."

"Eeeep." The pizza guy's eyes bulged as the Grumble edged closer, murder in his blank eyes. He back-pedaled to get some distance between himself and the unclean thing before him. After that, he ran as fast as he could back to his rickety bicycle and disappeared round the corner of the street from which he'd come.

Pavlov closed the door and retreated back inside to face Freud. "Think about it for a moment, Comrade Freud. We are the dead; what need have we to break bread? It's nothing but a memory of our past lives. We are dead. We are in hell. What need of sustenance do we have? Even if sustenance was required, if you expire, you are sent to Reassignments, where you start your afterlife again. What other than immortality is that, Comrade Freud?"

"So, habit? That is your position on this point? That humanity, the spirit, the soul, the spark that comprises our desires, our will, our striving, is but a collective bio-organic programming imperative? That those habits we learn as we age and grow are merely instruction sets? That we are nothing but the sum of our experiential sets, codifying themselves along semi-programmed patterns of development?"

"Yes, indeed. I proved this while alive. And philosophically, I can prove it here. We are the dead, from countless ages past and future, groping toward whatever destiny yet exists for humankind. I have spoken with many men and women down here. For all, the past was bleak, the future was bleak. Always it was so, because we, as humans, continue to slouch down an evil path, rather than seeking a means to saner ways. We are wont to drive toward the worst solution in almost every conflict. Resolution occurs only when violence overcomes an opponent's resistance. I am unable to find even one example of cooperation ending a conflict, rather than force of arms. Humans speak pretty words about how the path of peace is more persistent, more desirable, yet we go not toward it."

"I am of a different mind in the matter. I feel hunger while I am in this world of suffering. I know that my body requires sustenance. Ergo, I feed. The food is horrible, but at least the body, fed, continues on."

"Think you on this, then: Is that indeed a body you inhabit? Is this indeed a corporeal world in which we suffer? I personally have not 'fed' in months—years since being down here. Although some do, *I* have not 'died' of starvation. The place itself keeps my body nourished, or malnourished. But my mind . . . it constantly seeks new resources."

"Fascinating. Truly, you have not fed?"

"Not a lick, not a drop; not for as long as I can remember. The first time I tried any of the slop down here, I immediately forswore all food and drink. Food is nothing but an addiction. Liquids in this fetid hell are no better than feces brewed in cesspools. Why would I want to inflict that upon myself? Hell is not a physical place, so why would the illusion of foodstuffs keep these engines of motivation moving? It's nothing but the mind throwing us back into our remembered patterns, patterns programmed into us from a very young age, and continued throughout our lives. Look at the divide between New Dead and Old Dead. The need to feed and drink is so strong amongst the New Dead, it's like an obsession; for the Old Dead, they make do with what they make do. If they can get by, they do so. The New Dead, on the other hand, assume that infernity is all about them. There lies the clear division between the two, Comrade Freud."

"Energy cannot be destroyed, only redirected, yes? If I concede your theory, then we exist within this ecosphere, an unknowable amount of space, energy and time. The things we feed upon, which feed upon us, are fuel cells that burn for each and keep us moving. You liken the New versus the Old dead to separate sociological composites that seek different means toward ends. I posit instead that their essential difference is their diverse interpretations of the cause and effects of such interactions. We all flow to the same point; we just see that point differently, and give it names, different structures of complexity or simplicity. We damned are defective. Our sins have proved us thus by bringing us here. Would you not agree, Herr Pavlov?"

"Hmm . . . that concept of sin is a tricky one. I surmise that neither of us truly believes that our life ideals sent us here; yet at the same time, we cannot grasp or accept the reality of the opposite place, yes, Comrade Freud?"

"Da, this is true."

The doorbell howled its scream of defiance once again. And again, Freud started, not expecting the violent squawk to blast suddenly from nowhere.

Pavlov moved to the door display panel, where he saw a young woman in dark clothes, her expression set in an artificial smile. She held pamphlets to give to whomever opened the door.

Immediately she began her tirade of prattle: "Do you have a moment to hear of salvation? The word of our Lord . . . Have you personally taken Him to your heart?" She gushed with enthusiasm, it bubbled, it burbled, it glowed upon her forehead, then suppurated as she continued: "He is the way, the word of true reflection and redemption in this horrid place. He will welcome all souls, all creatures, all things with the ability to differentiate good from bad. He has no agenda except to help all who seek assistance, every person down here has the right to—"

Pavlov did not wait to hear the name she longed to prattle on about. He interrupted her practiced speech with a harsh and grating, "*Excuse* me, miss!" One, who shadowed him like a second skin, poked his decaying visage past Pavlov's shoulder and stared at her.

Facing so much raw dissonance as One the Grumble embodied, she could not continue. "Um, yes, good sir?"

"Does that always happen, that putrefaction on your forehead?"

"Yes, sir, it does. I feel very strongly about the Word, and I must deliver it where I can, even though I suffer such malediction—"

"Right; I have no time for this. One! Eat her."

The Grumble launched himself upon the plainly dressed woman, biting straight away into her face, ripping her arms from their sockets, breaking the bones of her legs and shredding her abdomen, spitting bloody gobbets of flesh all over the street. Sharp claws tore through her rib cage, scraping against the pavement as they pushed meat and organs into his mouth; One threw back his head, gobbled up a stray piece hanging askew from his chin, and growled as he ate. In minutes, all that remained of her body was viscous debris scattered where One squatted. The blood quickly dried in the arid heat, its smell strong enough to make a soul gag. One looked around, perplexed for a second, then realized its task was done: one more body dismembered, and its uneaten remains sent back to the Undertaker's slab. Blood still dripped from One's face, droplets rolling down its chin, falling to the ground in fat, wet plops.

"Good boy, One." Pavlov slapped his thigh once, and One jumped to his side.

"Herr Pavlov, was that necessary?"

"Absolutely. Those preaching vermin keep assailing this work place. How will they learn to leave us alone if we don't show that they are unwelcome? I have no patience for their kind, who proselytize until the cows come home and still provide no up-step of the common weal. They blather on about this or that, yet never prove a single claim. Their path to this damnable place is clearly understood to be moot: they belong down here, and they deserve their fates. They dug their holes, now they keep filling them up with their own deaths again and again."

"You don't believe that a helping hand, an encouraging word fosters productive endeavors? You think these lost souls are irredeemable? Of no value whatsoever?"

"With that kind? Hell, no. Their kind will not change; they will forever be lapping at the boot heel of some loathsome upstart they deem worthy of aggrandizement. I have no time, no patience and no wherewithal to deal with their blather. They are in hell for good reason: pride, for one, and false virtue, for another. So some are here due to bureaucratic mismanagement or outdated statistical measurements of right and wrong. So what? The very definition of right and wrong hands is subjective and, regardless of taint, a matter of perception. Whose perception is the question. Or if not who, then what statistical parameters are poorly aligned. Proof? We are the proof—the consequences of those instruction sets gone haywire."

"I disagree with your assessment here. If, by your reasoning, we are here as a result of either our own wayward natures programmed into us by our experiences, or a result of statistical aberrations—margin of error—then by what *reasoning* are we here? If the individual has no means to acknowledge personal responsibility for actions undertaken, then there exists no choice in the universe, no free will. My understanding is that the very exercise of that free will is what either saves us from this fate, or sends us to this fate."

"We broke their rules; they have the stronger instruction set prevalent within that paradigm."

"*Who are they?* And what then? What purpose do we serve here? What value are we to the greater purpose of existence?"

"I did not say I know the purpose of the universe, I merely stated what I have observed. Scientific method insists that the observer changes this experiment. I do not have all answers; I merely have observations on the matter at hand."

The doorbell screamed from the wall, blaring its inconsolable isolation, and indelicate desolation. Freud jumped and furtively gazed at Pavlov, who promptly walked over to the door viewer once again.

In it he saw a youngish female in skirt and smartly matching blazer, felt hat on her head. Her skin shone pale;

she stood slightly hunched over. In her hand she held a covered wicker basket. She fretted over the basket, making sure she held it firmly, and safe from airborne contaminants.

"Ghoul Hide Cookies! Would you buy a box? We're out supporting our local Ghoul Scouts troop and . . ." She stopped only when interrupted by Pavlov:

"Are they made from real Ghoul Hides?"

"Absolutely, sir; nothing but the finest ghoul parts go into each and every cookie. Our goal is to create the most pleasurable cookie one can have. Ghoul Hide Cookies are hell's number one cookie treat; every household needs at least one box, three is even better. Share them, gobble them, toss them at poor orphan souls—They have countless uses, sir!"

"Fine; I'll take one box," said Pavlov.

She turned to hand him a box.

"What is going—Help!" the young ghoul screamed as One rushed out from behind Pavlov, cued by Pavlov's hand-sign, and began ripping the skin from her bones.

Again the Grumble stripped flesh from bone, plucking bones from joints, and rapidly disassembled the young woman, tossing her body, pulling it asunder; never attempting to consume a bit of meat or pint of blood. One was quickly coated with fresh blood, dripping from his hands to the elbows; deeply soaked in gore.

"I didn't say I was going to buy it; I just said I'll take one box. One, that's enough; she's expired by now."

"That was particularly harsh, don't you think, Herr Pavlov? And I just realized that we have not moved from this part of the building since we arrived. We talk a bit, the doorbell rings, you go out and reduce whomever has rung the bell to moist bits, and then we talk some more. Should there not be more to this cycle of interaction?"

"Something like that, ja; there should be, but we are bound by hell's dictums."

The doorbell rang again, the sound pummeling Freud's eardrums with its plaintive wail. Unprepared, Freud still jumped, but recovered quickly enough to stare at Pavlov, returning once more to the viewing panel.

This time the visitors were three dapper men in business suits. The first, bearded, thin, pale skinned, had rung the doorbell; the other two standing back three paces, hands on their belt holsters, were bald, tanned and looked comfortable despite the heat.

"Harrumph; I am the owner of this building and I've come to collect the rent. How will you be paying this month? In cash, blood, product, services? Come, come now, I haven't got all day; I've got lots of tenements to shake down. My men here will carry away our agreed-upon payment." He started through the doorway; but One stepped into his path.

"I'm grossly surprised by this particular interaction; it is a new variation on today's theme." Pavlov stroked his bearded chin. "Hmm."

"What the hell do you mean by that? Pay up your rent, or my boys will rip you apart."

"Amusing that you should use such a colloquial expression. I'd like to see you attempt to do that. You are not the landlord, since the Undertaker holds our lease, and has provided us the means to enforce whatever stricture we deem fit upon these grounds. Your claim is spurious and frankly laughable. I call your bluff: Try to come in here and remove anything." Pavlov bowed as if to invite the men inside. His other hand gestured first at One, then at the men.

One advanced quickly Pavlov, withdrawing behind the bulletproof glass, gestured to Freud to do the same.

"Boys, take this freak and rip it apart; and then rip the little guy apart, too. I wanna see what's in this joint, now," snarled the so-called building owner.

Obediently, his two thugs withdrew their firearms, and opened fire on One, who stood still as bullets flew through his body or ricocheted past to *spang* into the hallway wall behind him.

One mutely watched the three men.

"Uh, Boss; he ain't dropping."

"Well, then, shoot him in the head!"

The two thugs dropped their emptied clips, slapped in new ones, and opened fire again.

More shots hit One's head and upper body. Although gobbets of flesh from the Grumble's cheek splattered the floor with gooey bits, One never showed pain from the damage done him.

"Okay, enough of that. One, remove them!" Pavlov decreed. One immediately lunged through the doorway at the three men. He picked up the lead gangster, dragging him by the throat as he fell upon the other two thugs. One's assault dropped all three in a tangle of arms and legs, which he promptly began to rip and chew. The Grumble shredded all three gangsters, dismembering each in turn. *Smash, swipe, slash.* In minutes, the carcasses evaporated into thin air as the corpses returned to the Undertaker's slab.

"Very good, One; stand down. Comrade Freud, brazenly craven people such as those three are prime examples of those who'll assault any rampart of decency. Our job—our responsibility as intelligent souls—must be to return decorum back to our environment, be it hell or not. We are civilized; we can achieve communal goals and yet permit individuals to explore their fullest potential. These crass attacks are nothing but a disruptive confluence designed to wear our people down."

"Hmm, I don't know if that's what I would call this display. They attack, you rebut by increasing the stake of their attack tenfold. The heavy-handed tool you have, this 'Grumble', is a powerful instrument with only one objective, one dimension of responses. It can only destroy. Can Grumbles do anything else? I assume you train them, no matter what their 'natural state' might be."

"Indeed! Their natural state is completely aggressive. They attack anything that moves. They come from a hell called the House of Dust, set in darkness; a hell where only dust and Grumbles flourish. They have no defining purpose, or reason. I surmise that they exist as 'unused vessels of the Undertaker' for those souls not yet restored by the Mortuary. However, they are trainable. Hard work, lots of grueling repetition, but trainable by those means."

"To what end, though?"

"Survival, perpetuity, control through strength."

"Of whom?"

"Of everyone who is not us."

The doorbell howled again in the darkness, proclaiming gleeful discord and rattling through the rafters and beyond. Pavlov once more looked through the view pane.

He beheld a suited young man holding a clipboard. This soul was clean-shaven, of average height, medium build, with sandy hair and fingernails trimmed—innocuous in every way. Pavlov opened the door.

"Excuse me, sir," said the blond, "but would you answer a few questions about the neighborhood? We're conducting a survey in the area, to collect data for the local authorities to improve conditions. Can we count on your help, sir? I need only a moment of your time; a couple of minutes at the most." Polite, attentive and earnest, the young man had clear eyes and a wholesome attitude.

"I'm sorry, young fellow; you wish to *what*?"

"To hear your thoughts on the state of this community. My organization reaches out to all members of a community, hoping to bridge the gaps between what the damned want to accomplish and what can be accomplished. With the help of many souls, yourself included, sir, we can make changes that result in a better afterlife for all."

"You do realize we are in hell, and 'better afterlife' runs counter to the purpose of our incarceration here, yes?"

"Sir, just because obstacles exist does not mean that we cannot marshal the strength of the community by working together. The fact that we currently live in this awful place doesn't preclude our desire to improve things, to gather like-minded souls to work together to build a better underworld."

"Sounds insane to me."

"I would not know, as I never quite made it to University to pursue higher education; I preferred working with a community than with individuals."

"Yet you are an individual, speaking to an individual about individual issues. And as for education, I am particularly educated on this matter. So take it from me, one who is familiar with the specifics, your plan sounds insane."

"Well and good, sir. But, every team *does* have an 'I' in it, even if that is only 'me.' So we work with other individuals to build community; we cannot magically wish change into being."

"Clever, but trite. Learned. Taught at somebody's feet?"

"I don't recall, sir."

"So your views are as immutable as they are irrelevant? Your attempts here to engage, to ensnare, will meet with pain and displeasure. Was that your intent?"

"Most assuredly not, sir. If you won't comment, I'll leave and bother you no more. I apologize if I've caused any disruption or ill-will."

"So easy? You have already engaged in this attack, which must be countered. No exceptions. I did not make these rules, I merely abide by them."

"I am confused, sir; I see no attack, nor any rules broken."

"And that, sir, is the ball of thread you must untangle. One! Erase this one."

Pavlov stepped to the side as One lunged through the doorway. The budding bureaucrat screamed, threw his clipboard at the monstrosity bearing down upon him, then tried to run.

One grabbed the bureaucrat's arm and pulled savagely; the sound of popping tendons filled the alleyway.

The doomed soul dropped to his knees and sobbed uncontrollably as One ripped different pieces of his body from him and finally bit deeply into his skull.

Grumble teeth, sharpened by unknowable years of adversity, could not be stopped by necrotized flesh or bone. The bureaucrat perished quickly, decomposing into ooze and leaving another stain upon the road.

One, realizing his prey was no longer viable, returned to his station behind Pavlov.

"Why did you eliminate that one instead of letting him go? You let the first one go, why not this one?"

"They're all insane; they've all got notions in their heads that hell offers the possibility of a better afterlife. It's hell! There's no making amends, no reaching consensus, no ameliorating foul conditions; not here, not ever. If that were possible, through the millennia, with the billions of souls detained here, change for the better would already have occurred."

"That is a very dour outlook, very bleak. Depressing, even. Is that the only conclusion you draw from this encounter? Is there no possibility that the young fellow may have genuinely attempted something good, something community driven? Although all around us is hell, devoid of compassion, should we not, as human souls, bond together to create better conditions?"

"We do, we humans; we do precisely that! But these interruptions of concentration are not that; they are anything but that. They are gnats stinging the gazelle into impatience and vexation. If any Old Dead or New Dead truly meant to build better hells, I'd help them. However, they don't, they can't. Thus I respond with the only thing I have, which is death. I can give them no more than that. Besides, they'll do it all again, somewhere else, once they have been Reassigned by the Mortuary."

"Hmm. That does ring partly true. But it bodes ill for the stain permeating your own soul. Why insist on walking the same path to an end that brought them here? They fight, they rail, they lash out against the bonds that keep them damned, yet all roads lead to further damnation. Their character, as Heraclitus said when he was here, creates their destiny. Why keep extinguishing these souls? What does it gain? Where does this lead? How does this miserable, lonely existence help you? This is very distressing for me, knowing the little that I do of your history."

"I am fulfilling my role, playing my part; my hand is dealt. I cannot refuse to play Satan's game."

"Are you saying you have no choice, no free will, Herr Pavlov?"

"I am not. I am saying that my path is set, my choices already created by me. I am not only a creature of habit; I am a creature who has created habit. I have made my choices, and I abide by them."

The doorbell erupted in cacophonous dolor. Pavlov looked through the view pane and saw an unkempt, disheveled soul who might be fifteen or fifty, hair of indeterminate color, clothing covered with stains. Stocky of build, shorter than average, but agile, he could have had grace and strength, but despaired of either.

"Hey, dude; I'm, like . . . lost, man. Can you tell me how to get back to the freeway, man? I took a wrong turn somewhere. Whoa, dude. You got this great big scary thing behind you! Dude, that's awesome. Is it like—a pet? No, wait, dude: it's an awesome 'cosplay', right, right?"

"What the hell is this? Surely, this wreck cannot pits his wits against mine? One, dispose of this . . . waste. Shall loneliness and despair ever be my lot?" One rushed out past Pavlov and jumped on the disheveled visitor, bowling him over. The Grumble's weight kept the man down as his fists crushed the soul's chest.

The sound of cracking ribs echoed through the alley, followed by the sickening sound of One's fists pushing through flesh to soft tissue and pulling out organs and strewing them about. More stains upon the ground.

"I can't even believe that was someone considered to be a fit challenge to us; I am insulted."

"Please clarify. How does it matter which of the damned come here? Your pattern of interaction here is at odds with reason. Do you not see that you stretch for control over your environment? That you push to force your own inflexible view onto things? Is there no room for error? No way for those who approach you to leave, except by death? Why do you eliminate these visitors? I infer that this is a constant thing, that these interactions occur fairly regularly?"

"Yes, every other Sinday as a matter of fact; like clockwork. One choice leads to loneliness; the other choice leads to despair. I have no hope of a change; my punishment is set in brimstone."

"Herr Pavlov; there is always hope."

"No, Comrade Freud; there is *not* always hope. There is sometimes hope. Sometimes events, circumstances, variables enter into the ring of being, and create the possibility that events could take a different turn, approach parameters otherwise unattainable: companionship, even joy. Sometimes there is hope; sometimes, desperation, usually only loneliness, only one mind screaming in the void. We are in hell, it is the quintessential definition of hopelessness, the breath of the Void."

"Surely, you do not believe that. Hope, as they say, is eternal. It exists as a permanent component of the human makeup; arbitrary and unreliable, but part of our humanity. Even in hell, there must be hope; regardless of reason, hope exists."

"Of course hope exists, but this is hell. Hope exists as punishment. Concrete planning and forethought create only the 'possibility of something.' Possibility of the unattainable leads first to hubris, then to ruin, to loneliness and despair—which you have made your province and the nature of your abode. If you want an end to your misery, stop punishing all who come here for daring to suggest that loneliness and despair are not the alpha and omega of existence."

"Why, when they are the bedrock of my experience? I—"

The doorbell's yowl once more blotted out conversation. This time, when Pavlov looked through the view pane he saw an attractive woman wearing a business suit: white blouse, black slacks, black jacket. Long red hair billowed around and beyond her face. She held herself confidently, radiating resolute commitment. Pavlov opened the door and faced her.

"Hello, sir! I am campaigning in the area and I would like to ask for your support. Will you vote for me in the upcoming elections? With me as your duly elected representative, you can be sure I'm looking out for the welfare of my fellow constituents: better food, housing, respect. Yes, we all can do with more respect. Right, my friend?"

"Didn't we already hear this song from the survey guy?" Pavlov turned to One, who gazed back attentively. "Right, go ahead, One: make a mess."

As One jumped out from behind Pavlov, the woman screamed. She turned to run, but didn't get far.

One's inhuman strength drove him into her legs, knocking her flat into the street. Her face smashed against the pavement, blood sprayed from her eyes, mouth and nose.

One poked at the corpse as it dissolved back to the Mortuary, leaving behind one more stain.

"Well, that should be the last one,," Pavlov sighed. "Come, let's be off to the lower levels. We can discuss things in much greater length and peace down there." Pavlov turned around and began to walk into the cavernous building; the hollow shadows showed no hint of mercy or malice. Freud turned to follow suit, while One hulked at Pavlov's heel.

The doorbell sounded again, insistent in its attempts to wrangle chaos out of the comforting shadows and silence.

"Wait, that makes nine rings of the doorbell; this has never happened before. What the hell?" Turning around, Pavlov walked again to the view panel and looked out. He saw a short figure in a burlap robe, hood pulled over the head, hands tucked into the sleeves; most likely a male human soul, but other creatures lurked in hell. Pavlov opened the door. "Yes?"

"Hello; I am here as a result of the USUHC's past disruptions of my master's machinations. He is very displeased with you people; and has sent me to respond in kind. Now that we know where your facility is located, should I fail in my mission, we will continually barrage this place to make your stability crack, your house fall, your dependents crumble like clay in the baked sun." The small figure's voice spoke with a resonant rasp, like a wind whispering through pine boughs.

"Don't talk in riddles, little man. Speak clearly so that better men can make decisions based on real information."

The burlap-covered head cocked to one side as if considering; he pushed into the doorway, making Pavlov uncomfortable enough to retreat a few steps. Burlap hood turned Freud's way, then returned to face Pavlov as he barged through the doorway, saying:

"I told you: Merlin is unhappy with you people and your meddling in his affairs; I am here to retaliate." He pulled his hood back to reveal his hands and face. These looked wooden, as if the visage of an old man had grown from a tree. Wooden twigs for fingers and eyes like acorns rattling in wooden sockets peered at Pavlov. And winked. In moments, his body began to stutter and shake. Another step, and then another, and the wooden man crowded into the receiving room.

Still watching the intruder, Pavlov edged closer to the sidewall and his cluster of instruments.

The wooden man shook ever more violently. Suddenly, he lurched forward, the sound of his leg snapping audible in the enclosed room. The leg slipped out from beneath his robe, a deformed branch now rapidly decaying to ash. He gawped, stared Pavlov in the eye and lurched again. This time his entire body swayed, then fell forward, crashing to the floor. *Crack* went his wooden body as it hit the stone. The powdered leg, then his entire body, wafted through the air as the room filled with swirling dust eddying throughout the room.

"*Spores!*" Pavlov quickly smashed his hand against a small glass pane and pulled a red lever. Immediately an alarm sounded, accompanied by a red light that flashed insistently. Pavlov bent to the speaker grill, pushed a call button, and shouted directions before he retreated into a doorway leading deeper into the building and away from the vestibule.

"Fire control teams, to the main entrance immediately!" Pavlov yelled. "As we've practiced: Naphtha tanks four by four, on the double!"

The ashen cloud of dust spores swirled faster and faster, while Pavlov waited for his response team.

Meanwhile, ash seemed to multiply, to spin faster in the air.

An eyeblink later, four more Grumbles joined One, behind Pavlov. These carried metal tanks strapped by hoses to their backs. The hoses had small blue flames peeking out through their nozzles.

Pavlov pointed at the four, directing them into the vestibule proper. All four surged into the room, knelt in the doorway. There they painted the room with four separate streams of flame, dousing the entire room, setting the dusty air afire.

With the front door wide open, air from outside fueled the fire, turning the metal walls red-hot. The conflagration consumed everything in the room, including the four Grumbles with flame-throwers as Pavlov pulled the door shut behind them.

"Herr Pavlov; won't we need to go that way to get out of here?"

"No, Comrade Freud; we have other doorways. Wasn't that exciting? Just a taste of the attacks to come, or so the wooden one warned us. Somehow I find that prospect interesting, even exhilarating."

"You don't see, Herr Pavlov? You are stuck in a pattern, endlessly repeating the same set parameters, again and again. You must break that cycle."

"Why? Pattern is comfortable; understanding sits politely in its crock and provides the joy of knowing what is going to happen."

"But is not the reason we experiment to learn where we've been, what we do, and how we get there? To expand our understanding beyond the reaches of what we ordinarily see?"

"No. Thinking that way leads to madness, chaos, disharmony."

"Surely, you jest."

"Surely, but if I don't keep up appearances, what will the Joneses think?"

"I do not know who these 'Joneses' are. And I don't understand why what they think would have any bearing in this matter."

"That, comrade, is what I would consider a jest. Never mind. Come; let me show you the Grumble factory. On the way we can talk about many things. Do you know, they never let me experiment with cats; why do you think that was?"

Hell on a Technicality

Joe Bonadonna

"But alas, if I have not maintained my victory, it is God's fault for not making man
and the devil of equal strength."
—Victor Hugo, *The Hunchback of Notre Dame*

Somewhere in the inconstant, ineffable and invariably
infuriating environs of New Hell, shut inside his steampunk,
cinematically retrofitted new laboratory, Doctor Victor Frankenstein (whose brain now resides in the skull of his most
famous monster) prepares to lance a boil on the neck of his
patient. The sharp reek of ozone and scorched metal fill the
air as generators hum, transformers spark, and miniature
lightning from a large Jacob's Ladder snaps, crackles and—

Pop! goes the boil, spraying pus into the flask that the
doctor quickly presses against the open wound of his patient.

"Fuck—That hurt!" cried Giovanni Fortuna, alias Bad
Luck Johnny, a/k/a Johnny Fortune, one-time hitman for the
Chicago Mafia and now, in hell, one of Frank Nitti's tor-
pedoes. Johnny sat on the wooden examination table and

gritted his teeth while Doctor Frankenstein cleaned and bandaged his incision.

"My most heartfelt apologies, John," said the doctor, speaking in the deep, resonant voice of the monster he once created. Frankenstein wore a soiled lab coat, surgical mask and gloves, and a black felt cap. Although this cap resembled a yarmulke, it had two big ears attached and on its front boasted an iron-on decal of a cartoon rat wearing high-topped gym shoes, knickers and a waistcoat. The ensemble made Victor look like some huge, grotesque doctor in a children's hospital. He adjusted the wire-rim spectacles balanced on the tip of his nose.

"Tell me again about brains and this theory of yours, Doc," Fortuna asked.

As Victor Frankenstein prepared to lance a second boil on Johnny's cheek, he thought back on how all this got started: when he and Adam, his monstrous creature constructed of dead body parts, had hired Merlin to build them a secret, magical hideout in Pitt's Pendulum, the saloon they'd once owned and operated in Brimstone, Hellizona. The magician's price? To swap brains between doctor and monster. Thus, the brain of Victor Frankenstein now resides in the skull of the monster, and the monster's brain, Adam's brain, now inhabits the cranium of the infamous doctor.

"The brain is the center of it all, John," Frankenstein explained, "the seat of personality. Just as the skull houses the brain, the brain houses the mind. And at the center of the mind resides the soul. That is my theory. That is what I believe."

"Got it, Doc," Johnny replied with instinctive understanding. "No matter what bodies you two wear—you're still you, and Adam is still Adam."

"Precisely."

"You still believe Galatea and your Adam don't have souls?"

"Indeed I do."

"And you still think those two can get out of hell on a technicality?"

Victor nodded energetically. "Neither was sired by a man's seed and born of a woman's labor. They are artificial creations, constructs fashioned by the hands of mortal men. Souls are divine, created by the Big Guy Upstairs, as you call him. How and why Adam and Galatea are in hell when they don't possess souls must be the result of some over-sight, some clerical error."

"They committed murder, Doc. Galatea killed Pyg-malion. And who knows better than you how many poor schmucks Adam sent to the grave?" Johnny brushed dan-druff from the right shoulder of his purple zoot suit as if knocking off a cartoon angel whispering in his ear in an ef-fort to convert him to the paths of righteousness. "I think they're gonna need a second opinion."

With the sound of a champagne bottle being uncorked, the boil on Johnny's cheek popped. Victor, too slow with the flask this time, watched as noisome green pus sprayed the air. A small black fly with a white head then darted from the mouth of the opened sore and flew off somewhere, crying and begging for help in a high-pitched, pipsqueak voice.

"Holy shit—was that inside the boil?" Johnny asked.

"Afraid so." Frankenstein wiped sweat from his brow and accidentally knocked the cap off his head, revealing what it formerly concealed: his exposed brain, held in place by wire mesh that had replaced the top of his skull. Out of nowhere, flies immediately began buzzing around the exposed gray matter.

"For hell's sake, put that cap back on," begged Johnny, averting his eyes. When the cap was firmly back in place, he squinted. "By the way, where did you get that silly cap?"

Victor Frankenstein heaved a heavy sigh. During the showdown in Brimstone against Lemuel Gulliver and the Uncubi, when Gulliver tried to suck the essence out of Mary Shelley, Victor had saved her by attacking Gulliver and diving into a pool of hot lava, taking the madman with him. While he had no idea what befell Gulliver after that, Victor had ended up on Slab A. Bad enough to be trapped in that monstrous body, badly burned and scarred, but lying there at the mercilessness of the Undertaker added infernal insult to ghastly injury.

"The cap was a parting gift from Gorgonous, the Deputy Assistant Undertaker," Victor explained. "'To keep the flies away. Goodbye and have a nice day,' he told me. The bastard."

Released from the Mortuary and reassigned to New Hell, Victor next took a job as lab assistant to Doctor Faustus, laboring to find a cure for the epidemic of plagues unleashed by Erra and his maleficent Seven. Once he'd saved up enough diablos, Victor built Goblin Manor, his modest castle and library on Golem Heights, a new strip of land that appeared after Satan restored a portion of New Hell previously vaporized. Since its materialization, Golem Heights had become hot property, coveted by New Dead and Old Dead alike. From his Golem Heights laboratory, Victor set to work treating patients and experimenting with his own vaccine against Erra's plagues.

"So how come you ain't got no boils or junk and stuff like that?" asked Johnny.

"Behold this body that I made with my own two hands, John. I don't know if there's any room left on this accursed flesh to sustain another curse."

"Yeah, your shit's pretty fucked up."

While Victor cleaned and bandaged Johnny's cheek, the gangster who had left the land of the living in 1960 looked around, admiring the additions to the lab that the doctor had acquired since his last visit. Torches in wall brackets lit the laboratory and sent shadows scurrying about the high, vaulted ceiling. Walls of huge, blood-red stone were now covered with electrical panels and all manner of dials and meters, buttons and toggles, lights and switches. Tables sagged under an alchemist's arsenal of crucibles and alembics, mortars and pestles, jars, vials, Bunsen burners and distilling apparatus. Van de Graf generators, Tesla coils, nebulariums, cyclotrons, voltmeters, and much, much more were neatly arranged around the room.

"I like what you did with your new house of Frankenstein, Doc, but I—" Johnny suddenly gagged and then coughed up a handful of bullets from a Thompson submachine gun; the never-ending, self-regenerating hail of bullets that had ended his time on earth and followed him into his afterlife.

"Still spitting them out, I see," said Victor.

Johnny wiped his mouth on the sleeve of his suit coat. "You'd think with the boils and all, I'd catch me a break and stop hacking up slugs."

"This is hell, John. There are no breaks for thee and me."

"No shit, Sherlock. How long you figure on these plagues sticking around?"

"Your guess is as good as mine." Victor lowered his surgical mask, then removed his gloves and tossed them into the small fireplace. Almost instantly, the sickening smell of burning rubber permeated the lab. "Besides Faustus and me, Jekyll and Moreau are also working on a cure for these plagues. But now we have this new plague that causes in-stant death—but *not* immediate reassignment, turning the victims into pseudo zombies. It's all very perplexing."

"Plague zombies in hell? What a great title for a horror film," Johnny said, laughing. "Hell is sure in one helluva mess, ain't it?"

Bang!

The outer door bursts open and one of the New Damned, wearing frayed blue jeans, a tie-dyed tee-shirt, long hair and flip-flops, shambles into Frankenstein's lab. Foaming at the mouth, he moans and groans and staggers about, zombie-like. His face, neck and hands are twisted and deformed . . . flushing purple, then blue, then green, and finally yellow.

"The fuck? This one of them plague zombies?" asks Johnny.

"No," Victor replies. "One of my patients."

Johnny reaches inside his suit jacket, pulls out his Bolt .45 revolver, takes aim and squeezes the trigger twice, and—

"Quasi—Help!" Victor shouts.

—two bullets drip from the mouth of Johnny's gun barrel like drops of water from a leaky faucet, and fall to the floor.

"Damn it!" Johnny grabs Victor and drags him away from the intruder.

The damned hippy growls in anger when he spots Doctor Frankenstein and starts trashing lab equipment and tossing furniture and gadgets around the lab like some mad monster from an old B-movie.

"Help!" Victor yells again.

The Hunchback of Notre Dame drops from the vaulted ceiling, riding the top of a giant bell jar. His left hand grips the rope fastened to it and his right balances a tray bearing two glasses filled to the brims with neon-green wine. Neat as you please, the huge bell jar makes a perfect touchdown right over the maniacal longhair, trapping the unfortunate inside of it. Quasimodo, once bell ringer and now lab assistant, hops from atop the bell and sticks his landing without spilling a drop of wine.

"Your wine, *Docteur*," Quasimodo said, bowing from the waist and extending the tray. Still as athletic and agile as he was on earth, he ended in hell for the murder of Archdeacon Claude Frollo. The Undertaker, in a moment of kindness, pity, or canny cruelty, restored the hearing of that shapeless lump of human flesh.

"What the devil took you so long?" Victor asked.

"I had to let the wine breathe, *Docteur*," Quasimodo replied.

"I asked for water, Quasi. Not wine."

"'One drop of wine is enough to redden a whole glass of water,'" Quasimodo said with a wink, quoting another man named 'Victor' who had immortalized him in a novel.

Victor reached for both glasses and handed one to Johnny. "Drink," he said. "Good."

"That's cute," Johnny told him, gagging as he tasted his wine. "This crap must taste like sour blood, sulfur and monkey piss."

"*Oui,* and with just a hint of the vomit and bile," Quasimodo added.

Victor shrugged, guzzled his wine and smacked his lips when finished. "Since my dive into that pool of hot lava, I can't smell or taste anything anymore."

Johnny: "That's a blessing, no doubt."

Quasimodo: "If there can be such a thing as a blessing in hell."

Sudden, muffled sounds of pounding and wailing from inside the giant bell jar caused the trio to turn in unison.

"Holy shit!" Johnny swore.

Inside the bell jar, the long-haired freak howled and beat his fists against the glass sides. Blood poured from his ears, nose and mouth. Then his eyes bulged and exploded, spewing all sorts of nasty and ghastly bits of gore and flesh against the inside of the bell jar. An infernal instant later, the hippy collapsed on the floor.

"Quickly now, Quasimodo," said Victor.

The Hunchback of Goblin Manor set his tray on the table, grabbed the rope and started pulling on it, lifting the bell jar off the floor, then raced to the other side of the room where he tied the end of the rope to an iron ring set in the wall so the bell jar hung suspended from the ceiling.

Victor rushed over to examine the corpse. Johnny and Quasi joined him.

"What's the verdict, Doc?" asked Johnny.

Victor checked for wrist and throat pulses. "Why . . . he's dead, he's dead! By all that's unholy, now I know what it's like to play Samael. I am twice cursed and twice damned."

"But that cannot be," said Quasimodo. "His body is not shimmering. It's still solid, still here."

"Holy shit, Doc!" said Johnny. "Did this punk on the floor here have one of the plagues?"

"No. He was clean," said Victor, his expression dark, his heart thumping with fear.

"This poor soul was one of the many the *docteur* inoculated with his Victor's Vaccine," Quasimodo explained to Johnny.

"How *many* is many?"

"Somewhere in the vicinity of seven thousand or so," Victor said sheepishly.

"Leapin' fuckin' Lucifer!" said Johnny. "Do you know what this means?"

Victor shook his head and tried to control his shaking hands, but his body trembled and he began to weep.

Quasimodo shrugged his better shoulder.

"It means that every damned soul in hell who was given your vaccine might be dead or will soon die, Doc—and possibly never show up in the Mortuary," Johnny said.

Victor wept harder. *I swear by Apollo the physician, and Aesculapius the surgeon, likewise Hygeia and Panacea, and call all the gods and goddesses to witness that I will observe and keep this underwritten oath, to the utmost of my power and judgment.* "My vaccine . . . it failed! It's another curse!" he wailed. "Once again I have betrayed the inviolability of Hippocrates' sacred oath."

"We don't know that yet," said Johnny. "But if it's true, you're in a hell of a lot of trouble."

Victor collapsed in his chair, shaking like a lost soul looking upon the true face of His Satanic Majesty, wailing and weeping hysterically.

Quasimodo pulled Johnny aside. "Were you vaccinated?" asked the hunchback.

"I was going to, but I think I'll take my chances," Johnny replied. "What about you?"

"No, *mon ami*. I do not trust in such things."

"Now listen," said Johnny. "First, hide this body someplace where you guys can keep tabs on it, to see if it vanishes or rots. Second, I want a list of everyone Victor inoculated with his vaccine. I'll use it to check records and find out if any of his patients died and ended up on Slab A—or not."

"Fucking Murphy's Law," said Quasimodo.

Victor Frankenstein howled like a banshee being castrated.

"Tell me about it," said Johnny.

*

The crimson vault over New Hell is stained with shadow and echoing with the cries of the damned, their voices bleeding together in a hellalulu chorus of rage and agony as Erra's various plagues and maladies sweep through the streets like the wrath of the Almighty, which indeed they are. Old Dead and New, the infamous and the mundane—some already infected, others fearing they'll soon be struck down by this contagion sent from Above—go about their business as best they can, as they have always done and shall forever do, here in the unhappy hereafter.

Galatea, Pygmalion's bride, widow and murderer, still the most beautiful and desirable woman in all infernity, walked quietly beside the love of her life in hell, Adam Frankenstein. Today she'd dressed like a goddess of ancient Greece, wrapped in a long, flowing lavender gown. Her pink skin, so much like fine Italian marble, glowed with health and youth. Neither she nor Adam had thus far shown any symptoms of any plague. Perhaps they were immune, she wondered, she mused, she hoped. After all, neither of them had been sired by man and born of woman, thus were probably in no way human at all. This conceit animated their discussion.

Adam Frankenstein, garbed in 19th century Swiss hunting clothes, held Galatea's hand. His broken leg, which he had received trying to escape the attack on Brimstone, Arizona by Lemuel Gulliver's former allies, the Uncubi, had healed quickly; thereafter, he jogged daily to stay in shape.

"Pygmalion carved you from stone," Adam reminded her; *his* brain, *his* thoughts and words, came forth in the voice of Doctor Victor Frankenstein. "Thus, I believe, you are not human, having not been born of flesh and blood, but of stone."

"Are you saying I'm a rock demon?" She punched him in the arm. "Thanks a lot."

"Well, they *are* immune to the ills that flesh is heir to."

"And what of you, love? You inhabit Victor's body." Galatea watched the handsome face of Doctor Frankenstein adopt a thoughtful expression while the brain inside that head, the brain of Frankenstein's monster, contemplated her words.

For a long time, Galatea and Adam did not know the fate of Victor after he grabbed the vampire-like Gulliver and, holding him, dived into a pool of hot lava. But Mob enforcer Johnny Fortune learned that Victor had been reassigned and was now living and working in New Hell. As for Gulliver, whose plan to establish his own little kingdom in hell had been thwarted . . . rumor whispered he was now a piece of furniture in Satan's office.

"Interesting," Adam said. "If Victor is right and the brain *is* the seat of the soul, and I do, indeed, have a soul . . . then what of this body I wear? Is it soulless? Or not?"

"Good question," said Galatea. "Now what if the heart, and not the brain, is the seat of the soul? You inhabit Victor's body, and we all know that he was damned for daring to play the Almighty. Therein may be more conflict between brain and heart than usual."

Again, Galatea studied the handsome face and fine body of the Swiss doctor while Adam pondered her words. Although his form pleased her aesthetically, it was Adam, and not the doctor, whom she loved—before Merlin, that cambion who was a virtuoso of mischief and misdirection, had switched brains, turning the doctor into his creation and creature into creator. Frankenstein's monster had attracted her from the moment they first met: Adam and she were two of a kind, unique in all levels and circles of hell, so far as she knew: constructs made by the hand of mortal men; artificial life, human and yet not human. And if they possessed no souls, then perhaps they possessed something different, something more or less than immortal souls. Whatever it might be, this resonance had brought them together, united them in love and entwined their eternal fates.

"This is all so damned upsetting," Adam told her. "I wish Merlin would agree to put our brains back where they belong—each in the body belonging to it. Maybe then this issue of who's who, and do we have souls, and whether or not we can get out of hell can be easily resolved."

"Fret not, my love," she said.

"But what if this panel of so-called experts can't help us? Or they refuse?"

"Then we seek a second opinion."

They retreated into their own burrows of silence and continued on their way. Galatea studied the multitudes of damned they passed en route to the Hellexandria Memorial Library, where she and Adam were to go before a board of scholars who hopefully could solve the riddle and answer the question of whether or not they had souls, and what should be done with them if they did not.

"But you believe, you *really* believe we don't have souls?" Adam stared at her, through Victor's intense blue eyes, so full of hope.

Galatea smiled and squeezed his hand. "Yes, that is what I believe, my love."

"Then perhaps we can indeed get out of hell on a technicality."

And therein was the rub: Galatea was a realist: With souls or without, she believed there was no way out of hell for them. Each had committed crimes against mankind and the Almighty, crimes to damn them for eternity. Subject to her self-inflicted curse, she could exist in the afterlife of hell: such was the price for wanting to be human, for falling prey to human emotions, especially those of jealousy and rage and a thirst for revenge. In her mind, she perceived herself unquestionably human. What else could she be? In life she had been a woman in love; she'd acted as multitudes of humans before and after her had acted, men and women who had loved and been betrayed, as Pygmalion had betrayed her.

"Still, I'm not so sure about all this," said Adam.

In spite of her doubts, she would not dash his hopes. "Not to worry, love. Things will work out as they should."

"This is hell, Galatea. *Nothing* works the way it should."

Galatea sighed and walked on in silence, still clutching his hand.

As for Adam . . . had that poor creature not also proven himself human? Flawed, brilliant, childish, open-hearted, shy, vengeful and murderous . . . . The construct called Adam was as complex as any mortal sired by the seed of Man and nurtured in the womb of Woman. He was monstrous because he had been made monstrous and had been too feared and misunderstood ever to be looked upon as anything *but* a monster. His crimes and his sins had earned him his eternal season in hell. And yet she knew he hoped he'd be found lacking a soul and thus unfit for afterlife in hell. Galatea loved him all the more for that fiery hope burning inside him, a beacon of promise. However, what she feared more than eternity in hell was their ultimate fate, should she and Adam—or one and not the other—be found wanting in soul. To her knowledge, only one soul had ever been released from hell. But one soul *had been* released. Without souls, no damnation or salvation could be had. So what price, to be judged lacking a soul?

"Perhaps you should return to Hades. I'll only bring more torment and misery into your afterlife," Adam said after a time. "You belong with the Old Dead and their finer sensibilities."

"I belong with you, my love. And we belong together," Galatea told him. "Now stop talking like a demon's ass. We're almost there."

Damned souls scream and shout, moan and wail. Galatea notices something untoward in the intersection near the library, a disturbance unfolding around a beat-up old catering truck parked at one corner. Painted in scintillant green, brown and yellow across the truck's side is the hel-logo, *Tarta-R-Us*.

"What is that, Adam?" she asks, noticing a gaggle of damned gathering around the truck.

"Fast food," he replies. "They're selling *tortas*—Span-ish flat bread. But either they misspelled the word or thought to have some fun with the name."

"Why anyone bothers to eat anything is beyond me. Food in hell is so disgusting."

"Unnecessary, too. But old habits are hard to break."

Lost souls start running away from the truck, many car-rying grease-stained bags of foul-smelling food. It's clearly a major panic attack among the damned.

"Get away!" one damned fool yells to them. Galatea recognizes the man as a very minor poet from ancient Greece named Philocles who'd written verse that won a rigged con-test over Sophocles' Oedipus Rex and been damned for it.

"Run away! Run away!" shouts a former 21st century president of the United States.

As frightened hellizens rush past her and Adam, Galatea sees the reason for their panic.

Two damned souls, a barefooted old man and a young woman in ragged coveralls shambling around one side of the catering truck, lurch into view. Flesh drops like melted wax from their bones, maggots pour from their orifices; their jaws hang slack, dripping with foaming saliva, yellow vomit and green bile. The woman stumbles about like a baby try-ing to walk for the first time. The man tries to speak but only mumbles incoherently, as if his tongue has been cut from his mouth—and then his tongue falls from his mouth.

Adam, handsome and brave in Victor's body, steps in front of Galatea, to guard and protect her against the two plague-infected hellbillies. "Back away slowly," he whispers.

Without a word, Galatea takes careful strides backward, still clutching Adam's hand; he has become her shield against these two disgusting and rancid souls who stagger toward them with arms outstretched, a pair of zombies from old horror films such as Adam watched on late-time hellivision.

"I think we should take the word of that president and run away—*now*," she said.

No sooner had Galatea spoken than seven Uncubi arrived on the scene. Two carried wooden tridents, four were armed with lariats. The seventh Uncubus, whom Galatea recognized by the union badge hanging around his neck, snapped orders like a drill sergeant trying to recite poetry. Within moments the two plague victims had been lassoed, roped and tied. Task completed, the Uncubi then stood at attention while their captives struggled, biting and chewing on their bonds. Crowds of curious damned gathered around, rubbernecking now that danger was past.

Galatea called out to the badge-wearing Uncubus. "Mister Up! Mister Up!"

Glancing toward her, the New Breed demon waved to Galatea and hurried to join her and Adam. Mister Up was the hetman of the Uncubi—the unpublished poets and authors who had sold their souls to Nephilim, thinking they were romancing the Muses. Totally naked, having been made androgynous by the Undertaker, Mister Up and the Uncubi had heads and faces fashioned from an infernal hybrid of human and pteranodon; wriggly worms instead of hands and fingers; their bodies were flickering images from an old black and white television set.

"Hello!" said Mister Up, a/k/a the Unknown Poet. In life he'd possessed an eidetic memory, but in hell the Undertaker had taken all his memories from him, leaving him with only rudimentary recollections. Mister Up had attained union stewardship of the Uncubi when their former hetman, Kilroy Bass, was slain by Johnny Fortune. Once rebels involved in Gulliver's plot to overthrow Satan, the Uncubi now worked for Jimmy Hoffa.

When hundreds of Uncubi arrived to form a perimeter around the Hellexandria Memorial Library, Adam asked, "What's going down, Up?"

The Unknown Poet bobbed his head and laughed with a sound like a crab clacking its claws. "With riots breaking out all over New Hell, and these new plague zombies appearing, His Satanic Majesty believes another attack on the library may be in the works." He pointed a wrist of wriggly worms at his tribesmen. "Mister Hoffa ordered us to stand guard."

"Plague zombies?" asked Galatea. "Like these?" She pointed to the two wretched hellizens struggling to get free of their restraining ropes.

"Yes," said Mister Up. "It's the new plague: causes death, but not immediate reassignment. When these victims die, they get right back up again and stagger away, putrefying as they go about whatever business near-mindless things may have. After a few days, they dissolve in a flurry of maggots and finally end up in the Mortuary, bits, pieces, maggots and all." He nodded his pointy big head toward the captured plague zombies. "See?"

Galatea and Adam turned to watch as the body of first one and then the other damned zombie melted like ice cream left out too long. Maggots, gobbets of half-dissolved flesh, and chunks of bone formed a noxious, yellow-green stew on the sidewalk. Shortly after that, the grisly remains shimmered and vanished, leaving behind only two wet spots on the ground.

"Cool thing is," said Mister Up, "even their clothes end up on Slab A. No muss, no fuss. I'm surprised you haven't heard about them."

*

Sitting at a desk in one candlelit corner of his laboratory, Doctor Victor Frankenstein types into his Crapple Slablet and ponders his eternity in hell.

So much harm have I done in life—and now in hell. I sought to explore powers unknown and reveal to all mankind the mysteries of creation. But what have I truly accomplished? I wanted to create a being both beautiful and wise, but gave the world the vilest creature in nature. And now I wear his flesh for all eternity.

Outside, in the vast distance, explosions and gunshots invade the *sanctum sanctorum* of Victor's laboratory as Old Dead and New battle for control of the Golem Heights. Erra's plagues have brought not only physical torment to the damned but mental affliction as well. Fear and madness reign in New Hell, and the situation grows desperate.

Distracted by the noise, Victor looked up from his screen and turned to the buxom, black-haired beauty sitting on the stool next to his desk. He was delighted to know that she remained untouched by any of Erra's plagues. "When do you wish to leave?" he asked her.

Wearing a red tee-shirt, tight black Mangler Jeans, and faux-leather motorcycle jacket and boots from "Hell Bent for Leather," (not affiliated in any way with *Hell Bent*, the hit play written by William Shakespeare and Christopher Marlowe), Mary Wollstonecraft Shelley pointed to Victor's Slablet, folded her arms and said, "As soon as you can finish up here. I don't like the members of that board Adam and Galatea have to face. Those two are going to need our help."

"Are you coming with us, John?" asked Victor.

Leaning against the wall next to the desk, tossing a lump of coal from one hand to the other, Johnny shook his head. "Nope. Nitti's got another job for me. Besides, why in hell would I ever wanna get outta hell? I like it here."

Victor pointed to a brand new pustule on the right-hand corner of Johnny's upper lip. "For starters, there's Erra and his plagues."

"You know me. I roll with the punches." Johnny was the only person Victor knew in hell who did not want to get *out* of hell—not even for free. "Where's that stiff I told you to stash?"

"Up in the bell tower, where Quasimodo hid him."

"He didn't shimmer and vanish yet?"

Victor squeezed his eyes shut. "No."

"And it's starting to stink up the joint, as Johnny would so eloquently put it," said Mary.

Johnny winked at her. "Mary was kind enough to help me with this, Doc. But it don't look none too good." He stopped playing with the lump of coal, pulled a parchment scroll from the inside pocket of his suit coat, then set it down upon the desk. "Here's the new list."

Victor reached for the scroll, but did not pick it up. "And?"

"Sorry, Doc. Bad news," said Johnny. "Almost every damned soul on that list has taken the last train to Boot Hill. Of your seven thousand patients, only a few hundred have popped up on Slab A, and another thousand are still missing in action."

Gulping a rising tide of bile, Victor asked, "Could they have gone . . . elsewhere? To some other level or circle of hell?"

"They could be anywhere," Mary told him. "Or no-where."

"What—what of the others?" Victor asked in a quaver-ing voice.

"Five thousand bodies have been collected and brought to the Mortuary," Mary replied.

"And they're all as dead as Dante. As *morto* as Mil-ton," said Johnny.

"But we are in hell, *mon ami*," said Quasimodo. "We are, all of us, dead."

"But these stiffs are *really* dead," said Johnny. "Their souls may be gone. Their hell-made facsimiles of flesh and bone are rotting away just like stiffs are supposed to do when they get ripe. Odds are they ain't gonna be reassigned."

Victor's hands begin to shake as he remembers some-thing Mary once wrote. He returns his attention to his Slab-let and types: '*I was seized by remorse and the sense of guilt, which hurried me away to a hell of intense tortures as no language can describe.*' Then he types something of his own: *Here, in the very heart of perdition, I have created nothing but further horrors, and now, even the final death of nonexistence. Oh, twice damned am I!*

Finished with the day's entry into his digital diary, Vic-tor clicks on *Save*, turns off his Slablet and places it on the shelf hanging on the wall, above his desk. He stares at a small vial containing a green, glowing mucous: the last of his Victor's Vaccine. Lying next to this is a bright and shiny new hypodermic needle. Hippocrates' words return to haunt him: *I will comport myself and use my knowledge in a godly manner.* Victor reaches for the needle when the Slablet, the latest in Crapple's infernal gizmos and gadgets, bursts into flames.

Mary hops off the stool as the Slablet burns. Johnny dances aside. Victor pushes his chair away from the desk. And Quasimodo swoops down from above, swinging from a rope like a jungle ape-man, holding a glass pitcher in one hand.

"Water!" cries the Hunchback of Notre Dame, dousing the burning Slablet with brackish water. He lets go of the rope, lands on his feet and finishes putting out the fire. But it's too late: the Slablet is warped and melted beyond repair. All Victor's notes and musings—lost forever.

"I cannot win. I can never win," he moaned, removing the mouse-eared cap from his head and fanning his exposed brain.

"In hell, there are no winners," said Quasimodo. "Not so long as Erra and his seven little madmen run amok in this cathedral of everlasting rue and woe."

"That was quite an entrance, Q," said Mary.

The hunchback set the empty pitcher on the desk and bowed in a most theatrical manner. "*Merci, oh belle dame.*" He picked up the ruined Slablet and studied it. "Perhaps it can be salvaged, *Docteur*?"

Victor replaced the cap on his skull and adjusted his spectacles. "What do you know, you garrulous little gargoyle?"

"I do know that 'a one-eyed man is much more incomplete than a blind man, for he knows what it is that's lacking,'" said Quasimodo, quoting from the novel that made him famous. He offered the Slablet to the doctor, who shook his head and turned away as if in disgust.

"Oh, take it away. Take it away," said Victor.

Quasimodo tossed the gizmo into a handy trash bin.

Victor picked up the parchment scroll, studied it, and put it down again. He pulled his hair and wrung his hands. "Giving life to the dead was easy, but undoing the evil I have worked, the sins I've committed . . . that is a task only heaven can perform. And heaven, as ever, is silent." It all hit him then. "Oh, dear—what have I done?"

"You've done nothing wrong, Doc," said Johnny. "This is hell, remember? We're already dead. If anything, you've actually done some good. Think about it."

"*Think about it*? Think about what?" asked Victor.

"You may have given peace to six thousand souls, *mon ami*," Quasimodo explained. "Maybe you have given to them the way out of hell, no?"

Victor swung around on his hunchback assistant as if they were mortal enemies facing each other in combat. "You clown, you fool! I've given them nothing but death!"

"For some, better true and final death than a never-ending afterlife in hell," said Mary.

"That's true, Doc," said Johnny. "Your vaccine could be the only exit from hell."

Victor pounded the desk with his fists. "But they were not given a *choice*, don't you see?"

"They came to you for help," said Johnny. "You explained to them that the vaccine was still in the experimental stage, and you didn't know what the side effects might be. But they didn't care. They just wanted protection from the plagues. They *chose* to be inoculated—you didn't twist their arms or hold a gun to their heads."

"But would they have chosen to be injected with my serum if they knew the end result?"

"They took the chance, *Docteur*," Quasimodo argued. "They accepted the risk factor and chose inoculation. Think on this, *n'est-ce pa*? Your vaccine was the only hope they had."

"Yes, and we can sell it to all the damned in all the hells," said Johnny. "We'll give the poor bastards a choice between eternal suffering and self-euthanasia."

"Call it what it is, John," said Mary. "Suicide."

"It don't matter," said the gangster. "We're already in hell. And maybe, just maybe, the way everything is all fuck-eyed and cocked-up around here, suicide in hell means the opposite of what it does in life."

Quasimodo scratched his hump. "You mean to say—suicide as a way *out* of hell?"

"Sure, why not?"

"Suicides always end up back on Slab A," Mary pointed out.

"But what if the vaccine destroys the *soul*?" Johnny persisted. "Look at the cadaver that's rotting away in the belfry. Look at the ones in the Mortuary. That's proof enough for me. Where there's no soul, there's no reassignment. Victor's Vaccine kills the damned and kills 'em dead." He placed a hand on the doctor's shoulder and squeezed it gently. "See what I mean, Doc?"

Victor shrugged his shoulder free of Johnny's hand. *What if it is true? What if I have found the way to bring final and lasting death to the damned? I can be free—free of all guilt and remorse and eternal torment! Free of hell and its house of eternal horrors!* He glanced at Mary. "'But soon, I shall die, and what I now feel be no longer felt. Soon these burning miseries will be extinct!'" he wailed, quoting from her most famous novel.

Victor grabbed the hypodermic needle and was reaching for the vial of green serum when Mary shouted, "Stop him, John!"

Johnny snatched the vial off the shelf. "Oh, no, Doc. You need to make more, a lot more, before you shuffle off to your mortal buffalo coil or whatever."

"No!" Victor shouted. "Oh, let me die, let me die, let me die."

The lab equipment now hums and crackles into life. Cyclotrons spin. Jacob's Ladders and Van De Graff generators flash with sparks. Arcs of lightning spring from Tesla coils. Machinery hums and glows, glass tubes boil with liquids, electrical currents charge through the coiled tubes and conductance. The sizzle, snapping hiss and sparkles of ozone and its sharp odor fill the lab and Goblin Manor.

"What the fuck?" Johnny says, his voice sounding as if it comes from the bottom of a well.

The outer door opens and a darkly handsome Roman-nosed man walks in, the heels of his shoes clicking on the stone floor tiles. He sports a black, pinstriped suit, black shirt and white tie. Over that he wears a long white lab coat.

"John!" says Victor.

"What?" asks Johnny Fortune.

"Not *you*—this is Doctor Polidori."

"Hello, Victor. How are you, Mary?" says John William Polidori, author of *The Vampyre*, one-time physician to Lord Byron and friend to Mary and Percy Shelley. He committed suicide and landed in hell in 1821.

"What brings you here?" Mary asks.

"I'm working with Faustus," Polidori replies. "Victor has something I need."

Victor frowns suspiciously. "And what, may I ask, is that?"

"This." Polidori snatches the vial of Victor's Vaccine from Johnny's hand.

"Hey! You can't have that!" yells Johnny.

"*Al contrario, Giovanni*," says Polidori. "You humans . . . none of you have ever been worthy of salvation, much less damnation. No, obliteration is all your wretched race deserves. Oblivion is what you have earned."

When Quasimodo moves to take the vial away from Polidori, the Italian doctor snaps his fingers and the lab is bathed in blinding crimson light.

Surrounded by the light, Victor sees nothing but Polidori. "What is the meaning of this?"

"They will forget I was here," Polidori tells him. "They will forget all about your vaccine and the patients you inoculated. For them, there is no vaccine and none of this ever happened. But not you, Victor. No, you shall never forget."

Something with icy feet crawls up the length of Victor's spine. "What do you mean?"

"I mean just this, Doctor: you will remember your formula, your vaccine. You will remember the adverse and fatal side effects it had on so many of your patients. But you will never be able to recreate it. You will remember your grief and remorse, and all that you have wrought. You will never be able to speak of it, to write of it, to tell anyone about it. It all stays locked away inside your head." Polidori laughed and snapped his fingers. The crimson light vanished. "Have a nice Sadderday." He snapped his fingers again, and then he, too, vanished.

"Victor? Victor!" said Mary. "What's wrong?"

Victor turned around to face Mary, Quasimodo and Johnny, all staring at him. A sick feeling came over him, and his belly squirmed as if he'd just swallowed a handful of live worms.

"Are you okay, Doc?" asked Johnny.

How could he tell them? He tried . . . he stuttered and stammered, but the words wouldn't come. And he knew it would be useless to attempt a written explanation, to try to communicate in any other way. A powerful spell had been cast over him, it seemed, a hex or a curse. Alone he was, with no one in whom he could confide, forever *unable* to tell of these events.

A feeling in Victor's heart turned into a grim thought in his head. Remembering that his Slablet was now a melted piece of junk, he took the lump of coal from Johnny's hand, raced over to a bare patch of red brick wall and, using the coal, scrawled:

"Untold secrets, now revealed,
No sane reason for truth concealed.
Disappointment, harsh and deep,
Faith, no more, is mine to keep.
Heart turns cold, begins to weep,
Lost soul heavy, hides in sleep."

The others read his words and exchanged worried glances.

"What the fuck does that crap mean?" Johnny wanted to know.

Quasimodo shrugged his misaligned shoulders and shook his misshaped head.

"Victor? Are you all right?" Mary asked. "Victor? We have to leave."

His heart heavy with guilt, with a pain in his lost soul like no other torment he had ever experienced, Victor asked, "Are we going to the library now, to meet with Adam and Galatea?"

Mary shook her head. "We have an errand to run first."

As they turned to leave, Johnny pointed to the floor. "Hey, Doc. Is that new? I've never noticed those before."

Victor, Mary and Quasimodo looked to where Johnny pointed. The heart and soul of Doctor Victor Frankenstein shivered with cold.

Leading to the doorway, burned into the stone tiles, were seven footprints.

Seven *hoof* prints, to be exact.

*

Adam Frankenstein sits in a poorly-lit, windowless basement room under the Hellexandria Memorial Library. On a rusted examination table, he swings his legs as he buttons his shirt. Seated at a nearby table at the front of the room, five doctors of philosophy and medicine deliberate amongst themselves. A moderator stands at a podium, looking bored. At the hands of these infernally eminent doctors, Adam has suffered a series of physical examinations to make Torquemada envious. Now he endures a tedious Q & A session quickly degenerating into arguments among these wise men and their moderator, each more concerned with proving the validity of their own theories than determining, once and for all, whether or not Adam and Galatea possess souls.

Galatea fidgets in one of the chairs facing the panel of doctors, chewing her nails as Adam, sitting on the rusty metal table, remains patient and stoic. She wishes that Mary and Victor were there with them, if for no other reason than comfort and moral support. Her turn on the examination table is next, and she fears the worst. All she wants is to take Adam's hand and flee through the two doors at the back of the room. They never should have come here.

The moderator of this panel of five putatively distinguished polymaths is Imhotep—ancient Egyptian architect, engineer and physician, former High Priest of the Sun God, Ra. He yawns and looks at his tiny wrist sundial while Adam's interrogation continues. Rene Descartes, French philosopher and mathematician, father of modern philosophy, rises from his seat at the table and approaches Adam. Yet seated are Leonardo di ser Piero Leonardo, painter, sculptor, inventor and all around Renaissance man; Plato, mathematician, student of Socrates and founder of the Academy of Athens; Aristotle, philosopher and scientist, former student of Plato and one-time tutor to Alexander the Great; and last (but not least), Hippocrates, ancient Greek physician and the father of western medicine.

Smoothing his mustache and combing slender fingers through his long hair, Descartes points at Adam. "Open your mouth and say *ah*."

Adam blinked several times and then opened his mouth. Descartes pulled out a flashlight and used it to peer down Adam's throat. Next, Descartes examined Adam's eyes and ears.

"Well?" asked an impatient Imhotep, rubbing foul-smelling, synthetic palm oil over his shaven skull.

"*Mon collègue*, it is just as I have always stated: the soul is located in the brain," answered Descartes. "The mind, the soul, interacts with the body at the pineal gland."

Leonardo grumbled something *sotto voce* and then lapsed into silence.

"Do you mean to state that the soul is unitary and that the pineal gland is the seat of it because it, too, is unitary?" asked Aristotle.

Descartes nodded. "I think, therefore it is."

"Codswallop, I say! Codswallop!" said Aristotle. "If you had bothered to read my *De Anima* you would know that the soul consists of three parts: matter, form and the combination of both. The heart is the seat of sensation and cognitive functions. For example, when one loses consciousness upon excessive bleeding, many emotions are experienced viscerally—a gut feeling or emotional reaction."

"That is such a load of *asino merda*," said Leonardo.

"Gentlemen, please," said Imhotep. He turned to Adam. "Where do you believe the soul is located?"

"According to Doctor Frankenstein, it's located in the brain," Adam replied.

"And you agree with that?"

Adam nodded. "Frankenstein is my father. He knows best."

"All well and good, I suppose," said Imhotep. "And what do you believe, Galatea?"

"I believe whatever Adam believes," she said, not wanting to tip her hand by stating flat out that she believed neither she nor Adam had souls.

"What the lovely Galatea has said is called faith," said Aristotle. "It is also a pronouncement of love. Humans have a vegetative soul, a sensible and rational soul, capable of thought and reflection. Faith and love come from the heart. Therefore, the soul lies within the heart, not the brain. And there are three kinds of soul—"

"Your *De Anima* is based on the *logos, thymos* and *eros*, Ari—concepts you stole from Plato," said Leonardo. "Plato, speak up, man! Defend yourself!"

Galatea's anxious eyes shifted to Plato, silently studying his hands and fingers the whole time. She knew that he was still shaken, at a loss as to how to cope with the dissolution of his friend, Frederick Nietzsche. He had not yet fully recovered from his own mistreatment at the hands of Lilith.

Plato squeezed his eyes shut for a moment, then stared at Leonardo. "You, sir, know nothing of me or my work.".

"My prognosis is that the soul will grow apace in all living creatures," spoke Hippocrates. "I say we use lead pipes to drain Adam's chest of all fluids and abscesses, so we can get to the heart of the matter and prove that the soul—his soul—is located in the brain."

The proceedings were getting out of hand. Galatea couldn't take much more. "Sir, I beseech thee! Please, do not do this."

But everyone ignored her.

Leonardo pounded the table. "The soul is located above the optic chiasm, in the region of the third ventricle and the anterior ventricle, which contains the *senso comune*—"

"Disproved!" shouted Hippocrates.

"The soul resides in the heart," Aristotle argued in a most reasonable tone. "I'm the first genuine scientist in history, and the rest of you should kiss my hairy ass in gratitude."

"Drink hemlock and die, Ari!" said Leonardo.

"That was *Socrates*, you buffoon!" said Aristotle.

Imhotep: "I wish I had invited Kant and Horus, instead of you scarabs."

Descartes: "They'd probably Schopenhauer late, as usual."

Leonardo: "And you Kant put Descartes before Horus."

The French philosopher acknowledged the Italian painter's pun with a slight nod. Hippocrates let out a raucous laugh. Plato giggled like a schoolgirl; pulling out a clump of his beard, he said, "'Poetry is inspired by the Muses.'"

Galatea cast a worried glance to Adam, who smiled back and gave her a thumbs up sign. But his positive attitude did not give her much hope. This meeting wasn't going well at all.

Leonardo rose from his chair as if he'd sat on a tack. "I suggest we perform a series of anal probes on Adam."

"You're a moron, Leo," said Aristotle. "Furthermore, you are a sodomite."

"I was acquitted!" Leonardo reminded him.

"Leo, Leo, Leo," said Hippocrates. "We all know that only daddy's money and the de' Medici clan got you off the hook for that."

"What the fuck do you know, you quack?"

"I know that you, sir, are no Michelangelo."

Leonardo howls like a madman and leaps onto the table, attacking Hippocrates. They fall to the floor, fighting like two kids in a playground. Descartes, Aristotle and Imhotep join the brawl. Plato remains in his seat, counting his fingers and humming a song.

Adam now gifts Galatea with a helpless and worried look. Galatea rises to her feet, her anger and frustration at boiling point: this farce had been in progress all day.

"Enough! Stop this at once," she demands. Her voice echoes through the room, full of explosive rage. The philosophers cease fighting to stare, fearful of her anger.

"Galatea," said Imhotep. "You have no right to disrupt this court of inquiry with your—"

"Shut up!" she told him. "All of you: *Stop* this madness at once and sit down." She waited while the dueling doctors resumed their seats. "Adam and I care nothing about where the soul is or is not located," she said flatly. "We came here to learn whether or not *we* possess souls. But all we have learned is that you are a congress of arrogant, petty and jealous poseurs."

Leonardo leapt to his feet. "How dare you insult this august body of lofty minds and godlike intellects? Who in the name of God—"

Thunder growls angrily, rumblings that shake the floor and walls and ceiling. Bursts of lightning pop on and off like flashbulbs from the cameras of old-school paparazzi.

Leonardo, Imhotep and the other doctors and philosophers duck for cover with their arms over their heads.

Adam hops off the examination table and rushes to protect Galatea just as the outer doors swing open with an explosion of bright, golden light:

"*Silence, all of you!*" bellowed a deep, commanding voice.

When Galatea turned to face the new arrivals, a warm feeling of peace and comfort filled her heart. Tears welled in her eyes and a smile stole across her beautiful face. "Mary! Victor!" she cried, running to embrace them. Adam joined them, hugging them all.

Then Galatea stepped back to look upon the tall, ethereal being in the glowing white robe who had entered the room with Victor and Mary. The face of this supernal personage possessed a beauty no mortal artist in heaven or hell could ever capture on canvas or in stone. Thence came the scent of a pure, warm summer's day which now permeated the room.

"This is Altos, hell's own Volunteer Angel," Mary said to Adam and Galatea.

"He has agreed to decide the issue of whether or not you two have souls," Victor explained.

Galatea curtsied like a gentlewoman. "Thank you, good sir."

Struck mute by awe, Adam wiped tears from his eyes and bowed his head in respect.

Altos smiled at them. "Please, be seated." When they had resumed their seats, he turned to Imhotep and the panel of doctors: "Gentlemen, with all due respect . . . you are no more than a gaggle of mad scientists and a bombast of pompous devils. Therefore, I discharge you."

Imhotep stuttered. "But . . . but . . . but. . . ."

"No arguments, now," said Altos. "The location of the soul, what it is, and whether or not Adam and Galatea possess souls are not within your providence to know. Learned men you may be, but you are wrong: the soul is neither cardiocentric nor cephalocentric. Now leave us, please. Your work here is done."

Meek as sheep, Imhotep and the doctors filed out through a side door. Plato giggled and nearly spoke when Aristotle grabbed him, cupped a hand over his mouth and dragged him from the room.

"Let's see now," Altos said after the doctors had gone. "Adam and Galatea, you wish to know whether or not you possess souls. And if you do not, then how is it that you are in hell. Yes?"

"Yes, sir," spoke Galatea. "Might there be a chance that we were damned by error or oversight? Perhaps some flaw in the system that condemned us?"

"Please, call me Al," said the angel. "So you hope to get out of hell on a technicality?" Then he stared at Galatea for so long that she wasn't sure if the wrath of heaven was about to bless her or strike her down. "Tell me, Galatea, do you consider yourself human?"

"What kind of question is that?" asked Mary, giving Galatea's hand a reassuring squeeze. "Of course she's human!"

Without hesitation, Galatea replied, "I have ever longed to be human. Aphrodite may have turned my body from stone to flesh . . . but my heart remained unchanged, I fear. I walked through life as a thing unliving and unable to love."

Altos frowned. "And yet you killed Pygmalion, your husband, for coveting another."

"He was masturbating before another statue he'd carved and fallen in love with. I was insulted. I was jealous. I was hurt!"

"Dear Galatea," Altos said, "to feel such pain, to experience jealousy and anger . . . these are human traits, human emotions. It is the heart that feels, the heart that suffers. It is the heart that makes you human."

Galatea sat back in her chair.

Mary wrapped a comforting arm around her. "Then what is your judgment, Altos?"

"Because she is human, Galatea does indeed possess a soul."

Adam took hold of Galatea's hand, kissed and then clutched it to his breast. Galatea looked upon him with loving eyes, his brain forever trapped in the body of Doctor Victor Frankenstein. "And what of Adam, good sir?" Galatea whispered. "What of him?"

Altos studied Adam for many long moments, angelic eyes boring into the eyes of the damned. "Murder and mayhem you committed in life, Adam," he finally said. "Fear and terror you instilled in the hearts of many. You were shunned and betrayed, unloved. Rage and vengeance burned in your heart. These are not divine emotions: they are evil and human and thus, possessing them and being human, you also possess a soul."

"So then we are damned and deserve our fates?" asked Adam.

Sadly, almost reluctantly, Altos bowed his head in affirmation.

Galatea began to weep, and although Adam and Mary tried to console her, she remained inconsolable.

The knowing eyes of the Volunteer Angel slid from Galatea to Adam and back again. "How mutable are the feelings of mortals, and how wondrous, this clinging love you share, even in an excess of misery."

"How perceptive," Mary said, a voice edged with anger. "You condemn and praise in the same breath. What does an angel know about human love, and what sacrifices are made in the name and cause of love?"

Altos frowned at Mary, but his voice was not stern. "I know that a cold heart deserves no mercy. In Adam and Galatea, I see only the warmth and light of love."

Galatea gazed upon the angel, who was even more beautiful than she. "To love without selfishness, without condition, is all I've ever wanted. But only in hell have I found such love."

"And the form of the man you love, his face and body . . . does that matter to you, Galatea?"

Galatea looked at the monstrous body made by the hand of Doctor Frankenstein, that huge patchwork body of pale, nearly translucent flesh; of surgical scars, electrodes, ill-fitting clothes and hobnailed boots was, to her, noble of bearing, Homeric in stature . . . so beautiful was it in its grotesquery. But no longer was this Adam's body. Now it belonged to Victor . . . and the doctor's body now belonged to Adam, his construct, his son in all but flesh and blood. "I fell in love with Adam," she said. "And I would love him no matter what he looked like."

Altos stepped back, folding his arms, and looked with great kindness, even sadness, upon Adam and Galatea. "You are both unique in all creation. And such love as you have for one another must in some way be rewarded."

Victor removed his mouse-eared beanie and fanned himself with it. No flies came buzzing round; no one spoke a word against him. "What do you mean?"

"It means, Doctor, that in this particular case I have it in my power to bestow a gift—the gift of true and everlasting peace," said Altos. "I offer the peace of oblivion. No more pain. No more suffering."

Everyone lapsed into silence, shocked—except for Mary. "And no more love? Back to Nature will you send them, into nonexistence?"

"Only one of them, dear Mary," said Altos. "The gift is offered only to one. And they must choose between themselves."

"This isn't fair, Altos."

"This is hell, Mary."

Mary turned to Galatea and Adam. "Do you understand what is being offered here?"

Adam cast an uncertain and hopeless glance to Galatea. "Take the angel's offer. Be free of hell and all its evil, ugliness and woe. Go into everlasting peace, my love."

Galatea smiled and caressed Adam's cheek, for her heart was untroubled by this offer; she was at peace with herself and with her fate. In the very heart of damnation she had found redemption and salvation: true, pure, eternal love. She had no need for any other answer. "If Adam will have me for eternity, then I choose hell," she said. "But you, Adam—you who have never known peace . . . now is your chance."

Wrapping a loving arm around her, Adam said, "It's better to exist in hell and know love than not to exist and never know love, especially the love of Galatea."

Altos laughed—a sound like birds singing. "I thought so."

"This is not what I had hoped for them," said Mary, wiping tears from her eyes. "But I'm happy we shall all serve our endless season in hell together."

Now Altos turned to Victor. "Since I am still in a generous mood, Doctor, I will be happy to undo Merlin's handiwork."

"You mean . . . put my brains and Adam's brains back in their original bodies?" asked Victor.

"Yes, I do."

"I . . . I really am at a loss for words." Victor fumbled with his spectacles, removing them to wipe his eyes. "The love between Adam and Galatea is the only pure, clean thing I have ever seen in hell. Such is worth something, is it not, Altos?"

"Indeed it is," said the Volunteer Angel.

"Victor—do you realize what you're doing?" asked Mary.

"Oh, Mary, surely *you* understand? Galatea deserves to love a man, not a monster. And Adam deserves what I could never give him in life—happiness."

Galatea understood: this was Victor's gallant act of love. This was also his own, most personal way of atoning for his sins. Hell wasn't punishment enough; Frankenstein as well as his monster needed this form of self-flagellation to unite the two in payment for his crimes against Man and the Almighty.

"Then you choose to remain as you are, Doctor?" asked Altos.

"Yes," Victor told him. "Let me remain and truly *be* Frankenstein's monster."

Galatea began to weep. "Oh, Victor."

"Father, no!" Adam cried.

"Hush now, children," said Doctor Victor Frankenstein. He winked at Altos. "You know, I've grown quite accustomed to this body. It's rather well built, if I do say so myself."

*

Although Victor was pleased by the way things had turned out for Adam and Galatea, he'd hoped Altos would rule in their favor. He held hard to the belief that their being in hell had been some sort of glitch in the system. Perhaps the lovers' damnation indicated a backhanded slap from the gods of hell, for their masquerading and aspiring to humanity. He couldn't say for certain. Surely in hell, as it is in heaven, the immortal soul is the greatest gift, the dearest treasure.

If so, the ravenous lords of perdition had scored a victory by stealing the ultimate prize away from the Almighty.

He considered everything: his life; his crimes; his sins. He thought of his vaccine and the harm caused by it. And he considered what further harm it might still cause, now that the drug had been stolen by Satan. Victor tried considering his entire life and afterlife, but it summed too much for him to process.

He had other things on his mind now, unspeakable secrets he'd agreed never to reveal.

Today, if hell has days as men understand the passage of time, the damned are fighting in the streets.

Under this cloak of chaos, Victor and Mary, accompanied by Adam and Galatea, leave the Hellexandria Memorial Library to make their way toward Golem Heights and Goblin Manor.

The Uncubi are deployed in full force, guarding the library against attack, but Mister Up, the Unknown Poet, is nowhere in sight.

Riots break out all over New Hell as plague-infected souls panic and run amok while plague zombies shamble about, attacking the uninfected. The broadcast media and antisocial networks are filled with sharpies hawking remedies and immunizations. Every street corner has a pitchman selling some concoction, spell, talisman, potion, pill or poultice to the most dimwitted damned souls. Brand names such as Tophetrin, Purgatussin, Charon's Cure-All, Plutophen, Pandemodium, Acherminophen, Hadestatin, Stygiatropin, and Elixir of Erebos are shouted and touted, filling Victor's head with painful echoes, making him dizzy. He knows what is being offered by these vendors, knows where these therapeutic and prophylactic medicines have originated, and that knowledge weighs heavily on his soul.

And thus it begins, he thought. *Or ends, for some lucky few.*

"Looks like everyone has something they believe will protect or cure you from the plagues," said Adam, stating the obvious.

The monster never was the sharpest knife in creation's drawer.

"This must have all started while we were locked away in the library," said Galatea. "Things are getting worse. Vandalism and fires and violence—total madness." Weary, sad and afraid, she let out a sigh and clutched Adam's hand even tighter.

"Look, there's Doctor Polidori, just down the road," said Mary. She led the way, crossing a street littered and cluttered with refuse, debris, and even a body or two; some shimmered and vanished, obviously on their way to the Mortuary. Others remained, and before their eyes began to rot.

As they drew closer to Polidori's tiny wooden stall, Victor could read the hand-painted sign: "Poli's Practical Potion." This was the shop of the *real* John Polidori: Victor, as did most of the damned, knew or at least suspected that HSM loved to wander in disguise among his subjects, much as did Shakespeare's *Henry IV* or *Henry V* (he could never remember which).

"Hell-o, Mary! Hell-o, Doctor Frankenstein! Hell-o to you all," said Polidori. "Would you care to buy a bottle of my Poli's Practical Potion?"

"What's it good for?" asked Galatea.

"Why, it's good for what ails you!" said Polidori. "It'll fix you right up."

"For the plagues, no doubt," said Adam.

"Oh, indeed, indeed," said Polidori. "Manufactured by Avernus Labs, right here in New Hell. Not only will it prevent a body from being infected by any one of the plagues, it will cure you of any that you already may have contracted."

"Cure you or kill you," said Mary.

"Ha! That's a good one!" said Polidori.

Victor's stomach swallowed his heart. Polidori was selling a bootlegged version of what could only be Victor's own vaccine, stolen from him by Satan.

No cures waited here, no vaccinations—only the possibility of oblivion, of nonexistence—what nostrums Altos had offered to Adam and Galatea. But *they* had been given a choice. For the damned fools who purchased this and the other medicines, no choice existed. Victor had no doubt the elixirs were part of some master plan of Satan's. But how could he tell anyone the truth? How could he explain? How could he warn anyone? Victor himself languished under a satanic compulsion to silence on this subject unto eternity. He must suffer alone and in silence, in full knowledge of what he had wrought. He broke out in a cold sweat and began to tremble.

Nor shall any man's entreaty prevail upon me to administer poison to anyone; neither will I counsel any man to do so.

Mary glanced at him, her face crinkling with concern. "Victor? Victor—what's wrong?"

Doctor Frankenstein moaned and fell to his knees, weeping hysterically.

Convalescence

Michael H. Hanson

"In a hospital they throw you out into
the street before you are half cured,
but in a nursing home they don't
let you out till you are dead."

— George Bernard Shaw

The howls of pain from the one hundred residents had reached their nightly crescendo, though this wasn't saying much as it is always night in hell's St. Rictus Nursing Home.

Administrative Geriatric Nurse Martha Jane Canary, better known as Calamity Jane during her terrestrial life as an American frontierswoman, professional scout, and occasional nurse, rubbed her tired eyes and took a moment to take stock of the always stressful daily parameters of running hell's infamous retirement home.

Jane's demon housekeeping staff had barricaded every window and entrance on the first floor with an effective dirt, gravel, and boulder landfill that was seven feet high. They were in the process of finishing blocking the balconied periphery of the second floor with stacked sandbags. The remaining four floors had all windows and sliding glass doors locked and secured. This security reinforcement had been ongoing for many months and looked ready to withstand a years-long siege if necessary.

Jane climbed up into the crow's-nest atop the rest home and surveyed her surroundings. She raised her specially modified Sinchester repeating rifle and used the sniper scope at full magnification.

Outside, tens of thousands of plague victims continued to march toward St. Rictus from all directions. Pouring in from every corner and dimension of greater hell, they represented thousands of years of human history. First BC Roman citizenry stumbled beside twenty-second-century AD AmeriCanada citizens; fifth-century AD Olmec priests bumped elbows with Shang Dynasty house maids; nineteenth-century AD Zulu warriors walked beside mid-twentieth-century AD French soldiers who died at Dien Bien Phu, and on and on.

What had once been a huge surrounding lake of boiling spittle had now been reduced to a mere still-effective moat. Hundreds of advancing and decaying damned souls had been filling the depths of the lake with their inexorable advance this past year. Oblivious to the pain, or simply not caring, they trudged forward, their bodies boiled down to skeletons, or less, by the bubbling spittle.

A quick calculation told Jane that the lake would be completely filled with bodies inside of another year. And then, St. Rictus would no longer be an island, and therefore subject to direct assault from the endless onslaught of insane plague victims looking for miracle cures, and respite, at what was rumored to be the last bastion of hope . . . her nursing home.

The original hell-plague released by Erra so long ago had since mutated into a broad swatch of viral and bacterial horrors that had now spread across every square inch of hell. What had once been long-avoided chambers of horrors—the clinics and hospitals of hell—were soon overrun by hordes of plague victims willing to submit to anything to ease this ultimate suffering.

Two months ago, Jane received the final communications from the other surviving health facilities, just before they were destroyed in orgies of madness and terror. St. Rictus had one of the most horrific of reputations across hell, and as such was a much avoided locale by most damned denizens. Rumor held that even to be within viewing distance of it might curse one into becoming one of its eternally suffering residents. And yes, this belief was not without its merits. But now, so long after the vicious plagues had swept back and forth across the realms of hell, this last-standing structure had become the dark beacon of hope for all plague survivors. Whether through mumbled dialogue, rough sign language, or the simple herd urge to follow those stumbling in one direction, the damned were now drawn to St. Rictus as if it were the ultimate lodestone.

Jane smirked for a moment then lowered her rifle. This was no time for these kinds of musings. Tonight was St. Rictus' annual Strawberry Ball, and nothing was going to prevent Jane from making it a success.

*

Jane, wearing her white buckskin boots, leggings, and jacket, with her Sinchester slung over her shoulder, headed for the first of the three large bays that housed St. Rictus' residents, the Blue/Purple room.

"How we doing, Lill?" Jane yelled.

Running up and down the one main aisle splitting the double row of beds, Lillian D. Wald, wearing a late-nine-teenth-century AD nursing dress and bib, and famous in her lifetime for contributions to human rights and being the founder of American community nursing, snarled.

"I need more buckets," Lill said, "too many draining abscesses today."

Lill followed this up by dumping two large buckets of bloody yellow pus out a nearby window.

The floor, walls, and ceiling were all colored a rich, aqua blue. The sheets, blankets, and resident gowns were all dark purple. Each resident was a man or woman who appeared withered and aged beyond human capacity, right at the very edge of potential longevity. Each wallowed upon their cots, groaning in agony under the weight of weak lungs, failing bladders and bowels, severe arthritis, and rampant bedsores.

One small demon, brown, hairless, humanoid and about three feet tall, skipped around on its hopeless duty of mopping up the very slimy and filthy floors.

"Strawberry Ball starts tonight," Jane yelled, "don't forget your mask."

A momentary smile appeared on the short, Caucasian woman's face.

"Wouldn't miss it for the world, Jane."

Next, Jane entered the Green/Orange room.

The floor and walls were covered in orange spirals, while bed sheets and resident smocks were all a bright, al-most neon green. The residents themselves, a wide variety of races, creeds, and colors, looked not unlike those of the last bay.

A short woman with tied-down dark brown hair and wearing a dark, mid-nineteenth-century dress, was running up and down the aisle, constantly readjusting the restraints and straps which held down every single one of the residents under her care. Most of the patients howled, drooled, and rolled their eyes in such a way that it was clear they suffered from all manner of mental illness.

"Howdy, Dix," Jane said, "what's the good word?"

Dorothea Dix, one time creator of the first generation of American mental asylums and who, during the Civil War, served as Superintendent of Army Nurses, frowned.

"Tell the shop these straps are not holding up," Dix yelled, "the leather is rotten and keeps snapping."

"You got it, sister," Jane said.

Biting her lower lip, Jane didn't mention where the so-called leather was harvested, and that there simply wasn't enough time to cure it properly before cutting and transportation upstairs for this bay's never-ending demand.

"Strawberry Ball tonight, Dix," Jane added, "don't forget."

"Oh, I'll be here all right," Dix replied.

Jane trotted into the third and final bay, the White/Violet room.

The floor, walls, and ceiling were all polished pale marble, whereas the bed sheets and resident robes were colored violet.

The single attending nurse, a short woman with olive colored skin and long ebony hair, wore a short violet tunic with leather sandals. She moved quickly between cots and fed her patients from a large satchel of dried herbs.

"Hello," Jane said with some reservation. Her reticence was one of respect, as this particular nurse was one of the old dead.

"What do you want?" the nurse replied curtly. "I'm busy."

"Just wanted to remind you about the Strawberry Ball," Jane replied.

Metrodora, ancient Greek female physician and author of the oldest medical text known to have been written by a woman, *On the Diseases and Cures of Women*, sighed.

"Yes, yes," Metrodora said, "I remember. It will be a welcome distraction. On your way."

Jane frowned at the inappropriate dismissal, but left without further comment. Time was flying and she needed to double check supplies for the party.

Five minutes later, Jane exited the creaking elevator that had dropped her six full floors, beneath the kitchen, workshops, and laundry, right to the farm caves.

It took a few moments for Jane's eyes to adjust to the poor lighting, from hundreds of oil lamps that seemed to stretch off into infinity. Where the oil for the lamps was rendered, Jane didn't want to know, though she could guess. The endless cave walls, dark ebony and smooth like polished ebonite, reflected very little illumination. After a while, Jane could see three figures cultivating three long rows of strawberries. She approached them slowly.

"Wow," Jane said, "looks like you timed them perfectly."

The three figures, all women and all dressed in long black robes, stood up. One glance was all Jane needed to see they were of the old dead. Their eyes, the darkest bronze, reflected ages of wisdom and dark knowledge. All had dark olive skin, and long black hair tied into coils like snakes about their scalps.

The shorter two walked up to Jane and gave her a quick hug.

Agamede, twelfth-century BC Greek physician acquainted with the healing powers of all the plants that grow upon the earth, and Agnodike, fourth-century BCE first female Athenian physician, midwife, and gynecologist, both laughed.

"I will have the crop picked within two hours," Agamede said, her black teeth, stained by some root she constantly chewed, smiling broadly. "So, is Metrodora happy with my latest herbs?"

"Yeah," Jane replied, "she's stuffing her ward like a bunch a turkeys."

"And the strawberry mead," Agnodike added, "will be second only to ambrosia."

Jane's eyes were drawn momentarily to Agnodike's forehead. Her curly locks had been intertwined with bright silver charms, each one an ancient demon/deity long since forgotten by most of mankind. A loud cough caught everyone's attention.

"Yes, Merit Ptah?" Jane said.

Merit, towering over all at a height of six feet, was an early physician from the time of ancient Egypt and most notable for being the first woman known by name in the history of the field of medicine. This most ancient of these old dead, silent as ever, pointed to the strawberry plants and Agnodike and Agamede quickly went back to their duties.

"Yes, well," Jane mumbled, "I'll leave you to it."

Walking back to the main elevator, Jane could feel Merit Ptah's large glistening eyes boring into her backside.

*

Kneeling in the crow's-nest, Jane took a bead on two plague victims that looked like they might actually make it across the boiling moat of spittle.

Two quick plasma discharges exited her Sinchester rifle and connected with the floundering swimmers. Instantly, their heads exploded and their corpses quickly sank beneath the surface of the bubbling spit.

Jane patted the stock of her weapon, content with the modifications made to it last year. Its interior was now a near perfect recreation of a twenty-third-century AD Marsguard Marine Blaster. Its Prometheum power cell was good for another thousand shots. Music emanated upward through the roof and Jane quickly climbed down the main ladder to join the festivities below.

The party was in full swing. All of the demon staff were dressed up as multi-colored harlequins and were engaged in a variety of athletic dances designed to entertain the bedded invalids. Streamers of white and pink were strung everywhere, throughout all of the resident bays. Every resident had a party cap forcibly strapped to their heads, and music blared from overhead speakers. Jane smiled as the chords of late nineteenth century AD ragtime filled the air.

Entering the Blue/Purple room, Jane studied the suffering patients. It was quite a punishment, all right. Every damned soul in St. Rictus had been someone who had preyed on the elderly during their lives. Also, each one of these suffering bastards had died before the age of forty, and thus had never known the ravages of old age. Jane nodded her head slightly, thinking this punishment was most just.

One the far side of the bay, two figures were just finishing handing small paper cups of strawberry mead to the patients. The shorter of the two, wearing a blue mask, was obviously Lill. The much taller figure, wearing a red mask and pushing a cart covered with several large pitchers of strawberry mead, could only be Merit Ptah.

But what the hell is she doing up here, Jane thought, *she's never been above ground as long as I've been around?*

Before Jane could shout out a greeting, Merit pushed her cart out of the bay.

Lill stepped forward and offered Jane a small paper cup. Jane smiled and waved off the treat.

"Naw," she said, "I don't get mine until everyone else has had a drink. First to order, last to profit. That's my motto."

Lill nodded and slowly sipped her drink until it was emptied.

"Uh, excuse me, Lill," Jane said, "I want to talk to our red-faced colleague for a moment."

Lill shrugged her shoulders and Jane quickly walked out.

Entering the Green/Orange room, Jane got tangled in some too-long streamers as she saw Merit helping Dix serve the last of the mead to this bay's patients, pouring the drink into their mouths. Dix was wearing an orange mask. By the time she got disentangled, Merit had pushed her cart out of the room toward the last of the bays.

"Hello, Jane," Dix said, "care to join me in a drink?"

"Saving myself for last," Jane said. "Say, something else that Merit is up here with us mortals, huh?"

"Indeed," Dix said while joyfully quaffing her mead, "not much of a conversationalist, though. I couldn't even get a hello out of her."

"Right," Jane added, "well, happy Strawberry Ball."

"Happy Strawberry Ball," Dix shouted to Jane's re-treating back.

Jane trotted into the White/Violet room to see Merit serving residents strawberry mead at the far end of the bay while Metrodora, wearing a violet mask, was handing out paper cups a mere three feet away.

"Metrodora," Jane said, "all going well?"

"Of course," Metrodora said. "You seem flustered. Is the horde outside worrying you?"

"No more than usual," Jane replied. "So, umm, you don't find it strange that Merit has left her lair to join us this year?"

Metrodora looked up quickly and lightly bit her lower lip. "To be honest, she does seem to be avoiding me. Oh well, an ancient like her is always moody. Who knows? Maybe she was getting lonely down below."

Metrodora followed this up with a chuckle just before she downed a cup of the strawberry mead.

Jane smiled and spotted Merit pushing her cart out to the main hallway. Feeling the beginnings of dread forming in her gut, Jane spun on her heel and jogged after Merit.

"Happy Strawberry Ball, Metrodora," Jane shouted.

Out in the hallway, Jane didn't spot Merit at first, and then she saw figures at the far end, down by the main eleva-tor. Walking quickly, she saw strawberry mead being poured into cups and swallowed. Confused for a moment, Jane sud-denly realized she was looking at four figures.

"Who the —?" Jane murmured, and then it hit her. Three of the figures wore the black robes of Agnodike, Aga-mede, and Merit. *Then who is the other tall figure in the red mask and robes*?

"Stop!" Jane yelled, but the red-masked figure had disappeared into the elevator, whose doors closed quickly.

"Merit," Jane said, "who was that?"

Before Merit's lips could more than part, her eyes opened wide and she gasped, grabbing at her throat. Immediately, Agnodike and Agamede did the same. In moments they were all writhing on the floor, groaning in agony.

Jane could only stand there in shock as the three ancients died amidst painful contortions and vomiting.

The sound of terror ripped at her mind and Jane instinctively ran back toward the last patient bay she had left.

On the floor, Metrodora lay contorting as blood drained from every orifice in her body. On their beds, her patients writhed in agony worse than anything they had suffered before. Jane stepped forward and her eyes grew wide in shock. They were not all suffering from the same sickness but somehow, some way, each seemed to be dying from completely different yet horrific conditions.

Jane ran into the next bay and found the same with Dix and her residents, all of them displaying the end stage symptoms of any number of plagues.

Jane sprinted past this horror and into the third bay. Lill was rolling on the floor in agony, her body covered in bleeding, open, pus-filled sores. Her residents were much like the others, suffering a mind-boggling variety of contagions.

Forcing down the madness that threatened to overcome her, Jane sprinted back to the elevators.

Merit, Agnodike, and Agamede each lay in a pile of putrescence, their damned souls no doubt on their way to the Undertaker's slab. Jane punched the down button and gritted her teeth. Moments later, a loud ding announced the elevator's arrival.

Furious, Jane dashed into the elevator and punched the glowing lavender button for the deep basement farming level. Immediately, as the doors started closing, a figure moved from the darkness and tackled Jane.

Long fingernails stabbed at her backside, some of them even managing to cut through her buckskin clothing and into her flesh. Loud, insane cackling echoed painfully in the elevator and Jane's ears. The weight of the attacker was oppressive, and Jane could only assume it was the imposter in the strawberry guise who had bushwhacked her.

With a loud grunt, Jane got her feet up under her and stood straight up with all her strength. The effect was satisfactory as the attacker was tossed up and away to slam painfully against the opposing elevator wall. Jane spun around and gasped.

It can't be, she thought. But it was.

Standing in the elevator, not four feet from her, was the cackling, craze-faced Welcome Woman, a horrid figure that Jane had not seen since her very first day in hell. The Welcome Woman was dressed in dark rags and Jane just as quickly realized that this abomination wasn't the intruder she was tracking. How or why this infamous greeter of damned souls had appeared here, at this time, was beyond Jane's comprehension.

"What's the matter, sweetie," the Welcome Woman cackled, "too good to give us a kiss?"

Jane swung her Sinchester rifle off her shoulder and shoved the barrel at the abomination's toothless mouth. Before she could pull the trigger, though, the Welcome Woman yanked the rifle away with amazing speed and strength, and smashed it against the nearby elevator wall, breaking it in half. Next, she leaped forward and tackled Jane once again to the floor.

Jane's right hand slid down into her right boot, pulled out a long, nasty-looking bowie knife and shoved it up through the Welcome Woman's throat right up into her brain, the point just sticking out of the skull.

Jane stood up and stepped over the hideous corpse as the elevator doors opened. Stepping into the vast ebony farming cave, she saw that over half of the innumerable oil lamps had gone out. Overhead, a single electric emergency light had been turned on. It emitted a ghastly scarlet glow that twirled in a circular fashion, giving everything a frightening blood-like cast.

Standing ten feet away was the imposter, standing tall and still wearing the strawberry robes and bright red face mask. In one hand the figure held a half filled pitcher of strawberry mead, and in the other, a long-necked goblet.

"I don't need a rifle or knife to stomp you," Jane shouted.

As she got closer a strange chill ran up her spine, something she had not felt in a very long time.

Several yards later Jane stopped in her tracks, standing mere feet from the intruder. His robes were the ridiculous costume she had picked out days before, but the mask, the horrific red mask made of harsh angles and frightening ridges, was not a mask at all. It was a face, one she had not seen in years, and it wore the ghastliest of smiles.

"Surely you are not surprised," he said.

Jane could only nod her head mutely.

"Your sins are legion," he added, "and you thought you could just hole up here, safe and secure in your hubris and arrogance, achieving some kind of joy and sense of accomplishment as all of hell suffers?"

Jane nodded her head once again, and somehow found the strength to reply.

"You can't make me drink that," she said.

"Listen," he said.

Jane cocked her head, and suddenly noticed a distant pounding sound.

"Like tens of thousands of bodies smashing against the walls, doors, and windows of your stronghold," he laughed. "Oh yes, they'll swarm inside in minutes and soon will be down here, legions of the doomed begging and demanding your comfort and respite, and only you, Jane, yes, only you left to face them all, the combined surviving plague victims of hell. Will you help them, Jane? Will you nurse them all? What will you tell them to ease their endless suffering?"

The truth of it all welled up in Jane like a bomb about to burst.

"Go ahead, face them all, Jane," the great deceiver said, "or . . ."

Jane accepted the proffered goblet of strawberry mead and drew it to her lips while speaking one final epitaph as if it were a toast: "And darkness and decay and damnation hold illimitable dominion over all."

Calamity Jane tilted her head back and hungrily swallowed the collected plagues of hell.

Hell Noon

Paul Freeman

She strolled into the room as she always did, her heels echoing on the worn wooden boards as she sauntered across the floor. Holliday sat in a leather armchair, smoke spiralling into the air above him from a cigar burning in an ashtray by his side. He watched in rapture as her purple showgirl dress slid to the floor. With pursed red lips and a come hither look in her eye, she stepped out of the puddle of silk and lace. She'd piled dark curls on top of her head, like some ancient Greek goddess—he'd seen enough of them in hell to know what one looked like. Holliday was not a man ever accused of disappointing a lady. He stubbed his cigar and stood up to join her.

Before he could lay a finger on her, she twisted his arm and flicked her leg. In an instant he was on his back, panting, arms outstretched as if he had been crucified to the floor. She stood above him, one foot on his chest, pinning him down. His gaze crawled up the length of her nylons, focusing on a tantalizing glimpse of caramel-cream flesh at the top of her stocking. He yearned to reach out and touch the soft skin of her thigh, to explore her secret places, to feel comfort and exhilaration from the warm moistness. But he daren't move.

His eyes wandered up, over the curve of her hip and across her heavy breasts, close to spilling over the corset struggling to keep them contained, to the raven-dark curls cascading over her shoulder. Her full red lips parted in a sneer. His gaze continued toward her round, black eyes, full of contempt. How he hated her . . . how he loved her. No, not love, how could he love someone who despised him so?

Lust. He wanted to fuck her, he wanted to rip her clothes from her, to push her naked body over a table and hear her scream his name as he reamed her from behind. He wanted to be the dominant one, to hear her beg. Beg for what? For him to stop? For him not to stop?

Then he realized she had a pistol gripped in both hands. How had he not noticed it before? Because he was like a fly trapped in a spider's web, already intoxicated by her venom, poisoned by passion. He'd looked down that dark chasm often enough in life; to face it again in death seemed, somehow . . . unfair.

"Don't!" he pleaded. He didn't want to face the end again, not before he had sampled her forbidden fruit one more time. He imagined her skin would taste of butterscotch melting on his tongue.

She pulled the hammer back with her right thumb.

He squeezed his eyes shut and flinched when she pulled the trigger. He counted; one second . . . two seconds . . . three seconds . . . nothing: no boom, no excruciating agony. He opened his eyes and she was laughing. She spat once, he watched it fall, felt it land on his face, felt its wetness dribble down his cheek. She turned her back on him then, retracing her steps across the floor.

Once. Once she had let him fuck her. On his first night
in hell; but even then she had pushed him away before he
climaxed, left him burning with the agony of unfulfilled
passion. Whenever he let down his guard—on any day,
any minute of any day—that memory tormented him. The
unbridled joy he had felt, exhilaration released in wave after
wave as he hammered into history's most desired courtesan.
Her presence every night mocked him, his reminiscences'
a constant reminder of that one savored, ecstatic moment,
never to be had again, an eternity of want to look forward to.

He sighed, picked himself up off the floor and followed
her out of the backroom. Of course, she was gone by the
time he entered the main bar area of the Tombstone Saloon.
One group of patrons sat around a polished wooden table.
The saloon looked empty, otherwise. Holliday pulled out a
chair and joined the group. Sitting directly opposite him was
a diminutive man with a long luxurious beard.

"Are you ready to play?" asked the Russian novelist
Fyodor Dostoyevsky, rolling his 'R's.

"Aye, deal the cards, boy." Holliday turned his gaze
on the Irishman, Eoghan Ruadh Ó Néill (the spelling and
pronunciation had been hellicized to Owen Roe O'Neill).

John Henry Holliday—commonly known in life and
in hell as Doc Holliday—picked up a tumbler of whisky
and swallowed the amber liquid in one gulp. "Hellnation!
This stuff tastes like a skunk pissed in rat shit and put it in a
glass."

"This is hell, boy; that's as good as it gets," O'Neill
said with a grin. "Is your wee dalliance done for the evening
then?"

"Dalliance? You call my nightly torture a dalliance?
No crueler a torment has been devised than the unsated

frustration I am afflicted with nightly." Doc snatched the bottle of Old Helltucky Burnbon from the center of the table and refilled his glass.

"I think you will find there are many, many worse punishments to be had in hell," Dostoyevsky said. "Besides, seeing a sexual liaison to its natural conclusion is not such a good idea in hell."

"Aye, Zeus's curse," the big Irishman added. "Every ejaculation a burning agony of poisonous spiders and hungry scorpions." He shuddered at the thought.

"You ever think that her nightly visitations are her punishment and not yours?" said Martha Jane Canary, the only woman at the table.

"Aye, good one, Calamity," O'Neill guffawed.

"Don't call me that," she said with a scowl.

"Come now, please, dear lady and gentlemen, let us return to our game," urged bewigged John Montagu, 4th Earl of Sandwich. The English aristocrat suddenly burped. Then, before the embarrassment disappeared from his face, he retched.

The other four watched in silence, a mixture of fascination and disgust flickering across their faces, as Montagu clasped his throat. After several more choking sounds his reddening cheeks began to expand. His mouth opened wide.

Then, like a newborn babe slipping into the world to take its first breath, a fat cockroach slid from his open mouth and plopped onto the table before gaining its many feet and scampering away.

"Sweet divine Lucifer, that gives me the willies every time I see it," O'Neill said.

"Hell's a bitch," Holliday said quietly, although it was unclear if he was referring to his own torment or Montagu's.

Montagu snatched a lace handkerchief from his cuff and wiped his mouth. "It amuses His Satanic Majesty to torment me with the constant regurgitation of beastly insects, he calls them sand-roaches . . . very droll, I'm sure," Montague, soldier, politician and inventor of the sandwich said before swallowing a large whisky.

"Are we going to play cards or not?" Dostoyevsky began shuffling the deck.

"Aye." The big Irish warrior threw a diablo to the center of the table. "I'm in."

Each of them threw in a coin. The Russian began dealing the cards.

"Damn, but this thing itches something awful," Montagu complained, pushing back his powdered wig. A fat millipede crawled out from beneath the wig and disappeared down the back of his neck.

"You have a wee . . ." O'Neill began, but stopped when Montagu shifted the wig to reveal a nest of crawling insects atop his head, all slithering and sliding over one another. "Never mind."

"There, that's better," the aristocrat said once he'd settled his wig.

Holliday picked up his cards; aces and kings. That was no surprise, he always won. Nevertheless, every time he picked up a hand his heart would beat that little bit faster, hoping, always hoping that he'd hold a losing hand. An odd wish for a professional gambler, but for a man who thrived on beating the odds, who lived for the surge of adrenalin that came with a win when the possibility of losing all seemed inescapable, the certainty of victory was as cruel a blow as the inevitability of defeat. Nay, worse: the bitter taste of the hollow victory left nothing but ashes in his mouth. His Satanic Majesty was truly a master at inflicting the cruelest cut.

"I knew a lad who lost his soul in a game of chance," O'Neill said. "He was young and foolish and couldn't see his opponent for who he really was, so blinded was he by all the riches he thought to win."

"Was it you?" Calamity Jane asked.

"No, girl, I've committed far worse deeds in my lifetime to earn my place here in infernity. The worst of which was marching a band of six thousand *ceithern* and *gallóglaigh* to the gates of Hell. . . . Oh, but we were a grand sight that day. A countryman of our dear friend, the earl"—he favored Montagu with a nod and a wink—"gave us an ultimatum: 'To hell or Connaught'. We chose hell." He laughed then, a hearty rumble that made his chest shake.

"I know to whom you refer, dear boy. A hero in my land, a devil in yours," Montagu said as another cockroach peered out from beneath his wig.

"Aye well, twas a long time ago. And now we all reside in hell, where friends are enemies, and enemies are friends." He picked up the bottle of Helltucky Burnbon and refilled his glass.

"Where friends are enemies, and enemies are bigger enemies," Holliday added grumpily before suddenly erupting into a fit of coughing.

"Deal the cards," Calamity Jane said; but before a hand was dealt, a loud knock on the door interrupted their game.

"Who in hell is that?" Holliday turned toward the closed door, irked to have the game interrupted.

"Dear boy, it could be anybody," Montagu said.

"Who's there?" Doc shouted out.

"We need a doctor," a male voice answered back, "we got us a sick man out here." The door cracked open. Outside, the light shining down from Paradise turned the dusty street an eerie crimson, making the road look like a river of blood. A stetson-wearing head peered through the opening.

Doc Holliday, gambler, drinker and gunfighter in life, stood. "You got the wrong doctor, friend." For Holliday, the moment just before the draw becomes an almost spiritual event, when all else is blocked out and life is condensed into a single moment. In a split second he can feel the rythmic beating of his heart, hear nothing but the indrawn breath of the other man, see nothing but the narrowing eyes of his opponent. Time stops—the twitch of a nostril, the quiver of a lip—and explodes to life as iron slides free of leather. Noise, smoke and confusion tear assunder that most tranquil of moments, distorting the reality of time. Many citizens of hell prefer to arm themselves with modern weaponry rather than use the killing implements of their own era, but Holliday was a traditonal sort of man and would always favor the familiar tool of his trade. "I'm a dentist."

Gunfire. Smoke and flame from an antique barrel in fighting condition. A deafening report.

Like a wave bursting across the shore, reality crashes in. "What in hell have you done?" Calamity Jane stands, gawping at the mess of blood and flesh lying outside the door.

Montagu jumps off his chair and runs toward the entrance.

"Don't go out there," Holliday calmly says, still pointing his smoking gun.

"Sweet Lucifer, boy, that was an awful impulsive thing to do. The man was only askin' for a wee bit o' help." O'Neill stood beside Calamity.

Meanwhile, Dostoyevsky shuffled the cards and drank his whisky, as if a man had not just had his brains blown out and sprawled in his own pool of blood in the dusty street.

"He's infected with some kind of contagion." Holliday holstered his gun. "I heard some folks talk of pockets of hell being overrun by a plague, a terrible curse afflicting the souls of hell, a malady of weeping sores and oozing boils. Out here, in frontier towns like Helldorado, we're generally the last to hear of such doings."

"Aye, well . . . that's well and good, but yer man there came with friends." O'Neill nodded toward the corpse.

Mere seconds later a loud crack sounded, followed by splinters of wood showering his head. Before anybody reacted, another shot was discharged, smashing the half-raised glass in Dostoyevsky's hand.

Calamity Jane snatched her Winchester from where it rested against the wall and returned fire, while the big Ulsterman turned over the table for them all to hide behind.

"I say, old boy, you had better take cover," Montagu called to Holliday as he dove behind the table.

To the others, it appeared as if Doc Holliday had gone into some kind of trance, but in actual fact he had seen something he didn't like and was scrutinizing the corpse of the man he'd shot.

"Get out of the darn doorway, ya big galoot!" Calamity Jane cried. Her words and the cracks of gunfire gouging splinters out of the wooden floor around him brought him to his senses. He rolled across the room and crouched down behind the upturned table.

"Well, ain't this just a pickle," he said with a grin.

"You're enjoying this, you old coot." Jane's eyes narrowed as she flung the accusation at him.

"Just like old times."

"With some exceptions," O'Neill said as he pulled a shotgun from beneath his fur-lined cloak, its barrel sawn short for better concealment. The Irishman stood and blasted the entranceway with a spray of buckshot, firing both barrels in quick succession. Holliday stood beside him and walked step by step with him as they closed the distance on their gang of attackers, both of them firing—reloading—firing again.

"*Yeehaw!*" Calamity stood behind them picking off assailants with her Winchester. Pretty soon the torrent of gunfire from the street grew silent. O'Neill continued firing through the door at anything that moved . . . or looked like it moved. There wasn't a building on the opposite side of the street with a window remaining, or a store sign left hanging straight. One unfortunate cat barely made it out alive, vaulting over a side gate minus half its tail.

As O'Neill went outside, Holliday held back, gun trained on the street, watching for any sign of movement. Bodies lay scattered in the dust. He craned his neck over the threshold and could see the Hell Kay Corral at the end of the street. Red dust hung in the air, clouding the wooden buildings and walkways as Paradise cast its crimson smirk over the frontier town.

"An explanation, dear boy?" Montagu joined Holliday in the doorway, while Calamity Jane moved to the window, all the while sighting down her Winchester. Dostoyevsky righted the table and poured himself a drink, using the last unsmashed glass.

Holliday pulled a thin cigar from his top pocket. He struck a match off the sole of his boot before bending toward the flame. "Urgh," he groaned as the unique flavor of anything smoked in hell hit the back of his throat. "O'Neill! Get off the street," he called out to the big Irishman.

The onetime Ulster chieftain didn't hear Doc's warning as he searched the small frontier town for any more would-be bushwhackers.

"Why ain't those bodies relocating to the Undertaker?" Calamity Jane pushed past Holliday.

The gunfighter grabbed her arm and pulled her back. "Don't go out there," he said.

"What is the matter?" Dostoyevsky asked as he too stood and crowded into the doorway.

"Look!" Holliday pointed toward the body of the first man he'd shot. Its leg twitched.

"Well, I'll be a darn tootin' hornswaggler!" Calamity Jane said.

"Please repeat." The Russian novelist looked at her quizzically.

"O'Neill, dear boy, perhaps you should return to the inn," Montagu summoned the Irishman wandering uptown.

The body suddenly sat bolt upright.

"Get yer Satan-damned ass in here!" Calamity Jane roared. O'Neill finally turned back toward them. All around him, corpses began reanimating and dragging themselves up out of the dirt.

"Fuck," was as much as O'Neill could manage before he started running. He burst into the saloon with once-dead bodies shambling after him. Maggots crawled all over them, sliding out of every visible orifice, while their sickly-green skin flaked and eddied behind them.

"I do not understand. These men are dead! They should be on the Undertaker's slab waiting for recycling," Dostoyevsky said.

"Must be a symptom of the plague," Holliday answered as he held the doorway until O'Neill was inside, then slammed the door shut.

"This is Satan's doing?" the Russian novelist asked.

"No, I don't think so: something about a curse."

"I do not like it," Dostoyevsky answered.

"No? Nor do I, my friend."

"There's hundreds of 'em collecting out there. They must be coming in from all over the Dead Plains," Calamity Jane cried out from the window.

"I think it would be wise to relocate," Montagu said.

"Aye, ya got that right," O'Neill agreed.

"We could leave by the back door. With enough of a head start, we'd easily make it across the desert. New Bodie's not that far away," Calamity Jane said.

"Aye, that could work, girl. We'll need to get word to Wyatt Earp and let him know what's going on here," the big Irish chieftain agreed.

"No," Holliday said. They all turned toward the gunfighter. He suddenly doubled over in a fit of coughing. When he came back up he wiped a trail of blood from his chin with the back of his hand. "You would think the malady what put you in the ground in the first place would at least have disappeared in death. Not so," he said.

"Why are you so set on staying put?" Calamity asked. As if to remind them of the urgent need for speed, banging began, so hard it made the door shiver, followed by a chorus of wailing groans.

"I can't do it, Jane, I can't leave here."

"Why would you choose to stay here, dear boy? Have you not noticed what is outside that door and doing its utmost to get inside?" Montagu asked.

"Choose? You think I have a choice?" Holliday's voice rose. "Don't you get it? This, all of this"—he took in the room with a wave of his hand—"His Satanic Majesty put me here: the saloon, the town, the girl, even all of you are here at his pleasure and to torment me. He thought I was having too good a time in New Bodie . . . as if anyone can have too good a time in hell."

"Huh?" Calamity Jane scratched her head.

"Each of you is among the most renowned gamblers the world has ever seen. He brought you here to play out whatever game he has in mind for me."

"But we can come and go at will—" Montagu began.

"Hey, this is my torment. You can get your own," Holliday answered.

"Those things will kill us once they get through that door. I ain't that keen on goin' out like that," Jane said.

"Then go. None of you are trapped here."

"They're going to kill you too, boy," O'Neill added.

Holliday shrugged and glanced toward the door. Just then there came the sound of smashing glass, and a deathly-white hand appeared through the window. Holliday drew his Colt and reloaded the cylinder, spun it.

"You can't stand alone against those things." Tears were forming in Jane's eyes as she spoke. Her downy upper lip quivered.

"Now don't you start coming up with stupid notions. All of you can get out of here now. And you should. Don't wait on me. I know where I'm goin'. I'll give your regards to the Undertaker." Holliday grinned, a death's-head grimace.

"Wait! I have an idea," Jane said urgently. The doors creaked from the weight of bodies pushing instinctively against it, as their putrefying brains tried to figure out how to climb through a smashed window. "What if you get there ahead of them?"

"I don't follow," Holliday said. A crash signaled one of the diseased souls had managed to fall through the window. A maggot-riddled, puss-oozing reanimated corpse shambled toward them. A blast from O'Neill's shotgun sent body parts spinning in every direction.

"Doc, if you are sent to the Undertaker's slab, then surely the hex put on you by HSM will be broken and you'll be relocated elsewhere." Her voice shook with panic.

"Can we hurry this up?" O'Neill called over his shoulder as he reloaded and continued firing through the windowframe.

"But at what price?" Dostoyevsky asked.

"He's going to end up there one way or another," Montagu said, Calamity's nodding head showing that he followed her logic.

"I don't know." Holliday sounded skeptical.

"Go now! Backroom," O'Neill roared as a huge crack split the air. The double doors at the main entrance crashed in. They raced to the backroom and slammed the door behind them. Directly opposite the door was a small square window; outside sprawled the dusty terracotta desert.

"Okay," Holliday said.

"What?"

"Do it."

"*Me?*" she gasped.

Doc Holliday looked into Calamity Jane's dark brown eyes; he could see doubt and confusion there. She hadn't thought through her plan to its inevitable conclusion.

"I trust you," he said, taking her hands in his. Suddenly there was a boom, and a spray of blood splattered Calamity's face.

Oh, he thought. He still held Jane's hands as he slumped to his knees, no longer able to feel his legs. His last thought was to wonder who had shot him.

*

Calamity Jane stared open-mouthed as Holliday slumped to the wooden floor. Standing behind him, Dostoyevsky tucked a small pistol into a holster under his arm and covered it with his coat. "We do not have time for discussion," he said pragmatically. Behind him the door bulged inward.

"Out the window, now!" O'Neill shouted over the din of groans and splintering wood.

The Ulster warrior left last, exiting through the small escape route, firing a blast into the horde as the door crashed inward before leaping through the window.

"What now?" Montagu asked, once they were all outside.

"Just run. Don't look back," O'Neill said and set an example by running toward the desert.

They ran, each of them alone with their thoughts as the light from Paradise cast an eerie red glow over an ocean of parched earth. Dust dried out their eyes and clogged their chests, making them want to vomit. Exhaustion burned their muscles and clouded their vision, but still they ran.

Calamity's heart ached as, over and over in her mind, she replayed Holliday's final moment. His blood still stained her clothes; she imagined she could still smell his cheap cologne. She was finding it hard to understand the depth of her feelings. She wasn't in love with him, never had been. He had looked after her since she'd arrived in hell, kind of like a big brother. She hadn't realized how deep those feelings ran.

They stopped when they could run no more, collapsing on an incline from where they could see a dust cloud rising upward.

"You'll see him again." O'Neill sat down beside Calamity.

She hid her emotions and turned a blank stare on the Irishman. "The Undertaker could relocate him anywhere." She shrugged.

"Somehow I get the feeling he'll find us," answered the Irishman with a grin.

"Look!" Dostoyevsky pointed toward the swirling mass of cloud. "The Hell Cattle, circling New Bodie."

"Aye," O'Neill answered, "a herd of man-eating cattle eternally stampeding around the outskirts of town. We'll have to figure a way to get past them." He turned a hard gaze on the Russian. "Listen, when we get into town, there'll be a lot of questions asked, especially about Doc. Be careful what you say to the Earps, about how Holliday met his demise . . . at least until we've figured things out. They were friends. . . ." Trailing off, he turned his gaze toward the distant town.

*

Doc Holliday opened his eyes. The first thing he noticed was the pain . . . perhaps not pain; more like searing agony.

He tried to move his arms but quickly realized the source of his torment: his hands were nailed to the floor. This time he really *was* crucified.

"Dear God in Heaven help me," he whimpered. His blasphemous curse brought a thunderous reaction from His Satanic Majesty, making the whole building rock and shudder so much Holliday thought it would collapse on top of him. *Stupid! Never utter His name.*

Holliday tried to remember what happened, to think his way past the pain. Someone had shot him from behind. His last sight had been the look of shock on Calamity Jane's face. They'd had a plan. He was supposed to go to the Undertaker and be relocated. Funny how plans never work out the way you want them to in hell. His was a bitter lesson: never think to outsmart HSM. He turned his head at the sound of footsteps making the floorboards creak.

"Well, who's been a naughty boy?" a sultry female voice asked.

He craned his neck to see who it was. He groaned then, only now noticing he was naked and as vulnerable as a newborn babe. *Not now.*

"Oh, that's not your decision," the courtesan answered, reading his thoughts. "We're going to have such fun, you and I." Her ruby red lips parted in a smile.

To Holliday, she looked like a she-wolf regarding her next meal. "Let's see if we can set some of Zeus' creatures free. I'm told the agony is excruciating." She laughed as she knelt beside him and took him in her hand.

"No!" Holliday cried, feeling himself stiffen. His eyes widened as two massive leathery wings unfurled behind her. "Succubus," he gasped.

"Awww, you look so sweet when you're in pain." She leaned in close then. He could feel her hot breath on his face. "You're all mine now."

*

"What was that?" Calamity stopped, the others bunching up behind her. A mournful cry drifted on the hot desert wind, quickly filling the space around them and turning that cry into a desperate wail of anguish and despair. Beyond the wail, farther off, sounded faint laughter, slowly magnifying as if someone had turned up the volume for their ears alone.

"Just keep going." O'Neill pushed them onward. "It's none of our concern."

"Do you think Holliday is still on the Undertaker's table?" Calamity asked.

"No, girl. With the luck that man has, he's already sitting in the fanciest hotel in New Bodie, cleaning out the casino and winning the hearts of the ladies. I'll wager he'll be sitting there waiting on us when we arrive."

She nodded and smiled and turned her back on Helldorado for good.

The Judas Book

Jack William Finley

With typical annoyance, Frank Nitti read the handbill that had stuck to his shoe as he crossed through a back alley on his way to the Hall of Injustice. "Some people never learn," he grumbled and stuffed the damp paper into his pocket.

Upon reaching his office, Nitti removed the damp and crumpled paper and spread it on the desk of his reluctant partner, Elliot Ness.

"I *told* you we should have iced that treacherous bastard. I *told* you he'd just cause more trouble."

Ness eyed the paper which read: 'Coming soon —"Escape from Hell" by Judas Iscariot. Learn the story of a group of daring scientists who escaped from hell and how Dr. Walter Freeman and Meister Eckhart plan to free everyone!'

Ness rubbed his forehead and sighed. "And you think a trip to the Undertaker would have changed any of this?"

"Woulda made me feel better. I'd settle for that."

Ness shook his head wearily. "Well, I guess we better go talk to this Doctor Freeman and his pal Eckhart before things get out of hand and we catch hell from the bosses."

The so-called Lobotomist, Walter Jackson Freeman II, M.D., wasn't hard to find. Within the hour Nitti and Ness were knocking on his door. Nitti, quick to use violence at the least excuse, looked down at the .45 auto in his beefy mitt and grumbled to Ness, "We should have brought shotguns for this."

Ness shook his head. "He's a doctor, for Satan's sake. We don't even know if he's gonna cause us any trouble."

"We don't know he won't. He's an egghead. I keep tellin' you these know-it-alls are always trouble."

A white-coated lab geek answered the door and ushered the two investigators to the doctor's office. At his cluttered desk, Freeman looked the perfect stereotype: balding head, goatee; he embodied the whole package. The spitting image of an old-timey doctor in his three-piece tweeds, he was practically black and white, a turn-of-the-century textbook photo come to three-dimensional life but for his two distinguishing characteristics: his empty wire-rimmed spectacles framed a pair of ice picks driven into his eye sockets.

"Gee, I bet those hurt like hell," Nitti blurted, disconcerted.

"You have no idea," Freeman responded. "And I can see, after a fashion. Like antennae, the ice picks feed thoughts into my brain, the thoughts and feelings of all the patients I treated Above, in the earthly world. What can I do for you, gentlemen?" He gestured for the two detectives to seat themselves in consultation chairs before the desk.

"Judas Iscariot seems to think you have a plan to free everyone from hell," Ness said, taking a seat. Nitti remained standing, wandering the room, taking in all the details.

"Iscariot the Idiot. I wish he'd have waited. His announcement is premature, but essentially correct."

"So" —Nitti turned from a bookshelf —"another know-it-all who thinks he can save the underworlds."

"You say that like it's a bad thing, Mister . . .? I'm sorry, I didn't get your name."

"Nitti. Frank Nitti." Nitti stomped across the floor and slumped into one chair. "Not a bad thing, just dumb-ass. I've seen this song and dance more times than one of you chalk-board-filling eggheads can count, even using all your fancy-ass math. Gets old after a while. So give us the scoop. super villain. Spill your master plan."

"Is he speaking English?" the doctor asked Ness.

Ness smiled. "He tries to be witty. Forgive him. He lived an unfulfilled life as a gangster when what he really yearned to do was write comic-book stories for kids."

"You're a barrel of laughs, Ness. Go ahead, side with this nitwit. I can't wait to see how well that works out for the both of ya."

"So there *is* a plan?" Ness prodded Freeman.

The Lobotomist smiled and winced as his ice picks jiggled. "As a matter of fact, there is. I've spent a lifetime and more studying the human brain and consulted with others —notably the eminent Meister Eckhart who has studied the mind and human perception —and we have come to certain inevitable conclusions."

"Which are?" Nitti jacked upright and helped himself to a drink from the doctor's well-stocked bar.

"Existence can only have two possible forms, physical or mental . . . what you'd call spiritual. The absolute laws of science and nature decree that all things physical change over time. Energy can be, and in fact is to all intents and purposes, eternal but it can hold any given form for only so long before it too must undergo inevitable change. Entropy and decay are absolutes of the physical world. Only those things of the incorporeal, the mental, spiritual world can maintain their form indefinitely. If we abide in a physical world, that world can be changed, destroyed, and therefore escaped. If this milieu around us cannot be changed, then the only thing keeping any of us here is our expectations: we have bought into the lie that Satan, Father of Lies, is selling."

Nitti brought his drink with him to the desk and sat again in his chair. "Assuming any of your egghead crap makes sense, which I doubt, I still don't see how that helps anyone."

Doctor Freeman sighed. "Of course. You wouldn't."

Nitti glanced at Ness and grinned like a shark. "Remember what I said about shotguns?"

"Let him finish," Ness snapped.

Nitti shrugged and gestured with his drink-holding hand toward the doctor. "Please, Doc, go on. Sounds like this'll be amusing after all."

"Very well. Do try to follow. I know logic can be trying for laymen."

Nitti held his temper and nursed his whisky.

The Lobotomist sat back in his desk chair. "The human mind is simply incapable of conceiving the infinite. The concept is far too large, too complex. So we create the finite myths and physical forms that we agree upon, and surround ourselves with them to give the human race some context. Satan, or the Deceiver as he calls himself, and his minions tap into that collective unconscious and manipulate it to their own ends. They don't really control it, or no more than anyone else does. They sell us all a lie that gives form to our need for a collective delusion. Our plan —mine and Eckhart's —is to expose that delusion by using the current plagues."

"The plagues?" Now the Lobotomist had Ness' undivided attention.

"How you gonna do that?" Nitti wondered aloud.

The doctor smiled. "Everyone else is wasting their time trying to cure the plagues. We have made good use of ours, recruiting several assistants, not least of whom are Walter Heerdt, Bruno Tesch, Wilhelm Lommel and Wilhelm Steinkopf, all laboring under our direction to make the plagues more deadly."

"*More* deadly?" Ness tried to control his shock.

Nitti just frowned. "To what end?"

"Our goal is to make the plagues one hundred percent infectious and one hundred percent lethal. Perhaps we will even kill the Undertaker and His Satanic Majesty himself." He pronounced Satan's title with great scorn. "Even if we fail in that, the Undertaker cannot revive everyone, not all at once. Thus we'll prove once and for all that this . . . all you see around you has no real independent physical reality. In fact, the underworlds are no more than a mutually consensual dream state, over which each individual mind and spirit exerts equal control. So each makes his own hell, and thus in hell you get what you expect. We simply need to change those expectations. We need an event or series of events big enough to shatter the faith and belief that binds us all to infernity's rules. *We* are the manipulators of this place. Nothing holds us here but our own belief. We suffer only because we have been convinced that we deserve to suffer, and that we have no other choice. Eckhart and I will give free choice back to the people!" Freeman's voice boomed as if he were trying to reach the back rows of a lecture hall.

"Sounds like you're plotting revolution," Nitti commented.

"Yes. And so what if I am?"

Nitti looked at Ness. Ness shrugged.

Nitti drew his pistol and the .45 roared in the enclosed space of the Lobotomist's office.

Ness looked at Nitti. Nitti frowned.

"Well. This is new." Nitti craned his neck and grumbled as he looked about them.

Both Ness and he were now sitting before a red-felted card table. The rest of the room was white and empty. On the card table lay a note. Nitti picked up the note and read it aloud:

"'That's okay, I wouldn't have believed me either. But you do now. Don't you?'"

Nitti crumpled the note in his fist. "I really hate smart asses."

"This is bad," Ness added. "You just had a drink. What was it? What did it taste like?"

"What the hell difference does that make?"

"*What* did it taste like?"

"Whisky. It tasted like whisky. Best whisky I had since . . . oh. Shit. How much trouble are we in, Ness?"

"You haven't had a drink since you've been in hell that didn't taste like yak piss or worse, have you? Not until that whisky."

"Don't sugarcoat it, Ness. How bad is it?"

"How good was the whisky?"

Nitti scowled at him. "This strike you as a good time for jokes, Ness?"

"I'm not joking. How good? Better than you expected? The best you ever had?"

Nitti shrugged. "I dunno, G-man. Pretty good. Not the best, but very good. What difference does it make?"

"The difference," Ness informed him, "is that the Lobotomist is manipulating what we hear and see and feel. What we taste. If that drink tasted like something you'd drunk before that'd be bad, but if it tasted *better* . . . that's a whole lot worse."

"How do ya figure that, Genius?"

"If it's something you remember, maybe all Doctor Freeman can do is alter our memories, switch things around. If it tasted better than anything you remember, then he can implant thoughts in our minds. Do you remember seeing anything in the room you'd never seen before?"

"I never saw the doc before."

"But you did. We both saw his picture."

Nitti stopped and thought, then said, "You've got a point. As far as I remember the Doc's was just a regular office. Fancy, but then I expected it to be fancy so . . . No. I don't think there was anything that I *for sure* hadn't seen somewhere else before. You think this crazy Freeman can do what he says he can do —get souls out of hell?"

Ness shook his head. "I very much doubt it. We just stumbled onto this. If his scam were that much of a threat, the bosses would know about it, and they would have sent an army to obliterate everything, the Lobotomist in particular. I don't think he's that big a deal yet, but I think he's

working on it, and I think we probably oughtta stop him before he gets that far."

Nitti smiled. "Good plan. I love it. Only thing missing
is . . . *how*?"

Back at their office in the Hall of Injustice, Ness and
Nitti spent hours combing through every bit of information
available on Dr. Freeman and Meister Eckhart. Most of it
gave Nitti a headache. Finding clues had never been Nitti's
strong suit. None of what they learned could tell them how
or where Freeman had acquired his power to manipulate
minds, or what he planned to do with that power.

"None of this makes any damned sense," Nitti complained. "What's Freeman up to? What does he stand to
gain? That crap in the good doctor's office, what was that
about? It musta been a setup, right? So what was the point
of all that?"

"Wait. Let me see the note again."

"I threw it away. I read it to you, didn't I? It was BS.
Just taunting us. 'You didn't believe, but now you do,' some
crap like that."

Ness grimaced. "Maybe that's it. Freeman wants us to
believe."

Nitti shook his head. "I don't get it. What difference
does believing make?"

"Faith. Belief. Didn't you listen to what he said? Whatever power the doctor has, maybe that's where it comes
from. Maybe he's doing what he said he can do: creating a
shared delusion. The more people he gets to believe whatever version of reality he's selling, the more power he's got."

"Okay," Nitti replied slowly. "But power for what?
What's his goal?"

"I don't know yet. We need to find him. Not where he wants us to think he is, but where he *really* is."

"It was this dumb-ass book crap —'Escape from Hell' by Judas Iscariot —that started this whole thing."

"That's *it*!"

Nitti looked surprised. "What's it?"

"The book," Ness told him. "*That's* what this is about. Freeman is selling some crazy shared delusion and Judas' book is how he plans to sell it. You remember what Iscariot was like when we met him during the Pandora incident a couple years back —the most infamous backstabbing traitor since Brutus' crew. If minds give Freeman power, just think how much power he'd have if even one percent of the damned souls in infernity buy Judas' sales pitch in that book and believe in it?"

"That sorry sap is getting used again. It almost makes me pity the poor bastard."

With all the powers of Satan's Insecurity Service at their disposal, it wasn't long before two gray demons dragged a disheveled and bruised Iscariot before them in their Hall of Injustice office.

As soon as the demons remanded Iscariot into their custody and left, leaving two stinking slime trails behind, Ness said, "Okay, so, Judas, where do we find Doctor Freeman?"

Judas turned his face away, reluctant to meet their eyes, and whispered, "Freeman wants to help these poor souls. He wants to set them free. Why must you resist all attempts to make this awful place better?"

"Because it's a lie, you sap. He's just using you. He's using all of you. This isn't about setting anyone free. It's about power over them, and the Doc wants more than his share."

"You don't know that," Judas protested.

"And you don't know we're wrong," Ness countered. "Your track record at telling right from wrong isn't exactly unblemished. Give us a chance to prove we're right. Tell us where the Lobotomist is hiding."

True to form, Judas did.

But finding Freeman took some doing. Eventually they tracked him and Eckhart to one of the oriental hells, holed up in a cellar room that reminded Nitti and Ness of an opium den —except the bodies lying on sofas weren't stoned: they were dreaming, each one attached to some alien machine. The doctor was inside the machine, master of their dreams.

They collared Eckhart without much effort and he spilled his guts like he was committing hara-kiri. So much for honor among delusional megalomaniacs.

"The Lobotomist found this device in the deep desert, and brought it here. It allows him to share his dreaming world with anyone linked to the machine who has faith in the shared dream state."

"But I still don't understand *why*," Nitti said. "What's the point? What's Freeman after?"

"I think I finally get it," Ness told him. "You only have so much horsepower in any one mind. One mind can only imagine so much. He needs the dream to seem real. Escape only becomes real if they can forget they're dreaming. And the more the dreamier: the more who believe, the easier it becomes for more to believe. You ever hear of morphic resonance?" Nitti hadn't. "To pull off this scam, they need enough dreamers to keep their dream-world fresh and mysterious. He's bled dry the imaginations of his first group of subjects and needs Judas' book to recruit more devotees."

"So, it's all just a con then, there's never been any real physical escapes, just damned souls hooked up to a machine that convinces them they've broken out of hell?"

Ness shrugged. "I suppose it depends on your definition of escape. The card table we sat at looked real enough. The whisky you drank tasted real. It seems almost a shame to flush it all."

"You think they'd get away with it if we didn't?" Nitti asked.

"No. Not really. The book hustle is a bridge too far. They've called too much attention to themselves."

"They got too greedy," Nitti said.

"I suppose it's hard not to, when you're onto something as close to real escape as anyone here will ever get. Those patsies hooked to the machine *think* they're free, even if they're just kinda having a time out."

"So. What do you suggest we do, G-man?"

"The only thing we can do: Send them to the Undertaker and let him sort them out."

They burned Eckhart and the dreamers in their den, and Freeman in his machine. For good measure, they confiscated and burned every copy of Judas' book —after having torn off their covers and returned those to Damnazon, Bombs & Ignoble, and CremateSpace for credit —in a single huge bonfire.

The smoke burned their eyes. "In hell, the only real sin left is the sin of dreaming for something better," Ness mumbled softly.

On a hill overlooking the fire, Judas wept.

Writer's Block

Janet Morris and Chris Morris

"'Tis magic, magic that hath ravished me."
— Christopher Marlowe, *Doctor Faustus*

"'Tis now the very witching time of night, when churchyards yawn and hell itself breathes out contagion to this world," spoke Shakespeare in Kit Marlowe's ear, quoting *Hamlet* as the two of them spied a fabled doorway wrapped in shadow. Whenever cowed or overmatched, Shakespeare quoted Shakespeare, as if word could conjure life from death—and perhaps it would: this quote game was their mainstay when infernity waxed oppressive. As it did tonight.

"'Ugly hell, gape not!'" Marlowe retorted from his own *Doctor Faustus*. "What's behind that door we might not want to see, or taste, or bow our heads to greet. Read and beware what that sign says . . ."

Above the stairway down which they must descend to knock, a sign swung slowly in New Hell's fetid breeze, creaking back and forth:

'*Witch Doctor*' proclaimed the sign in flaking prideful letters. And underneath in cursive script:

'*Specializing in Magic, Witchcraft, Ghosts, Necromancy, Sorcery, Poisonous Plants and Omina.*'

And in even smaller script, on its last line: '*Final Causes.*'

"'This is as strange a maze as e'er men trod,'" mouthed Will from *The Tempest*, holding back, one foot upon the first step downward.

Kit pushed by Shakespeare and descended the first two darkened stairs, then turned to his friend: "*Now* you cower? Come on, Will. This gambit's your idea; not mine. A fortnight did we spend, finding our way to this storied doorstep. Nowhere in New Hell would do but here. Thus, here we be, in dark and rain to shirk a curse no worse than the cure for't."

"'I lodge in fear; though this a heavenly angel, hell is here,'" whispered Will from *Cymbeline*. Honest, at least, was William Shakespeare, atremble, affrighted to his core.

"Will, you yourself demanded this visit. ''Tis true: there's magic in the web of it: A sibyl, that had number'd in the world . . .' That's what you said we need. A sibyl." When Will balked this way, only his own words could move him, and these from *Othello* should do the trick. "So here we'll consult hell's finest quacksalvers."

"No. 'This rough magic I here abjure . . .'" *The Tempest* again, when *Othello* would better serve them both.

Kit squinted through the ruddy night, past Will and up toward pale Paradise glaring down spitefully, withholding heaven's light. "No sibyl? No rough magic, when it lies within our grasp? Then how about a witch doctor? A physician, some doctor of the doomed to save us both from hell's plaguing ills, manifold as sinners?" New Hell was awash in plagues of every sort, but none so rarefied as that afflicting Marlowe, or so hopeless of a cure. "Yet here we are, by your own contrivance, to consult hell's famous necromants and charlatans." Now that Shakespeare wanted to flee, Kit Marlowe would see this gambit through, to whatever end. "You insisted, you recall. I said my trouble's not worth all this. Writer's block will flee me in its good time. 'O, no end is limited to damned souls!'" Marlowe spat his own *Faustus* up into Will's face; only when two steps higher could they stand eye to eye. "Now the finding's done, and done. My cure but needs a sibyl to bring me back my muse, unchain my sickly heart to sing another day. In we go, Shak, or away to beg your lover Satan to give me my own magic back."

Kit never called Shakespeare 'Shak' except to remind him of his follies whilst alive, all those plays writ with Marlowe and with others under this name or that, and then signing his will '*Shak*speare'. But of all Will's follies, his dalliance with the Prince of Darkness galled Kit most.

Grumbling "'The prince of darkness is a gentleman,'" out of *Lear*, "You're not." Will took a step downward, then another.

With Shakespeare close behind, Kit Marlowe descended the remaining stairs two at a time and, on a landing deep with rotting leaves, pounded the brass knocker hard against the cellar's oaken door.

Which opened with a squeal to reveal a shop as stagey as he could have written it, complete with vines and cauldrons, jumbled shelves, beakers steaming over fires, a waist-high counter, and three figures robed in black.

Facing all, Marlowe hesitated, so that Shakespeare bumped him from behind. Off balance, Kit stumbled one more step, then another, wondering why he hadn't wanted to come here when Shakespeare so insisted, then couldn't resist the venture when Will held back.

Why hadn't he at least brought a weapon, a rapier, dagger, or even a letter-opener . . .?

"In," said a voice that matched a withered hand upon the door and a bristly chin under tangled hair. "I give ye leave, the both."

In they bumbled, Kit with Will's breath puffing against his neck, the bard's codpiece nearly banging his buttocks. "We're looking for a sibyl, a doctor—an end to some plague or witchcraft put upon my head." Best get right to the point.

The other two dark clerks were watching. One was male, Kit thought, ancient and wizened, bandy-legged, bones bending this way and that as Nature never meant, wrapped in linen blacker than night: broad head, sparse hair combed forward and a beard much thicker. His long nose divided a pair of owl's eyes and led to a mouth thin with age. From beside that one, and around the counter, came a face and form Kit had hoped never to meet again: a goddess, this one, tall and overripe, reeking of the grave. "Hail, Hekate," said Marlowe to the Judge of Erebos, sorceress, necromant, witchcrafter supreme across the vast underverse. He hadn't seen her since he and Shakespeare rehearsed their last play, *The Witch and the Tyrant*, when she'd stepped in as co-producer. Among the worst nemeses a soul could have in infernity was Hekate, with her penchant for drama. "I'm after a cure for writer's block. If you'll help me, Will and I can make our deadline; thus His Infernal Majesty will be well served."

"Deadline," snorted Shakespeare from behind him. Then: "Yes, keeper of the crossroads. Give us a laxative for the soul. Tell us how to unstopper Marlowe's mind, before his mouth dries up completely and his brain wizens like a raisin. We've plays to write for Satan, and little time to spare."

"*Help you two*? The two worst cozeners in all perdition? Why would I? For Satan's sake? For your precious plays? I'll give thee ghosts—you summon them oft enough. I'll give thee tempests, thou lovest those. I'll give thee floods, ye fools, to wash thee clean. Or would you prefer metamorphoses? Would you both croak like frogs upon the stage? Or hiss like asps—it suits your tempers? Or become ye fish? Can ye swim? Or fowl ——? Ye both lay enough eggs for it. But hear you this: you'll never fly above the rising tide of torment."

"Two customers, are you?" asked the bristly-chinned hag at the door, closing it with a sucking sound behind him and Will. "Cross our threshold of your own free will, you do. No wind at thy backs. Seeking a cure?"

"What are you called? Have ye names?" asked the palsied one, hobbling toward them, so frail that Marlowe wondered he could walk at all, and so slow. . . .

By then Shakespeare's lips were to Kit's ear, whispering caution. Kit reached back and brought Shakespeare up beside: "This is the bard of Avon, William Shakespeare. I'm Christopher Marlowe, a poet who's lost his Muse."

"Lost?" said the bristled hag, and stuck her warty nose near Marlowe's face. "Lost your Muse? Never happens. Passing strange. Lost, you say? Sure you ever had one? Had you hubris in its place? I give no Muses. I can give you a wind to whisper in your ear."

"I, too," chortled Hekate, "I'll give ye wind enough to flatten any playhouse in the whole of hell."

"No, no, please and thank you, Hekate. The last wind we got from you took me and Kit too far from home, if you'll recall. A long walk isn't what we need today. We need Marlowe to find his voice. We'll pay handsomely—immortalize you all in verse, if you'll but help us now."

The ancient soul kept hobbling toward them.

Hekate laughed like a serpent's rattle.

Shakespeare quoted *Macbeth* too loudly: "'How now, you secret, black, and midnight hags! What is't you do?'" He bared his teeth, glaring impatiently from cowl to cowl to cowl. "Can you help us? Spin a spell? Weave a charm? Vex a potion? Hex an enemy? Do any magics such as your sign outside boasts you can?"

"I can. I'll give ye a push toward destiny," cackled the bristly hag.

"I can," giggled Hekate. "But shall I? Aye, there's the rub. To do or not to do, that is the question. Whether 'tis nobler in the mind to suffer fools—"

Shakespeare howled, wounded more by her parody than any dagger.

At that moment, the crippled soul stopped shuffling and peered up at Kit with a gaze steeped in years, washed with tears, and piercing. Marlowe felt raped, his depths disturbed, his thought assessed, his heart measured, his chest squeezed. Winded, Kit gasped. "Who *are* you?"

"Aristotle. You'll excuse us our tardiness: with Erra's Babylonian plagues infecting all the hells our services are greatly in demand. I'm a doctor of what ails such as you—of biology, zoology, physics, metaphysics, logic—of aesthetics, poetry, theatre, rhetoric."

Shocked, Kit bumped Will's hip with his and muttered, "Doctor of theatre?"

Never to be bested rhetorically by anyone, Shakespeare said, "Aristotle? Did you know that in his famous play *Doctor Faustus*, my friend, here, said of you, 'Live or die in Aristotle's works'? Few have been so highly praised. Now you aid one who helped keep your name alive. Heal Kit, and we'll write more of you—in our very next play."

Tactics fit for Avon or London, not New Hell. Not for the tutor of Alexander the Great.

This ancient Aristotle ignored Shakespeare and limped yet closer to Kit. "So you're not here for fear of the plagues roundabout? Not looking for a prophylactic potion, herbs from Hekate's garden? Spells spun from witchery?"

"No," Kit said, wit gone nearly dry before this soul who struck him speechless with its probing gaze. "I studied you. Read your *Poetics*. Read *De Anima, Prior Analytics*. You were—*are* the first teacher. You taught a boy with a twisted spine how to conquer the known world. Teach me how to find my Muse."

"You are your Muse, your own prototype, your exemplar. Nothing is missing, aside from you, hiding from yourself. You must give in to love, and hope. Your heart is crusted with disappointment, embalmed in sorrow. So write your way free of that—write tragedy, if you must."

"That's all he ever does, mewling thing. I'll give him inspiration," said Hekate, chortling. "Here, Marlowe: Write ye a song for me, or you'll wish you had: a song for singing to the winds of war."

"I'll give him inspiration; I'll give him a war such as hell's never seen," said the bristly-jawed witch. "And this cure's free: You'll find your salvation where last you left it, writer boy." Then this crone threw off her black cloak and her tangled hair and spun round in her own maelstrom like a shapely cyclone come indoors, so that jars jittered on their shelves and dried herbs crackled where they hung. When the cyclone ceased, there stood Sin, Satan's daughter, tangy and green, dugs hanging, her belly reaching nearly to her knees. "And all I want from you, lover-boy, is a bow and a kiss on my sweet hand. . . ." Sin extended her hand to Marlowe.

Who didn't take it, or bend a knee.

Kit stood dumbstruck. Kiss that green hand and what would happen? Of all the powers in perdition, Sin's was the most unpredictable.

Shakespeare shook his arm. "Do something. Say something," whispered Will urgently.

"Yes, do something," said Sin. "Kiss my hand or kiss a raft of corpses from here to Above and back."

"Give us all a kiss," said Hekate, cagey. "Seal your pact, and get your Muse back."

"Get her back," urged Shakespeare.

"Get her back. Get her back," said Aristotle.

Kit went to bended knee to kiss the green and pungent hand of Sin, Satan's first daughter, yet fearing another whirlwind come to drop him and Will into a desert—or worse, deposit him far from Will and all he loved. For Sin knew him well and knew that Marlowe cared only for Will, wanted only to be with Will, to protect Will, until eternity itself ran down and time stopped still.

Just as Kit pulled his lips away from the fish-belly hand of Satan's daughter and let her go, he heard Shakespeare's voice, dimly quoting his *Antony and Cleopatra:* "'In nature's infinite book of secrecy/ A little I can read.'"

Sin whirled and the room spun too, so that all the jars and unguents and cauldrons and bottles, and the sign and the door, spun together into a racket and a white bright light, and then a maelstrom against which Kit struggled until he could grab Shakespeare by the collar. That done, he closed his tearing eyes against the blinding light and the deafening noise. . . .

His backside hit the ground with a thump. The noise was gone, leaving a ringing in his ears. The light was gone, leaving him blinking into nothingness. But still he held Shakespeare's collar.

For a moment he feared that Will's collar might be all he held, with its tatting and lacy trim. Still he could barely see: white afterimages of the whirlwind centered his vision; only at its edges could he detect shape and color and form.

As those shapes resolved, slowly, the brightness faded. He was sitting on his buttocks in the dark and the mud, in a stairwell that ended before an old oaken door with a rickety sign above, creaking and squeaking.

Beside him on the muddy ground sat Will Shakespeare, chest pumping, eyes tearing, his goatee littered with bits of herbs and spittle and glass.

Kit let go Shakespeare's collar when Will began to laugh. Shakespeare laughed until he nearly cried, until he held his stomach, until he panted a line from his *Macbeth*, "See? 'Hell is murky!' Just as I once said."

"Yes, Will, just as you once said." Cold comfort. Suddenly Kit wanted to upbraid his friend for leading them, once again, into dangers unreasonable for reasons best forgot. Now that Satan's mad daughter no longer loomed nearby, in hindsight all they'd suffered, all they'd risked, looked foolish.

"Forsooth, Kit, recall what you said about sin in Faustus—not meant for Satan's daughter, but fit for her: 'If we say that we have no sin,/ We deceive ourselves, and there's no truth in us./ Why then belike we must sin,/ And so consequently die./ Ay, we must die an everlasting death.'"

These Marlowe lines on Shakespeare's lips summed Will's peace-offering, after nearly getting them both blown into the Deep, or worse.

They'd both risked everything that mattered—one another—in this hell where only Milton could make himself at home. And for what? Because Will thought Kit's mind wasn't on his work? Someday, Kit would lose Will among the manifold hells of creation. Someday, Shakespeare's bold assurance would fail before Satan's schemes to split him and Will apart.

Will wanted Kit to have a malady hell could cure, not simply be afflicted by the devil's jealousy: Kit knew, in his heart, that Satan was the root of this evil that dried his tongue and made his soul hide deep inside him. Satan wanted to prove to Will that Shakespeare didn't need his Marlowe. But Kit couldn't say that, could barely think it. For Satan was unbeatable, here on his home ground.

So they sat there, silent, in the mud, next to one another while Paradise glowered overhead, watching.

After a silence far too long, Kit grudgingly offered Will a bit from *King Richard the Third*: "'O, no, my dream was lengthen'd after life;/ O, then began the tempest to my soul,/ Who pass'd, methought, the melancholy flood,/ With that grim ferryman which poets write of,/ Unto the kingdom of perpetual night.'"

Shakespeare said, "Kit, don't be angry. We've done it, just as if we were in *Macbeth*: 'A deed without a name.'"

When Marlowe made no answer, Will repeated the same thing a second time, and this time Kit joined in, for this line must be said by all: "'A deed without a name.'"

But they both knew the name of this deed they'd done today: its name was love.

From Perseid Press:
Excerpt from the new Heroes in Hell novel,
"Hell Bound", by bestselling author
Andrew P. Weston:

A Moment of Clarity

Andrew P. Weston

In the Juxtapose level of hell, Olde London Town was a conundrum at the best of times, a heady mix of the implausibly warped and secularly grotesque. Its denizens were the perfect accompaniment to their city; a stir-fried hotchpotch of condemned souls who took the geophysical and temporal irregularities of their hometown in their stride.

Everyday life here was as much an enigma as it was a challenge, and you'd think that, having lived here for centuries, I'd be used to it by now. Yet it still caught me unawares from time to time, the boundaries between eras being as fluid as they were temperamental. In this place more than any other, I'd discovered that even if you knew a surprise was coming, forewarned was definitely *not* forearmed.

As was the case regarding my current predicament.

Nimrod and I were en route to the Grey Friars. In the land of the living, Greyfriars had been the site of a Franciscan friary that existed from 1225 until 1538, in a northwestern part of the City of London, called St. Nicholas on the Shambles. That great establishment had included one of the largest conventional churches in the capital. It had also been home to a Studium, an extensive library of logical and theological texts so important it was rivaled only by Oxford University. It achieved a level of cultural prestige that drew people from all over the then known world, until Thomas Cromwell—a man who came to be a good friend of mine—ordered it seized during the English Reformation. Under his enlightened guidance, the Greyfriars estates were confiscated, the order itself was disbanded, and most of its monks banished or executed.

Of course, *we* couldn't let such a monument go to waste. And with a gothic twist, it became the perfect establishment for the truly irreverent.

The Grey Friars were now Satan's very own thought police, an unholy order of hermits who regularly vetted the ranks of the Devil's Children to weed out those with doubts or illusions of grandeur. Every Sinday morning, the pews of the High Church of Lucifer within the Friars' domain would be packed with blue suits and spooks, all of whom would undergo their regular *confessional* evaluation.

But the order also served another purpose.

The site had retained its archives and was now one of the largest publicly known repositories of occult knowledge and arcane mascots in the underworld, rivaled only by the Hellexandria Library.

The Grey Friars defended that vault and had placed the treasures in their care within the Cloister of Scourging, a great castlelike tower situated within a separate annex. Constructed on a mound built from the bones of those who died during the Great Fire of London, some one hundred years after the original monastery's passing, the cloister was protected by a series of enchanted wards, and a powerful temporal barrier. Of course, it was also guarded by the friars themselves, who were known to possess skills far more lethal than Shaolin monks tripping on amphetamines.

A heavy set of precautions, and yet all these measures were but a secondary line of defense. To reach them, you first had to pass the Knights Bridge, although the term "bridge" was rather a loose one in that it wasn't a literal construction of wood or stone linking one side to another. It was more an esoteric conduit from *here to there*, between *now and then*. A multidimensionhell link that spanned hydraspace to get you to where you needed to go.

Appearing much like a ground level mushroom cloud from a nuclear explosion, the Knights Bridge encompassed the Cloister of Scourging in a haar of literal thought-stealing smog. A brume so thick, so cloying, that unworthy individuals had been known to enter only to wander forever more, lost and alone.

And if the thought of facing such a barrier wasn't daunting enough, the entire pall was also protected by the Knights Tempter, an ancient heraldic order of warriors fanatically devoted to the glory of the Arch Deceiver and Father of Lies himself: Satan.

And to get where I needed to go, that obstacle had to be faced.

I stood outside the Old Bully—the main court of the Ministry of Injustice here in Juxtapose—and eyed the deceptively calm mists tumbling and twisting over and over on the other side of the street.

"Okay," Nimrod murmured. "What do we do now?"

"*We* don't do anything," I replied. Then I cocked my head at the murky film on the other side of the street. "*I*, on the other hand, have to go into that."

"Are you sure that's wise?"

"There's no point in us both having our minds screwed with. You've heard the horror stories. Anyone attempting to traverse the bridge must pass a series of tests. What they are, exactly, differs from aspirant to aspirant. But whatever you *do* contend with, it measures your physical, mental, and spiritual fortitude in a way that flays your damned soul bare. Not a pleasant experience for a denizen of hell."

"Then why risk it, Daemon? People like us are especially wicked and depraved. The stronger we are, the more profound the experience in there will be. Why don't you simply try to phase through, or generate a short-range portal? For fuck's sake, if anyone's strong enough, it's you."

"Because that *would* be suicide, my friend. Don't forget, that stuff has built in safeguards to prevent any kind of skullduggery. And if it was that easy, you'd get idiots like Tesla storming the place like hyenas on a fat juicy carcass."

Nimrod fell silent for a moment, then calmly stressed, "And yet, Cream and his cronies managed to breach the Sphincter and the Grumbles gate-room without much difficulty. And one of their clues led you here."

"I know. I've been worrying about just that point, because if they've found a way around shields like this, we're all in trouble."

Nimrod clasped me by the shoulder. "I never thought I'd say this, but thank Azazel for the Knights Tempter, then."

"I'll let you know." I returned the gesture. "Remember, that fog is designed to neutralize whatever enhancements a candidate possesses."

"So you'll be completely . . . ?"

"Normal? Yes. And I for one don't intend to have my head rearranged by a magically augmented club anytime soon." Pointing at myself, I tried to lighten the mood. "I mean, look at me. Would *you* want your features spoiled if you were a perfect specimen like me?"

"If I looked like you," Nimrod countered, "I'd be ashamed to be seen in public without a bag on my face. Two. Just in case the top one fell off!" His countenance suddenly became impassive. "But if you're afraid, I could always fit you with a set of baby reins to pull you back when you start crying."

I scanned his aura and could see he was attempting to mask his concern behind a humorous façade. I had to admit, I felt all emotional.

"Fuck off, you pussy! Sitting here talking about it won't get the job done. I've had enough of your drivel. See you on the other side."

I pushed myself away from the wall, strode across the sidewalk, and headed toward the gently undulating wall of mystery. Passersby checked their step as they realized where I was heading. Cars screeched to a halt.

Seizing on the lull, Nimrod called, "Can I have first dibs on your apartment when you die? I've always wanted rooms with a view."

I gave him the finger, stepped in . . .

. . . and froze.

I'd expected a gradual transition from light to dark, a sense of being progressively enveloped and transported in some way to a new location. But I didn't get any of that. In an instant, I was someplace else entirely.

A thick gray soup surrounded me. I couldn't see the ground beneath my feet, and when I extended my arms, my hands were swallowed whole, as if they didn't exist. Peering about me, I searched for a focal point on which to establish a poin t of reference.

Not a goddam thing. Has the trial started already?

Suddenly wary, I realized it would be best to clear my head, so I took a deep breath, calmed my nerves, closed my eyes, and listened.

Thum—thump, thump—thump, thum—thump . . .

The sound of my heartbeat dominated, its steady rhythm providing an anchor around which to ground myself. I didn't need a cardiovascular system, of course, but I'd always found the sensation soothing, as it made me feel something I'd never been—normal.

For some reason the enfolding brume exacerbated that beat. It grew louder, and then more distant, as if my heart had suddenly been transposed beyond my flesh.

Thum—thump, thump—thump, thump—thump . . .

Now I was puzzled.

It sounds like it's getting louder. Drawing closer in some way. But how . . . ?

I opened my eyes and was startled to realize the vapors had folded back to reveal an open tourney field, carpeted with thick, lush grass. White marquees formed a parade on either side of the meadow, each of them bedecked in red and gold pennants. In front of them, equipment racks had been arranged so that unseen champions might choose from a wide assortment of lethal-looking weapons. I completed a quick three-sixty and discovered there was even a fully decorated pavilion behind me, resplendent in the sunshine and festooned with ribbons and bows in the same heraldic colors.

The entire arena lay within a surrounding cocoon of milk-white fog, and despite my best efforts, I couldn't detect any other unliving soul.

Thud—thud, thud—thud, thud—thud . . .

I spun toward the sound, and a massive shadow detached itself from the mist at the open end of the field. My jaw dropped, for there, not fifty yards away, was an armored warrior atop a midnight-black charger.

Dressed from head to toe in steel, and with the distinctive scarlet and gold inverted long cross emblazoned across his surcoat and shield, I knew without a doubt that *this* was a Knight Tempter. The horse itself was huge, a courser; its broad chest and powerful body likewise protected by barding, spikes, and leather.

Armor and tack were coated in fine beads of moisture which glistened like diamonds in the imaginary sunlight. Staring at them, I imagined for a moment what it must be like to have to face such a daunting team in battle.

My thoughts were definitely jinxed lately for no sooner had I contemplated the notion than the knight lowered his visor, and raised his lance in salute. He then put his heels to his mount's flanks, and the horse jumped forward into a trot.

Mesmerized, I stood rooted to the spot and tried to fathom what it all meant.

Forty yards.

Their speed abruptly increased to a canter.

So, is this part of the process? Am I supposed to react . . . or not?

I chose to react and rolled to one side. As I came up, I unbuttoned my coat and threw back my hood.

Thirty yards.

Rider and steed altered trajectory, and the earth trembled beneath my feet. I gamboled again, and drew my scythe. By the time I had dropped into a fighting crouch, my weapon was extended and primed for combat.

Does he really want me to hamstring his horse? Or worse still, confront him directly?

They accelerated into a gallop. The beast snorted, its nostrils flared. Muscles bulged and the vibrations increased as divots flew. Like a portent of doom, the spear tip lowered.

Intuition kicked in.

No matter what's taking place, we're on the same side.

Twenty yards.

We're on the same side, we're on the same side, we're on the same side . . .

Despite the danger of the situation, my gut was telling me not to resist them. They were here to do a job. I had to work with them.

Ten yards.

Oh, bugger! I need a raise.

Against my natural instincts, I collapsed my weapon, stood tall, and threw my arms wide. At the very last moment, I squeezed my eyes shut and yelled, "I am no threat to you, or to the treasures under your protection."

It seemed like a good idea at the time, but my voice sounded as feeble as a wet fart flying in the face of thunder. As their shadow blotted out the sun, I decided I wasn't so sure anymore.

Shit! Shit! Shit! Sh-iiit!

"Oof-fuuuuck!"

The tip of the lance struck with the power of a runaway freight train. Piercing leather, fabric, skin and bone, it lifted me high off the floor and carried me through the air as if I were nothing but a rag doll. I couldn't breathe, I couldn't think. Nothing else existed except the pain of impalement.

Suddenly, the spear impacted against something hard behind me, and shattered. The shockwave ran along the length of the splinter still embedded in my body and multiplied the agony a thousandfold. As I slid to the floor, the knight disappeared, and an ethereal voice hissed, "Impressive . . ."

I landed in a heap, blood bubbling from my mouth and nose, and streaming through the fingers clasped tightly over the hole in my chest. For some reason, my self-healing ability didn't appear to be kicking in, and there was nothing I could do to staunch the flow. I threw my sight inward to assess the damage, and tried to stop my heart.

It was no use. I was locked within a mortal coil. A terrible, hollow ache crawled its way up from the pit of my stomach, only to give way to a wash of cold, prickly heat. My vision began to waver and recede. The strangest of sensations wrapped itself around me. All discomfort faded and without knowing why, I suddenly felt heavy.

It took me a moment to realize—*this is death approaching.*

"There you go, old boy. Not to worry."

I jumped as an unexpected voice intruded.

"Don't you worry now, I'm a doctor. I'll soon sort you out."

A doctor? What's a doctor doing here?

Strong hands flipped me over and commenced an examination of my injury. I tried to see who had come to my rescue, but my eyes refused to cooperate.

"Hmmm. That's a nasty wound, but I have something here that will take away the pain. I take it you're not allergic to anything? Penicillin, ampicillin, cyanide? Ha! Just joking, I don't want you fading away on me just yet."

Great bedside manner.

Whoever this guy was, he wasn't gentle. He lifted my head by the hair, laughed in my face, and then abruptly let go. I saw stars as my skull slammed back down onto the ground, but at least it helped to clear my sight. My vision wavered, and then came back into focus.

Someone was kneeling at my side. Dressed in a style reminiscent of a nineteenth century physician, he had turned away from me to rummage around inside a black case. It was adorned with a decorative motif—a silver skull and crossbones if I wasn't mistaken—and I could hear clinking, as if glass bottles were being jiggled together. Sure enough, my mystery savior removed two small test tubes from his bag, and hummed a merry tune as he mixed their contents together in a separate vial.

Next, he extracted a syringe from his pocket, complete with needle, and filled the barrel with an evil-looking green liquid. Turning back to me, he said, "Normally, I'd let you ingest this little concoction, but where's the fun in that?"

Cream! "How in the blazes . . . ?"

I attempted to wriggle away from him, but discovered I couldn't move.

"Now, now," he cooed, "just be a good boy and lie back. It'll all be over soon."

He loomed over me, and made a show of squeezing a drop of his foul brew from the tip of the needle. With a final leer, he stabbed down and impaled the side of my neck.

"That's it, that's it. Now I get to watch you die. Quite fitting, don't you think?"

A burning sensation exploded into my throat. Intensifying, it launched itself throughout my nervous system, quickly spreading into my heart, brain and spine. In moments, an involuntary spasm caused my teeth to clench, and my extremities started jerking with spasmodic convulsions.

Fury congealed across my brow, but all I could do was snarl at him.

Cream grinned in response and stooped to pick up my scythe. It responded to his touch, and began powering up.

Hey . . . ? That can't happen . . . !

A flush of realization washed through me.

This isn't real. It's part of the test.

A welcome sense of release trilled in the ether. It didn't last long, as the taste of rising bile forced me to flip over onto my hands and knees. I heaved, and vomited the contents of my stomach over the grass. Then, before I realized what was happening, my arms and legs commenced sinking into the ground itself.

Oh, for Azazel's sake, what now?

Wraithlike voices condensed out of the air, singing a hauntingly evocative refrain. As the melody clarified, the lyrics took on a whole new weight of meaning. Something deep within me responded to the call of the Knights Tempter.

They sang:

"We have seen the places you have been
And can never go again.
Though dark and windswept
And as bitter as a sea of souls,
A bosom awaits to welcome you home.
Once lost but not forgotten,
You will be enfolded once more
Within light's eternal embrace,

Where you will rest,

Forever free of burdens . . ."

The words faded, snatched away by the breeze. Nonetheless, their import remained.

A paradox of some sort? But how does that relate to me?

As I tried to work out what it all meant, the foundations of the earth beneath me turned fluidic, and I found myself freefalling through thick, white clouds. The wind howled as it hurtled past my face and as I broke free of the veil, majestic sunlight baptized me in coronal radiance. My insides heaved again, but instead of puking my guts up, my perspective shifted, and I somehow felt myself merge more fully into the unfolding drama.

A plummeting sensation seized me, body and soul, and sent me hurtling to my doom. Nonetheless, I drew comfort from an object grasped tightly in my right hand. I glanced to one side and saw a huge sword. It blazed like lightning, encompassing me within a violet and gold corona that bonded the blade to my flesh and inured me against the terrible drop.

Things happened faster. The rate of my descent increased. My internal alarm triggered. As I scanned the vicinity, something hurtled toward me across the vaulted sky, and the sense of danger peaked. Instinctively, I stabbed out. Glass chimed against glass, and a shower of prismatic light and sparks crisscrossed the heavens with glittering reflections.

My unknown adversary clamped his hand around my sword wrist. I returned the gesture and squeezed as hard as I could. Locked together, we tumbled out of control, over and over, each attempting to obliterate the other by sheer force of will. Vast ribbons of energy encompassed us in a living plasma field.

A suspended animation rush of impressions consumed me.

The terrible drop . . .

Pain.

Skin, glowing white-hot from devastating friction . . .

Intense agony.

Primary flight feather torn free by overwhelming drag

. . .

Excruciating, prolonged torture.

A vast pit of malevolence rushing up from below . . .

Plunging.

Light receding above . . .

Forever plummeting.

A moment of clarity as the truth of my predicament finally registers.

I've fallen too far!

The endless spiral, down and down.

An overwhelming surge of heat as I pay the price . . .

Depravation.

The silence of eternal midnight . . .

Soul-crushing grief.

The inevitable pressure of all-consuming oblivion . . .

Anguish compounded a thousandfold.

Then an unexpected voice stabbed out of the darkness.

"You are more than you appear to be . . ."

Then why do I feel so emasculated?

". . . so much more. Do you not realize who you are?"

Who I am?

"What you are?"

I am alone. Stripped, barren, and darkened.

"Then why tolerate it? It is unnatural."

I deserve it.

"But you are a god!"

Don't be ridiculous, I am nothing. Debased, corrupted, and tarnished.

"A Titan to rival the likes of Lucifer himself."

That is preposterous. Outrageous. You shouldn't talk like that.

"Why? You are a colossus amongst insects. Why shouldn't you release the potential so artfully obscured and claim what could be yours?"

What are you saying?

"Overthrow the pretender, Satan. Why do you think Erra and his personified weapons were dispatched? He is insufficient for the task."

Blasphemy!

"Take the throne . . ."

Treason!

"Assume your rightful place as lord of the underworld. Have you not personally consigned billions to such a fate? Who better to rule?"

No. Never!

Myriad images flickered toward me, each depicting the many realms of hell as they would be under the dominion of my governance. Desolate, inhospitable, and the epitome of pure misery . . .

It was magnificent. I felt emancipated, alive for the first time in millennia.

"This is who you were," the enticing voice cajoled, "and a portent of what you will become."

It was . . . it was . . .

A lie!

The very thought of it repelled me. Fueled by a sudden burst of unrighteous anger, I trembled on the brink of the Obsidian Rage, a deadly fury as harsh and abominable as all the levels of the netherworld combined.

"I know what you're doing," I roared into the night, "but you'll never break my resolve, Tempters. These are but fabrications sent to test my integrity. I refuse to play these mind games any longer. Now release me, or face Satan's wrath . . ."

My challenge pealed into the void.

"Very impressive . . ." hissed an unexpected voice above me. Its resonance echoed through the ether, then dissipated on the wind.

My skin tingled and I found myself standing on a narrow gravel pathway leading up a small incline toward a fortified tower.

The Cloister of Scourging, I guessed.

A hulking great brute of a man dressed in simple gray robes stood before a lowered drawbridge. Behind him, a portcullis barred the way.

The welcoming committee? Or another test?

The guardian radiated great power and authority. Although he appeared to be in his mid-forties, his aura betrayed the ruddy tinge of one who had served in hell for centuries. Arms like threaded tree trunks crossed a broad, finely muscled chest. A combat scepter hung from a worn leather belt about the monk's waist. Something about the weapon set my teeth on edge.

Eyes like two chips of stone regarded me in silence. I was surprised to note a look of astonishment tinged with respect in their flintlike depths.

"You made it then?" he stated.

"It would appear so."

I patted myself down to ensure all the bits were in the right places, and then turned to look about me. "*That* was one of the most unpleasant experiences I've ever had to endure, and believe me, I've suffered quite a few."

"It's supposed to be unpleasant," a brief look of anger clouded his face, "but sadly, not unpleasant enough, it seems."

"What do you mean?"

"I think it'd be better if I just showed you. As you've just tasted what it's like to face the Knights Tempter, you'll appreciate more than most just how daunting the task is. Hopefully, you'll put a word in with His Nibs and be able to divert the heat of his anger." He extended his hand. "I'm Friar Lemuel Tuck, the Warden."

"Friar Tuck? Seriously?"

Lemuel smiled. "No. Not that one. *I'm* the real deal, one of the nastiest bastards you'll ever have the misfortune to meet in the woods . . . but only if you cross me."

I grinned in return and took the proffered hand. Only then did I notice it was a different color to the rest of his arm. In fact, the stitching was exquisite, an outstanding piece of work.

I felt my fingers go numb through my gloves.

Unholy shit! How did he do that? "Did the Undertaker make this modification?"

"He did, on His Satanic Majesty's instructions." He patted the war hammer hanging from his belt. "If I didn't possess the *angel-hand*, I wouldn't be able to wield the power of Godsbane, my mace." He gestured along the path, and began to lead the way. "Please follow me, and I'll clarify a few things."

"I take it this all has to do with the reason why our Dark Father is going to be pissed at you?"

"I'm afraid so," Lemuel sighed.

He took a deep breath, and continued: "Tell me, would you say the Knights Bridge was a formidable obstacle?"

"Are you kidding?" I couldn't prevent a claw from scratching its way down the chalkboard of my spine at the mere mention of it.

"What did you find the most disconcerting aspect of your experience?"

I thought for a moment. "To be honest, being confronted by my nightmares made manifest, and being unable to do anything about it except let the vision take me where it wanted. How did they manage that?"

"*That*, dear Reaper, is due solely to the power of the mystery we protect—the Key of Sighs."

"Key of Sighs?"

"Yes. Despite your high standing, it's a closely guarded secret, and not something that you, even with your clearance level, would have heard of. Don't feel insulted, it's a need-to-know matter."

"I'm not, believe me. My current assignment is emphasizing all the time just how little I really know. Seeing as you've mentioned it though, what *is* this Key of Sighs?"

Lemuel shared a strange telepathic image with me. At first, I thought I was viewing an oval piece of stone, but on closer inspection the artifact had the texture of crystal, overlaid by the iridescent luster of a precious mineral.

"Is that a rock?" I murmured. "Silicate of some kind?"

"Believe it or not, what you're looking at is a hunk of the pearly gates themselves, taken during the original attempt to storm heaven. We call it the Key of Sighs because of what it can do. Anyone of sufficient strength of will can channel its divine nature to generate a sympathetic cosmic cipher—a key, if you will—and . . . *Shazam!*"

"No way! Are you saying it can breech the Divide?"

My guide merely flared his eyebrows.

Fuck me!

Then a certain notion struck me.

"But what does all this have to do with you? Or the Knights Tempter, for that matter?"

Lemuel responded by enlarging the psychic representation. The Key of Sighs circled idly, round and around, and as it did so I noticed what appeared to be two smooth areas along the upper quadrant of its surface. From my perspective, it looked as if a gem cutter had excised two portions from the chunk itself.

Lemuel explained: "As you can see, our Lord Satan had two slivers removed from the Key in order to augment its defenses. The surrounding miasma generated by the Knights is empowered by one of those flakes. Think of it as an environment laced by the very essence of God's Grace. A crux that acts as anathema to all who are hell-spawned."

I whistled.

The friar continued: "By its tincture, the Tempters are able to measure the physical, mental, and spiritual worthiness of all who seek to pass, for the Key searches out the darkest secrets of an aspirant's soul. From this, the Knights gain a foundation for each trial."

They certainly do! But I still had questions.

"And this is linked to your hand and the scepter?"

"Correct." Lemuel flexed his fingers and hefted Godsbane from his belt. "This weapon is forged from a subtle blend of medusanite and the second fragment of the Key. As

I mentioned, were it not for the angel-hand, I would not be able to wield its might in battle. Nor would I be able to do things like this . . ."

By now we had arrived at the portcullis. Lemuel took a moment to compose himself, and flipped the mace so its handle was uppermost. Then he pressed the heel into a small indentation next to an ornate ring-pull.

"Lan khol yé zélah (by all that is holy)," he intoned, "pa-the eyl e-na shavat (open to me now)."

"You speak the divine language?" I felt a familiar ripple of power, and the metal grating rose ponderously into the air.

"A necessary evil, I'm afraid." He looked resigned. "The enchantments about this keep are comprised of both divine and occult essence, not that they seem to do much good, as I said."

I gasped. "Don't tell me someone's stolen the Key?"

"No! In a way, it's much worse." Before I could ask him to clarify his remark, Lemuel gestured again and led me down a short flight of steps. We stopped before a solid oak gateway covered in metal studs and engraved with a host of cryptic sigils. The hairs along the back of my neck and arms stood up, and I realized we had arrived at the threshold of a powerful force field.

Lemuel removed a set of old-fashioned jailer's keys from a fold of his robe. He selected one, positioned it at the lock, and whispered a brief phrase in Hellanese. A spark of energy pulsed through the glyphs and I heard a loud *click*! The entrance swung silently inward to reveal a similar corridor and identical-looking door about twenty yards away down a short slope. Braziers, stationed within alcoves on either side of the passage, burst to life as we stepped inside.

From the way he approached the next obstacle, I thought Lemuel was going to adopt the same procedure as before, but I was mistaken. This time, he used the shaft of Godsbane to operate the lock—as he had at the portcullis—and uttered a single word in the divine language.

It was at the next gate that I spotted his pattern. The first doorway had been sealed by sorcery, the next by angelic wards. As such, Lemuel was patiently employing an overlapping strategy to overcome each successive barrier. We continued in this manner until, after more than fifteen minutes, we arrived at the final gateway.

This particular entrance was huge, and fashioned from two great leaves of very dark timber. I examined its texture, and determined it must be something similar to brazilwood, as the black grain was enriched here and there by knots of luscious red heartwood.

The outline of two opposing hands had been fashioned into the surface of each panel at chest height; one on the left, the other on the right. On this occasion, the protective shield was powerful enough to make me feel as if a million insects were crawling across the surface of my skin.

My guide turned toward me. "Prepare yourself, Reaper. What you are about to see has only been witnessed by a handful of denizens in all the levels of the underverse. You might find it a little . . . overwhelming."

"Don't worry about me. My heart is black through and through, and my soul belongs to Satan."

"Good to know. Nevertheless, I urge prudence." He winked. "You'll see why in just a moment."

Lemuel slung his scepter and removed a knife from the opposite side of his belt. He ran the tip of the blade across both palms. As rich scarlet fluid flowed from the wounds, he placed each hand against the outline of its corresponding re-lief upon the panels. Conflicting energy blazed to life, red on the left, blue on the right, outlining his fingertips in coronas of lurid light.

He uttered a single word: "Lem-esh (Lemuel)," then stood back and made the sign of an inverted cross in the air.

His blood soaked into the wood's dark grain before my very eyes, and when I glanced at his palms, I noticed the cuts had already closed over.

The background *buzz* cut off. The barrier dropped, as did the door; straight down into a hidden trench in the floor. My sensibilities were instantly assailed by the pure, unadulterated glory of my personal opium made manifest.

The Bālefire.

I staggered, and had to grasp the frame and lintel to prevent myself from falling.

A chamber lay revealed, similar in design to a one hundred yard vertical tube. The entrance I found myself occupying appeared to be the only one, and had been positioned at the exact center of the chamber's height. At a point two or three feet below the ceiling, the Bālefire erupted from thin air in a rush of pyrotechnic fury. It thundered down past our position to terminate in coruscating glory a similar distance from the floor.

I inhaled deeply, and felt my potential swell.

"Careful, Reaper," Lemuel hissed, "so much tincture in such a confined space may present unforeseen hazards."

He's right, of course.

It was only with the greatest effort that I was able to prevent myself from leaping in, there and then, to feast.

Lemuel must have guessed my intentions. A firm grip on my shoulder refocused my attention away from the rose-tinted wonderland before me, and toward something else. "Look carefully," he murmured, pointing with his other hand.

I adjusted my sensitivity to compensate for the presence of so much limitless might, and was rewarded by the actuality of what I'd already seen by way of psychic representation.

"Behold the Key of Sighs," Lemuel breathed in a reverential tone, "a most puissant icon, and one of the great mysteries of the Divide, for by its sweet solace is the prohibition between our realms maintained."

Gleaming like a many-faceted precious stone, the basketball-sized hunk of the pearly gates hung suspended within the matter stream like the personification of tranquility made manifest. Its surface glittered, as if it had been dusted by a thousand mirrors, and in those reflections I saw an echo of the power of creation. It revolved slowly, over and over around its own axis, and its hypnotic redolence called to me in ways I'd never imagined possible for one so dark-hearted.

The more I searched the mystery of its hidden depths, the more I found myself falling into it, meshing with it, and understanding the sublimity of its nature.

A dissonant tone grated across my nerves. Without thinking, I linked to the discord and manipulated the Key's position within the plasma strand. It twisted, revealing a portion of its surface that had been hidden. An ugly scar marred the beauty of its perfection.

"Bloody hell! Your thoughts presented a different picture. I thought you said an expert was employed to extract the samples for the defenses?"

"You are perceptive, Reaper. Rest assured, that wound was not caused by us. Our artisan was indeed skilled enough to take the cuttings without marring the Key's form or function. What you are looking at is much more recent, and here we come to the crux of our dilemma, for whoever committed this act of vandalism was making a statement."

"A statement, you say?"

"Of course. Think about it. They went to all the trouble of infiltrating one of the most heavily fortified locations in all of hell . . . and for what? Just to leave their prize where it was? Just so they could take a selfie and post it to Hatebook? No, they came here for a reason, and the realization of their plans involved a great deal of preparation. I dread to think what the bigger picture may involve."

Cream!

My visage darkened.

Lemuel noted my look of anger and moved closer. "You suspect someone of this outrage?"

"Is it that obvious?" I projected a sanitized précis of my dealings with Cream and his mysterious benefactors directly into Lemuel's mind, so he would better understand my recent frustrations.

He spent the next few minutes studying the specifics of the data, and then laughed out loud. "I see. *Now* it makes sense."

"What does?"

"Reaper, I suspect you've either been baited again, or left another calling card."

"Calling card?"

"Yes." He pointed to the Key once more. "Please focus more acutely and tell me what you see."

I did as he asked, and was surprised to discover something had been wedged within the crudely fashioned hole. Something small and shiny.

I frowned. "Do you know what it is?"

"Sadly not. For all our arts, none of us possess the might to withstand the pure essence of the Bãlefire. Even I cannot enter, for the presence of the angel-hand might cause the wards about it to drop, and give away its location to those above who seek to recover it."

"So this setup effectively veils the Key from you know who?"

"Amongst others, yes. That's why I need your help. Because of your *unique* heritage, only you can hope to withstand such fury without triggering a catastrophic reaction within the shield's integrity."

Lemuel's statement puzzled me.

"Hang on a second, what about Satan and his fallen angels? Surely they could have helped you?"

"His Satanic Majesty fears to approach, lest the mere presence of the Key prompts his ardor to attack heaven once more. Such a move requires careful strategy and execution, and he is determined upon certain success, next time. When he comes for this blessed device, it will be at the hour of his devising, not before."

"And Samael and his brothers?"

"In all truth, HSM does not trust them to possess such might."

But he trusts me?

I didn't know whether to be shocked, honored, or downright insulted. Regardless, something Lemuel had just said hit a nerve.

"How do you think our intruder managed to enter, then? From what you've intimated, the barricades surrounding this site are formidable. If they're breached, there's a danger they'll fall. Our burglar didn't want that to happen, so he took precautions. But why? And how *exactly* would he do that? I could list the possible candidates on one hand, fallen angels and their mystic weapons included."

"Ah, I see what you mean," Lemuel replied. Then, more quietly, "I fear the answer may lie in the realms of the forbidden. Things proscribed since the Time of Sundering. Understand, Reaper, I only discuss such matters now because I wish to ensure the security of the treasure in my charge."

"By that inference, I take it you're aware of contrivances that could do this?"

"Of course. As the protector of the Key, it is my function to know of everything that might present a danger. Having studied the factors of this incident closely, I feel we may be forced to consider one or two utensils that should have been vitiated long ago. Such as the Sword of Damocles, or the Mermaid's Pin."

"What do these artifacts do?"

"The Sword negates all power, no matter who or what the source. The Pin is able to pierce the strongest barrier. They can only be used by a mortal individual once, and even then at great cost. Both were ordered destroyed millennia ago."

Oh, fantastic. Another pile of shit I'll have to sort out along the way.

But I'd procrastinated long enough.

"Right, you'd better stand back while I get this show on the road."

"Very well," Lemuel replied, "but if I may be so bold? Be careful to keep your aura under control. If the Key registers your presence, I fear your fortitude may trigger the Divine wards, and that is something to be avoided."

"You don't have to worry on that account," I answered wryly, "the least I have to do with anything of heavenly origin, the better."

Yeah! I scolded myself, *you talk the talk, but how are you actually going to walk the walk, and pluck the item from the Key without touching it?*

I considered my dilemma from a purely practical point of view.

Physical exertion is out. If I make contact, it'll activate the stone and God's angels will descend on us like the proverbial avalanche, and damn the consequences. But if I use my hell-spawned abilities, that could also elicit an adverse reaction.

I scanned the interior of the bore from top to bottom. My gaze came to rest on the spot where the Bālefire erupted from hydraspace. Opening my senses wide, I tasted the resonance of the matter stream as it cascaded through the chamber, and followed it down to the point where it disappeared.

Of course! It's so simple . . .

One of my primary attributes was the ability to *phase* through the ether. To do so, I incorporated a proficiency to blend with the very quintessence of hydraspace itself. However, I never actually breached the event horizon, as someone would do if they teleported. Instead, I merely skimmed the threshold between dimensions in such a way that it allowed me to *jump* between two locations in close proximity almost instantaneously. The point being, my molecules would temporarily mesh with those of the exotic medium through which I was traveling.

And if my essence is blended with the Bālefire, it shouldn't trigger . . .

In an instant, I was there.

At one with the roaring, writhing monstrosity that was the very heartblood of the underworld, I allowed its essence to sweep me along in a tide of ferocity that took my esoteric breath away.

Part of my consciousness was aware of the expression painted all over Lemuel's face. My maneuver had obviously taken him by surprise. Fortunately, that didn't distract me from the task at hand. The Key of Sighs.

As the column of fire screamed down, it flowed across the dignity of the stone without generating the slightest ripple. Where the current impacted the mystery token, however, a violent eddy had been created. Swirling round and around, the miniature maelstrom concentrated the rush of energies so much that they threatened to vaporize the memento at any second.

Fortunately, that would no longer be a problem. Joining with the vortex for just an instant, I snatched the offending article from its perch. Then, indivisible from the plasma ribbon once more, I allowed the stream to carry me toward the terminus.

Moments later, I was back, standing beside a startled Warden, with a glowing—and exceedingly hot—souvenir in my grasp.

"Well, that was easier than I thought." *Makes a bloody change.*

Lemuel was dumbfounded. "How did . . . ?"

"Let's just say it's part of the unique heritage you mentioned. It's what makes me an effective Reaper. *Nowhere* is safe." I paused to carefully unfold my prize, and took a closer look. "Now, what have we got here?"

The item in my possession was different to the messages I'd been left before. Although written by the same hand,

and in blood, the author had somehow managed to stencil the words into a malleable, metallic, sliver of paper.

This stuff feels like gold leaf . . . but far more flexible.

It was a very delicate piece of work, and it made me wonder how the text had been inscribed onto the surface without damaging it.

My latest clue said:

Kill jars,
Pickled remains of past grievances,
Both great and small,
Marinating now upon their shelves,
Preserves of the most succulent variety.
Mine to savor when the fancy takes me,
Sweet rich marrow,
Toothpick finger bones,
Toasting your accomplishments,
And flensing the taste of you from memory.

"Well, well, well!" I fumed out loud. "It looks as if I'll be settling some old scores much sooner than I expected."

"Is this from that Cream fellow you mentioned?" Lemuel asked. "And more importantly, do you understand what it means?"

"Oh, I understand it all right. And it's close enough to Cream to count as one and the same." I turned to the Warden and shook his hand. For some reason, the tingle running up my arm was much, much stronger this time. "Lemuel, thank you for your assistance. I wish there was some way I could repay you, but I've got to get going. This clue tells me where I need to be. The sooner I get there, the better for all concerned."

Lemuel maintained his hold, and grinned. "Then there *is* a way you could repay me. Just fry the bastard who dared to make me look incompetent, and return the stolen piece into my care. None of us will be safe until the shard is reunited with the Key."

"I'll do my best."

"One thing more," he said. "Think of it as a parting gesture."

Before I could ask him what he meant, Lemuel muttered something under his breath. I felt an icy-cold veil of darkness wash cross my body. Everything went black for a moment and when I opened my eyes, I found myself standing on the sidewalk outside the Old Bully, right in front of a very surprised hell-hound.

"How the fuck did you do that?" Nimrod spluttered. He jumped back, his usual composure totally blown away.

"Do what?"

"You've only just this second walked into the mist on the other side of the street, and now . . ." His voice trailed off, and I grew quite concerned by the way he was staring at me.

"What's wrong? You look like you've seen a long lost friend after he's been away for years."

"That's just it, Boss, you haven't *been* anywhere. And all of a sudden you've appeared right beside me, glowing like a neon advertisement outside a brothel."

I stepped away and looked at my reflection in a window. Then I held up my hands. Power radiated from me in waves, and I was shocked to discover I was indeed surrounded by a rich, strontium-red nimbus.

It must have been my exposure to the Bãlefire.

I sent my senses deep inside. *And come to think of it, I do feel strangely invigorated.* "This is gonna come in handy."

"How so?"

I waved the latest clue in his face. "Thanks to the Knights and the Grey Friars, we've gained a lot of time. *And* I know where to go next. What say I use all this excess energy and take us there in style, right now?"

"Sounds good, but where are we going?"

"We, my dear friend, are going to make a very public spectacle of a self-styled crime lord who thinks that attempting to murder the Reaper won't have repercussions. You might want to get your sword out. I have a feeling we'll be in the thick of it as soon as we arrive."

Thank you for reading!
To see more books from Perseid Press
please go to our website:
www.theperseidpress.com